Loving The Small-Town Hero

A Small-Town Novel

Carla Swafford

Praise for Carla Swafford

"This savage contemporary is filled with action, deception, and emotional and sexual tension that leave readers panting right up until the highly anticipated climax."

— Publishers Weekly, starred review, for
Hidden Heat

"Exciting and breathtaking. Carla Swafford is an up-and-coming author not to be missed!"

— Sherrilyn Kenyon, *New York*
Times bestselling author

"Great writing and a truly wonderful love story. Will definitely buy [m]ore books from this author."

— Reviewer on Amazon, starred review, for
Fake Play

"...dark, erotic and dangerous... "

— RT BOOKreviews, starred review, for
Circle of Desire

Ebook ISBN: 978-1-956518-10-8

Paperback ISBN: 978-1-956518-11-5

Hardcover ISBN: 978-1-956518-12-2

Chapter One

Sitting in a graffiti-smeared cell on a Sunday afternoon wasn't what Molly Hicks would call a good way to end a weekend.

"Dammit, Molly! You gave me no choice. Even if you believe I deserve being shot, it's against the law. Hell, it's assault with a deadly weapon for that matter. Even worse, if you'd killed me. That's a capital offense. I don't think you want to take up residence at Tutwiler Prison." Sheriff J.T. Rogan held his arm across his chest, babying the wound in his shoulder.

She'd like to think she'd intended to pierce his cold, lying heart, yet her intentions had nothing to do with his being a crooked sheriff. Her temper had gotten the best of her when she discovered he'd arrested her brother for murder. So in the heat of the moment, she'd drawn her gun but then simply tripped.

She opened her mouth to reply, but he continued his rant. "For that matter, how does that help your brother? Everyone will say if the sister is stupid enough to shoot the sheriff, he obviously shot my deputy. Damn, that sounds like a fucked-up old song." Eyes dark as hell glared at her. So appropriate, as he was the devil incarnate.

Staring into the sheriff's cold eyes, her fingers twitched with a need to hold her hand up to swear she told the truth. Thankfully, the bullet had merely grazed his upper arm. What happened to his sense of humor? It had been an accident for goodness' sake. Why arrest her for being clumsy? The bullheaded man had acted all offended, but he sure relished throwing another Hicks in his jail.

Yeah, yeah, pulling out the gun was her idea, but it was his fault she was here anyway. *He'd* taunted her into firing at him.

Determined not to squirm on the hard cot, she kept her mouth shut. He wasn't ready to believe anything she had to say.

She'd grown up with a domineering father who enjoyed intimidating people. So she'd become proficient in not showing fear or doubt or he would run all over her.

J.T. leaned on the iron bars with his good arm, a hand clasping the rod above his head. She couldn't resist looking him over. What sane woman could? Shirtless with only a white bandage and sling, he hadn't pulled on another uniform shirt since the doctor earlier cut off the bloody one. Red and black tattoos over well-defined muscles captivated her stare. Easily six-three, with broad shoulders and crow-black hair cut military short, he kept the women of Sand City, Alabama, stirred up, contemplating the benefits of breaking the law just to draw his attention.

Her gaze returned to his.

"You know Big Joe will have your badge when he hears about this. I demand you give me my one phone call," she calmly said, unable to remain quiet any longer.

He narrowed his eyes.

She refused to drop his stare again. It was better than admiring how his khaki uniform pants stretched across slim hips beneath the black duty belt. Mercy. He was a fine-looking man.

"I took the liberty in calling your dad. He's sending Weasel over to pick you up." J.T.'s chuckle infuriated her. He knew how much she hated it when Big Joe sent his crony, Raymond *the Weasel* Beauregard, the third, Esquire, to pull her back in line.

"Finally," she flatly stated.

She wanted to say so much more but during her years away, she'd learned to control her mouth and temper. With a glance at his stark white bandage, she grimaced. Obviously, her temper still needed work.

From the look of his glower, his might require a little work too. Besides, why wasn't he pressing charges?

Hold it. Why look a gift horse in the mouth?

Living in a small town mostly owned by her dad did have an advantage or two. Most people would be surprised she rarely experienced it growing up. Her dad had believed in tough love and his children were required to follow all laws and his stricter ones. All of that and a couple of situations had forced her to leave home five years ago.

"Well, well, I do believe little Miss Molly has grown up." The statement by the man walking down the hallway to the cells pulled her scowl from the sheriff.

Raymond stopped beside J.T. and leered into the cell. Her dad's lawyer had always given her the creeps and the years away hadn't lessened the feeling. Some women probably considered him sophisticated with the gray at his temples, his manicured nails, and three-piece suits, but he oozed grease, as far as she was concerned.

Worry chilled her as she contemplated the pros of

staying in jail.

J.T. stepped back and nodded at Big Joe's lawyer. "Hey, Weasel."

"Don't call me that," Raymond snapped. Then he pulled at his vest and cleared his throat. "If you decline to call me by my given name, then you can call me Mr. Beauregard."

What got him all tied in a knot? He'd been called Weasel all her life. Okay then. Raymond it was, for no way would she call him Mr. anything.

"I've taken care of the paperwork with the clerk," Raymond continued. "So you can release Miss Hicks now, Sheriff." From the smirk on his face, she could tell he didn't think much of the new sheriff.

"What about Devlin?" She peeked between the bars to the cell next to hers. Her brother was still unconscious on the cot, legs dangling off the end, one arm hanging over the side.

"You know the judge hasn't set bail yet," said J.T., his tone dark and forbidding.

"He didn't kill your deputy." How many times would she need to say it?

"I told you, Molly, several people in the bar heard him threaten Mike. No more than ten minutes later they heard a shot, and my deputy was found fatally wounded outside the Sandbox Bar." His eyes narrowed as if warning her not to argue further.

"And you found Devlin passed out in my truck. No gun. No one saw who shot your deputy. I bet they didn't find any residue on my brother either." Threatened or not, she would make J.T. believe in her brother's innocence.

"Enough!" The lawyer stepped in front of Molly. "You don't need to help the sheriff in his case against your brother." Raymond turned to J.T. "If you're not pressing charges, you best release my client."

J.T. smiled as if he were imagining smashing his fist into the lawyer's slimy face. Not wanting anymore bloodshed, Molly stood and waited as J.T. unlocked the cell door and pushed it to the side. Straining to hold onto all of her self-professed control, she walked by the sheriff without *accidentally* joggling his wounded arm.

He reached out and gripped her arm, stopping her departure. She looked at the long fingers turning her skin a lighter shade and then lifted her gaze to dark eyes filled with concern.

"Go home to your daddy. He'll make sure you stay out of trouble." J.T. released her arm and turned away.

She watched his long stride. The urge to tell him where to go evaporated like steam off hot cement after a summer rain. Lord, she'd thought she'd gotten over that man. He was one of the reasons she'd left Sand City five years ago and not returned until a couple of weeks ago. Over the years, every time the thought of coming back entered her mind, she reminded herself she wasn't a masochist. Only one person was able to talk her into returning and he'd been arrested for murder.

"Molly?" Raymond the Weasel waited in the hallway for her to fall in line and go home to daddy. She had no idea why Big Joe had arranged for her release. No matter how she'd threatened the sheriff's badge earlier, her dad had never cared what happened to her. So why he would start at that moment confused her even more. Whatever. She'd let Raymond take her back to Magnolia Farms. It was past time to talk to good old dad.

"Let's go and see what Big Joe wants," she said as she walked out, head held high.

Chapter Two

J.T. watched through the window on the second floor as she marched toward Raymond's white Lincoln. Her tight jeans and skimpy red top showed how much she'd grown into a shapely woman. Little remained of the young teenager who'd offered to give him a blowjob behind the gym. She'd been spitting mad when he'd called her daddy to come and get her, and she'd sworn he would regret turning down her offer.

He rubbed the ache near his bullet wound—really a mere scratch—and chuckled. She was right, he did have regrets, but not for what she claimed. He'd regretted making her mad, though he enjoyed teasing her. Considering what happened last night, he'd remember to check her for a gun next time they came face-to-face. The woman had a mean temper. Hell, it'd been twelve years since he stopped her from sticking her hand down his pants. She won the prize in holding a grudge.

Maybe it had been a good thing Big Joe had kicked his butt out of Sand City all those years ago. That taught him a Hicks would always side with a Hicks. At the time, he'd never wanted to see her again. And once he'd graduated college and accepted the FBI's offer, he'd planned to never return to Alabama, and hopefully drive all thoughts of her from his brain. But fate had a way of playing with a man's mind.

Thinking of her long legs and well-endowed chest, well, he never managed to erase memories of their teenage clashes, especially since returning to Sand City. Chuckling in self-contempt, he shook his head. What had happened to the little sex kitten? It was obvious. She'd grown up to be a hell cat—correction— fascinating hell cat.

"Hey, boss, Big Joe called. You're to meet with him tonight to talk about Devlin." The deputy hung up the phone and walked across the room to stand beside him, gawking over his shoulder. "Did you see the rig she owns?"

"Rig?" He half listened as he struggled to pull on a clean shirt without jarring his shoulder too much. The newly formed scab could break and bleed, ruining another uniform shirt, if he wasn't careful. His gaze followed the Lincoln's path down Main Street until it disappeared onto Elm.

"Yeah, big semi. It has one of those extra-large studio sleepers with chrome wheels and more lights than a Christmas tree. That baby probably can sleep four. I bet she's had some wild rides in that monster."

The deputy's enthusiasm grated on J.T.'s nerves. He reminded himself his irritation had nothing to do with Molly taking men for a ride in her truck. Though he knew what type of perverts and cretins lie in wait at truck stops for a good-looking woman like Molly. His stomach turned with the thought of her driving miles upon miles alone and in some of the worst weather with no one to watch over her.

"Eddie, since you have so much time to speculate on

Miss Hicks's road life, you can take care of the filing while Janet's at an appointment and won't be back until tomorrow."

"Ahh, maaan." The deputy eyed the tall stack with distaste.

The department's only female deputy, Brooke McDonald, stuck her head in the doorway. No surprise. The woman wasn't shy about eavesdropping.

"Eddie, I'll do the filing if you'll take my call for Franny Osborne. She's complaining about goings on at the old Farley place."

"I don't know which is worse, doing the filing or listening to the wackadoodle ramble on about ghosts and such." He shook his head and then sighed. "Okay. I'll take a chance with Mrs. Osborne as long as she keeps her hands to herself. Last time I went into her house, she pinched my ass."

J.T. chuckled. "Just don't turn your back on her."

Deputy McDonald picked up the first file, grinning at the young deputy's red face. "I've heard she's the second richest person in the county next to Big Joe, so if you play your cards right, she might make you her boy toy."

Eddie appeared to take the ribbing in stride. He'd been near to inconsolable with Mike's death until they arrested Devlin Hicks. Brooke was Eddie's cousin and worked at keeping his mind elsewhere by keeping him busy. Besides, she loved baiting her cousin. Even with everyone's emotions in a dumpster fire, they were handling the death the best way they knew how, going on with life and working on gathering enough evidence to put away his killer for good. They would all miss Mike's dry wit and insightful advice. He'd been the senior officer of J.T.'s deputies and made sure everyone accepted an outsider as boss despite everyone expecting Mike to take the job after Bubba Hagley quit. Many of the city's civilians considered J.T. as an outsider regardless of growing up in Sand City. It was more to do with the fact he hadn't worked his way through the rank and file. Their acceptance strengthened his resolve to become sheriff and he was lucky to be part of such a good group.

One thing was for sure: Devlin Hicks wasn't a well-liked guy at the moment, and his daddy would pull strings to get bail set and hopefully would do it soon. Big Joe had already thrown enough money around to keep the press at bay for a few days, giving everyone a little relief while the investigation was ongoing.

J.T. had a hard enough time soothing the deputies' tempers as they would like nothing better than stepping into the cell and beating Devlin to a pulp.

Rubbing his shoulder again, he frowned. Did Big Joe have something to do with Molly shooting him? The man wasn't known for being the Big Manipulator for nothing. Everyone knew Devlin was his favorite child. His daughter was considered to be a liability the ill-tempered man had said good riddance to all those years ago. At least that was what the gossips said around town. One of the drawbacks or, some would say, perks of the job in a small county, people loved telling him their neighbors' secrets.

Molly claimed Devlin had passed out in her sleeper after leaving the bar. Her truck had been parked behind Bill's Diner, just a short walk from the Sandbox. She'd claimed she left the diner at closing time which was ten o'clock. When she crawled into her cab, she'd heard her brother's snoring. So someone was lying. Either it was the witnesses at the Sandbox, and they were more drunk than not, or Molly, who loved her little brother enough to shoot a sheriff to protect him.

Yep. Sand City...hell, the whole of Sand County had its secrets and this time no one was talking.

Chapter Three

Molly stood in front of Big Joe's desk feeling once again like a nine-year-old being disciplined for bringing home Bs on her report card. Only straight As were acceptable, as her dad told her over and over again. Whenever she'd brought up her brother's grades, she would find herself in more trouble. Per her dad at the time, little Devlin was too highly strung for anyone to expect the same grades, and besides, boys were to excel at sports.

Then her father would say if a girl wasn't pretty, her only asset for obtaining a husband would be her brains. As in, to trick them into putting a ring on it. He'd known the boys in school called her "The Molly Green Giant," and as a teenager, dates had been few and far between.

When she'd reached her senior year, she'd paid the school's quarterback to take her to the prom. It was worth every dime when she saw the head cheerleader, and top instigator in making her life miserable, throw a hissy fit in the middle of the auditorium. One of the few times she was able to use Daddy's money and make it worth the trouble to pay her dad back. By the time she'd entered college, several of the boys' heights had reached or surpassed hers. Thank God!

Yet really, who, besides her parents, had ever said she needed to get married? No one ever proclaimed them as modern thinkers.

"Girl, why is it Devlin gets in trouble in less than a week after you return home?" He leaned back in his oversized, black leather chair, his accusing glare filling her spine with steel. His white hair stuck out in patches as if he'd been pulling at it in frustration.

How did he know she'd been back in town before the shooting? She grimaced. Silly to think she could hide anything from him. The man knew everything going on in Sand City and the surrounding county.

Shifting her weight from one foot to the other, she grimaced. "You're quite aware one has nothing to do with the other, right? Merely coincidence I show up days before he's arrested." She refused to be sucked into his need to dominate everyone.

He stood, leaning over his desk as his body shook from anger. He pounded his fist on the desk. "Merely? Merely? There was nothing mere about his arrest! You get him out of there. Whatever it takes. You managed to get yourself out of jail easy enough. The least you can do for your own flesh and blood is to get him out of jail without bail being set." He straightened. His car salesman grin warned her she wouldn't like what he was about to say. "If I remember correctly, you had a thing for our new sheriff. Seeing as he's interested in you enough to let you go without pressing charges, I believe you can sashay that ass of yours and get your brother out too."

"Joseph!" Plump as the Pillsbury Doughboy and

possessing a voice of a little girl even at the age of fifty-six, Lisa Cooper Hicks's angelic face hid the soul of an army drill sergeant. Anyone who visited would say she feared no one at Magnolia Farms, least of all the man towering over her. "Devlin finally persuaded Molly to return home and what do you do? Try to run her off again. She took up for our boy. Goodness, the girl shot that sheriff you're trying to throw her at. He's mighty sexy with those tattoos and black-as-sin hair, but she's not his type."

"Woohoo! I'm standing in front of you, Mom. Dad." Molly waved her hand. "You can talk to me. And I didn't intentionally shoot him. It was an accident."

Molly knew her mom's tactics. The woman never used the direct route to get what she wanted. Sure, her dad was also a part of the reason Molly left all those years ago, but her mom was as guilty. Everyone knew Devlin was her favorite too.

"Get your hand out of my face. And don't get smart with me, girl." Her mom's harsh tone was tempered by her arms opening wide for a hug. The older woman's head only came to Molly's shoulder, causing her daughter to lean down. "We sure missed you. You know I expected you to email me more often after you got a laptop. Those people at the computer store promised me you could use your phone as an internet connection to email me back from anywhere. So you have no excuse. And heaven forbid if you used that fancy cell phone."

That was her mom. Mrs. You'll-Live-With-Guilt-Even-If-I-Have-To-Glue-It-To-Your-Forehead. And who knew what would happen if she told her mom the cell phone received calls as well as texts.

"I'm here now." Before her mom and dad plowed into

her again, she asked, "What's up with Devlin and his drinking?"

Her dad grunted. "He's just sowing his wild oats, having a good time. Mike always picked on him. Since high school the man was a bully."

Molly knew Mike Lindsey had been the deputy Devlin was accused of killing. What she remembered of Mike, even before she left town, was how easy-going the man had been as a rookie deputy. She doubted he'd changed that much. Her father always treated anyone who stepped on his toes as the ultimate villain.

Actually, she didn't remember her brother being a lush either.

"Devlin's twenty-six. At the rate he's going, he'll be all out of oats and you two will never be grandparents. Anyway, he should be past sowing wild oats." Her mom shot her a sharp look. Uh-oh, she was about to be told off if she didn't watch her mouth.

"Does that mean you're back home to find a good man to settle down with and make us some grandbabies?" Her mom's little girl voice sounded so innocent, but Molly knew she was making a point. Molly couldn't get away with picking on her brother's wild oats without explaining her own.

Before she could defend herself, someone knocked on the study door and then opened it. Perfect timing.

"Mister Joe, the sheriff's here and he said you'd asked to see him." Willy Mitchell, skinny and white-headed like his boss, winked at Molly and waited for permission to bring in the guest. Willy had worked for her dad as far back as she could remember. The man had to be over eighty, and from what she'd heard, wealthy enough to retire in luxury but he continued to work, year after year.

Big Joe was generous to those who were faithful and kept his secrets.

"Send him in. Lisa's leaving."

"I am?" The older woman placed a hand on one ample hip.

Big Joe's bushy eyebrows rose above twinkling eyes. "Now, Mama, I need to talk business with the sheriff. You know how particular us men can get about our egos. I need him willing to back down on this arrest business with Devlin." He held out his hand and her mom took it. "I promise it won't take long and I'll see you upstairs. Sugar, I'll give you one of those..."

Molly closed her ears to the rest. As kids, she and her brother had always covered their ears when their parents began with the sweet talk. Too embarrassing. Of course, the same was true when they argued. They could get rather risqué about what to do with body parts in their insults.

"Okay. You play nice with the sheriff," her mom said, shaking a finger at her dad, and then she turned to Molly. She hugged her again. "See you later, sweetie." And quickly exited, apparently thrilled about whatever her dad promised.

Molly refused to think more about that.

"Well, I guess I better leave too," she said. No way would she stay when the sheriff backed down. Everyone gave in to her dad's finagling and for some reason she hated to think J.T. would.

"No, you stay."

"What about his fragile male ego around a woman?" What was her dad up to? She really didn't want to be part of his conniving.

"You don't count."

That hurt. She could tell by his unchanged expression,

he hadn't realized the insult he'd thrown her way. Nothing had changed. Despite the talk about throwing herself at the sheriff, her dad regarded her as sexless. In his head, no female taller than five-five was a woman.

"To make sure you're straight on this, I'm not using my body to get Devlin released." She crossed her arms.

"Now, Molly Lynn Hicks, you do what I tell—" Then J.T. Rogan walked in and her dad closed his mouth with a snap.

The walls in the room pressed against her and the air warmed considerably. How in the short time she'd been away from the jail had she forgotten J.T.'s magnetic pull? He filled a room with his presence. Broad shoulders, dark eyes, and high cheekbones, he was a luscious delight to behold. Though the khaki-colored shirt he'd pulled on had long sleeves and hid the tattoos she'd admired, he still had a look of barely restrained civility about him. He'd ditched the sling as he held one arm stiffly to the side. It was as if he refused to show Big Joe any weaknesses.

"What can I do for you, Mr. Hicks?" J.T.'s deep voice filled the room.

His question was all politeness tinged with resentment at being commanded to appear before her dad.

She knew how her dad operated. He never asked.

"Release my boy." Big Joe sat back in his chair without offering the sheriff a seat.

"The judge will set bail tomorrow. I'm sure it will be an amount you can meet." J.T.'s back went ramrod straight as he widened his stance in preparation for the oncoming argument.

"That's reason enough to go ahead and let the boy come home. You know I'll pay the bail. It ain't like he's going to leave town. You helped get Molly released without charges, it should be easier to release the boy before bail is decided." Big Joe grinned, flashing straight white teeth. He acted as if the sheriff's cooperation was a given.

"Mr. Hicks, you helped me get elected and I appreciate that, but the people of Sand County and Sand City expect me to keep a suspected killer in jail until a judge decides otherwise. So he stays until bail is set. As for Molly, I decided not to press charges. What with the shock of her brother being arrested for murder, I was certain her family had enough to contend with."

Molly resented the fact she owed J.T. for letting her go free after only a few hours in jail, accident or not. Yet seeing him stand up to her dad was enticing. She really wished he'd given in to her dad's demands or acted like a donkey's rear-end. He was making it hard for her to stay angry. But no matter what she felt about him, he treated her like she was sexless. She bet he liked tiny, fragile girly-girls.

"You know you're becoming too big for your britches. If you're not careful, you might find yourself jobless and drunk, passed out on the side of the street like your daddy," said her father. Considering how many fingers Big Joe had in the town's pies—in other words businesses he did not own—and in turn, people's livelihoods, he could easily get J.T. fired.

"Well, sir, you might guarantee I lose my job, but I don't drink, so 'the passed out on the side of the road' part might be stretching it." The sheriff glanced over to Molly as if he expected her to add her two cents' worth.

Maybe the surprise on her face gave it away but she hadn't expected the son of the town's drunk to be a teetotaler. Of course, she never dreamed of returning to Sand City and finding he was really the sheriff either. From what she'd heard around town, he was like some hero, being a former FBI special agent and involved in saving some local people from a crazy mob boss. Who knew such a little town could handle so much excitement?

"Molly!"

Startled, she jerked her gaze from J.T. to her dad. "Sir?"

"Walk the sheriff to his car." Over J.T.'s protest, Big Joe added to her, "Remember what I told you."

Heat scorched her cheeks. He expected her to proposition the sheriff. If only he knew, her dad was asking her to consider the pros in committing patricide. With guilt prancing around in the back of her mind, she led the way to the front door as only distance would save the old coot's hide.

She stepped off the front porch and looked up. A couple of seconds passed as she immersed her senses in the scent of honeysuckle floating on the air and the billion stars twinkling above. She loved this time of the year.

"No need for you to walk me to my truck," the sheriff said as he trudged past her.

J.T.'s offer was tempting, but she was certain her dad watched them on his computer in the study. There were security cameras everywhere on the property. She'd rather not listen later to how she once again failed him.

"It's no problem. Wouldn't want you to trip and hurt yourself and sue." Why had she said something like that? True, her smart mouth was a byproduct of her dad.

"Does that mean you'll catch me?" His chuckle infuriated her. As she turned to tell him her feelings about saving his ass, she tripped.

Strong arms caught her as her cheek landed on a firm, broad chest. His effortlessness in breaking her fall and his steady heartbeat proved how little her nearness affected him. Goodness, her chest felt ready to burst from performing the cha-cha. Sure, she was embarrassed by her clumsiness, but she admitted she liked his arms around her.

Unable to resist, she inhaled the scent of starch and pure male. Oh my, he smelled better than the honeysuckle, and she savored the heat from the firmness beneath her cheek. She bit her lip to keep a moan of pleasure from escaping, and at the same time, she heard his sharp intake of breath. Was she wrong? Was he as excited by her nearness as she was from his?

Her fingers brushed a bulge near his shoulder. Oh, crap! His wound! *Dummy, you shot the fellow.* His gasp was from pain, not of desire. No way could he feel anything but disdain. Talk about delusional. She had issues.

A quick step back alleviated the urge to slide her hand down to explore what she'd already seen beneath his uniform shirt. At twenty, he'd been lanky, but the years had filled him out and he'd emerged a hunk of a man, even tall enough that she had to look up into his eyes.

"Sorry. I didn't mean to jostle your wound." She stuck her hands into her jeans' back pockets.

"I've had worse." He pulled an arm across his abdomen and held his elbow, taking weight off the shoulder as he continued toward his marked SUV.

She'd heard he'd been gut shot before leaving the FBI, an injury easily fatal from massive bleeding or infection. The pain he'd lived through had to have been excruciating.

Who had visited him in the hospital and helped with the rehabilitation? She'd been told his brother had died during the same undercover assignment and his father was a drunk who refused to speak to his only living son. Was there someone waiting at his home? She took a long blink to clear her thoughts. It wasn't any of her business.

Lord, being near the man might drive her crazy. Hell,

being in the same city would do it.

A few more steps brought them to his SUV and he opened the door. Before he slipped behind the steering wheel, he turned toward her. "Molly, don't let your father bully you into doing anything stupid for your brother."

Stupid? Her stomach clenched with hurt. And to think she felt all empathetic about his brother's death, his lousy father, and her shooting him. With that word—stupid—if she still had her Beretta, she'd shoot him through his ignorant heart.

"How could you say that to me? If anyone knew what lengths I would go to protect my brother, you should. I'm not the selfish, self-centered bitch you think I am," she said as she lifted her chin.

By God, she had changed since she was an ignorant teenager. Tears were easy to blink away. He wasn't the first to think of her like that. She stopped herself from saying her brother was the only human to care about her as she refused to sound pitiful in front of J.T. Before she could move, he reached out and grazed her cheek with the back of his finger.

"You know what I meant. Your father knows how you feel and he uses your feelings to make you act out. Just be careful." He dipped his chin in goodbye and then slammed the door.

What the hell? Did he think she was still in love with him?

Asshole.

She watched his taillights become smaller down the long drive until they disappeared. Rubbing her chest, the heavy ache bothered her as much as the heat on her cheek.

Yet, how could a simple touch bring back all the old dreams she had about a man who could never love her?

Chapter Four

Maybe J.T. had it right.

Molly shifted in the driver's seat and glanced into the back. Maybe she was stupid when it came to her brother. Her dad had made her promise to keep an eye on Devlin now that he was out of jail on bond. Lord knows, her brother didn't have the sense of a billy goat. The boy would drink mouthwash to get drunk if she didn't watch him. No one had to worry he would jump bail. He was too falling-down drunk most of the time. For the last week, he'd done nothing but drink booze and howl at the moon.

When she heard snoring coming from the studio sleeper, she relaxed. Finally, he was asleep. As soon as the sigh escaped her lips, someone knocked on the door and she scrambled to stop the offender.

She stepped out on the metal step into the late-afternoon sunshine. Her heart stopped. Sheriff J.T. Rogan stood in the alley behind Bill's Diner looking up at her with his white cowboy hat shading his eyes. She shook her head in an attempt to clear her lust-filled thoughts. No man should look so good in a uniform.

"Is Devlin in there?" he asked.

"Yeah, he's sleeping. He somehow found a bottle of Jim Beam and downed it before lunch." She remained on the top step, hoping her brother hadn't stolen the whiskey.

"I'll need to see for myself. He didn't check in today." J.T. placed a foot on the bottom step.

"What if I say no?" Some deep urge to irritate the sheriff kept bubbling to the top whenever he was around. Surely she'd gotten over her resentment of how boys treated her growing up, even the one in front of her, though he was no longer a boy. Pure hard-core man.

"Then I'll have to take you in for obstructing justice, and aiding and abetting." He wrapped his hand around the grab handle and took the top step, crowding her. Heat radiated wherever his body touched hers. She looked up and could finally see his eyes. The anger shooting out of their depths chilled her to the bone. "If you're covering for your brother—"

"Yes." The next second, she amended, "No! I mean, you can come in. He's asleep and I didn't want you to wake him. Please just peek inside but don't wake him." She moved out of the way and jumped to the ground.

The sheriff ducked inside after taking off his hat and kneeled on the driver-side seat, leaving the door open, and then leaned over to look into the back. He stared for a few moments and turned his head, checking the rest of the studio sleeper before stepping out, closing the door softly behind him.

"Okay. Be sure to tell your brother not to miss another check in. He needs to lay off alcohol." J.T. put his hat back on and headed toward his marked SUV. "And tell him he needs to stay at his dad's place. He's too close to the Sandbox and some of the regulars would like nothing better than to catch him in an alley."

If Molly didn't know better, she swore he acted as if he couldn't get away from her fast enough. Was he afraid she'd attack him?

She sat down on the bottom step, and once again watched as he drove away. Why was she constantly seeing the tail end of his SUV? What was it about the man that made her heart flutter after twelve years?

Make that seventeen years. She'd been eleven when he spoke to her for the first time. He'd been her white knight, taking up for the gangly girl being made fun of by a bunch of kids at the park.

Four years older, he looked like an action hero with long, black hair, sunglasses, and no helmet as he rode a dirt bike between the picnic tables.

She was one of those girls who started filling out early and her mom had recently bought her a bra. The boys teased her about the undergarment outline beneath her T-shirt and kept snapping her back strap. Almost in tears, she'd blindly swung at the troublemakers. At the same moment, J.T. sprayed gravel on the boys, and then jumped off the bike, hollering threats as they ran away.

When he took off his sunglasses, hooking them in the neckline of his T-shirt, he sauntered over to her. She still remembered what he'd said.

"You okay, kid?"

She nodded.

He touched her cheek. "Don't cry. Those bastards will regret the day they hassled you." His grin faded when her tears continued. "Wait and see, you'll grow into those long legs and they'll come sniffing. Be sure to make them beg to touch your feet."

She hadn't understood what he meant, but she liked his sweet tone. No one talked so sweet to her.

He'd used the corner of his T-shirt to clean the wet streaks off her face. She'd giggled as he chucked her chin before cranking up his dirt bike.

"Thank you," she shouted over the whining bike noise, her voice cracking.

"It was nothing." Then a plume of smoke was all she could see of him. Like magic, he was gone and she knew her life wouldn't be the same.

It hadn't been *nothing* to her. Her crush had grown and grown as she matured and filled out. The problem was, the only guy she wanted to kiss her feet, or any part of her body for that matter, wouldn't give her the time of day.

Chapter Five

J.T. shifted in his seat. Eddie had been right. From what he'd seen three days earlier, the huge RV-like sleeper could easily hold four. Hell, she could hold an orgy in that monster. Not only bunk beds—double-sized on bottom and twin-sized on top—it had a small sink, mini fridge, and stove with a flat-screen TV in one corner above a short counter and what looked like a shower near the back. J.T. shifted again as he watched the semi parked behind Bill's Diner. He wished Molly had followed his instructions and sent her brother home. This morning, his office had received a call about a disturbance behind the diner. Most likely one of Sand City's citizens had decided to take justice in their own hands and punished Devlin.

On driving up, he didn't see anything to be concerned about. So he sat and waited. The sun high overhead had him rolling down the driver-side window. As the minutes passed, nothing but his imagination occupied his time, conjuring up who Molly invited into her spacious sleeper and what they did. With her pretty girl-next-door looks and long legs, he imagined she rarely got lonely. He bet when she unbraided her hair, the mass of golden brown reached beyond the small of her back.

Well, he better check on her. Just to make sure she was okay. He unbuckled his seat belt and grabbed his hat. When he looked at her truck one more time, he shook his head. Who was he kidding? He wanted an excuse to see her again.

He opened his SUV's door at the same time a scream exploded from inside her truck. Pulling his gun from its holster as he tossed his hat on the front seat, he ran and jerked open the cab door. He slipped between the steering wheel and driver's seat, aiming his gun at the culprit.

Wide chocolate-brown eyes stared at him from a pale face. She stood near the bunks in a black bra and thong. Yep, her hair reached the small of her back. Every drop of saliva left his mouth.

"What are you doing here?" she asked.

Was she pulling one of her stunts on him again? He swallowed. "I heard a scream..."

As she opened her mouth to explain, a gray mouse darted from under the bunks and ran toward the cab. Molly screamed again.

"You're afraid of a tiny mouse?" J.T. locked the safety on his gun and holstered it as he began laughing.

"I hate the filthy creatures."

She shivered and then looked down at herself. Her face reddened as she turned her back to him. He liked that view too.

"Oh, crap!" With a quick jerk she pulled a blanket off the bunk and then wrapped it around her shoulders. "Quit staring! Get out!" Facing him again, she pointed toward the door.

"I just can't believe Ms. Molly Hicks, who shoots sheriffs without flinching, is frightened of a small rodent." He crossed his arms, smiling. The blanket teased him to examine again. One long thigh peeked between the cloth, daring him to touch and see if her skin felt as soft as it looked.

As she opened her mouth to make one of her usual smart-aleck comments, the mouse ran across the floor and over her foot. She screamed once again and jumped into his arms, dropping the blanket.

He held her tightly as her arms clasped his neck for dear life. Unable to control himself, he laughed so hard tears came into his eyes.

She began beating his chest. "How dare you laugh at me? It's not funny! They carry diseases." Her face turned a brighter shade of red but J.T. wasn't sure if it was from anger or embarrassment.

"I'm sorry, but you have to admit this is so unlike you. I never thought..." He chuckled as he sat on the edge of the bottom bed and gazed at her. She felt good in his lap. With one hand he caught both of hers. They continued to stare at each other, nearly nose-to-nose. He recognized what was happening between them and she probably did too.

The satiny skin beneath his hands registered. Nothing felt better than a curvy, velvety soft woman in his arms. With each wiggle of her behind, his body demonstrated how much he appreciated her movements.

"Be still," he whispered with a groan.

"No," she whispered. Her eyelids dipped and then she kissed him.

She tasted of peppermint, so sweet he wanted more. He released her hands. She wrapped her arms around his neck. Grabbing a handful of her silky hair, he kissed back, his tongue exploring and wanting more. The woman knew how to kiss.

In an effort to regain his breath, he dropped his mouth to kiss the tender spot behind her ear before returning to her mouth. He nipped at her full lower lip and sucked the tender flesh into his mouth.

His hand covered one plump breast, and he liked how there was more to spare. With a jerk of the lace, he exposed one breast, giving his mouth access to a brown nipple. He tongued and drew on the hard nub as she moaned. Lowering the other side of her bra, he took a second to admire the sight of her hard nipples, perfect and more than handfuls. Leaning down he sucked hard on the newly exposed breast as he pinched her wet nipple and she arched into his mouth. Yeah, he liked her in his arms.

When he felt her hands fumble with the buckle of his duty belt, he inhaled, steeling himself for what was about to come. He pressed a kiss to each breast and released his grip of her hair, feeling ashamed of his earlier roughness, then grasped her hands before she could unhook and unzip his pants.

"Molly," he demanded. She struggled against his hold, pulling her hands away and resumed her task. "Stop! We can't do this," he said a little sharper than he intended. He grabbed her wrists.

She shuddered and looked up with haunted eyes. What was wrong with her? Her actions were of a desperate woman. She was pretty enough to catch any person's attention, and with her luscious body she could easily keep their interest. Did she act like this with everyone she wanted?

"Why not? We're single and over twenty-one." Tears began to well up in her eyes.

Damn. The last thing he needed was her crying again.

And to have stoic Molly emotional was more than he could handle. He was never good at comforting women. He preferred her mad.

"First, I'm on duty and, second, I'm not going down that road with you again." He gently placed her on the bunk and stood, tucking his shirt back into his pants, and then buckled his belt. Swiping nonexistent dust from his pants, trying to give her some time to straighten her bra and cover herself with the blanket, he did his best not to look. Again. Plus he needed time to get his body under control, some of the hardness to diminish.

When he felt it was safe, he glanced at her. Her face was pale but no tears marred her cheeks. Instead of a blanket, she'd pulled on a robe and was covered from neck to pink toenails in the material he knew was called chenille.

Forcing his eyes from the lovely sight, he stepped out of the studio into the cab and reached for the door handle.

"By the way, where's your brother? The locator said he was in your truck." He was late checking in per his schedule.

"He's at the diner, waiting for me to meet him. He's allowed to go there by himself. You might check the GPS location again. It's probably showing he's ten feet from my truck. I am parked behind the building."

He needed to kiss that smirk off her face. Damn it. He gritted his teeth and nodded.

Yeah, her brother could go to prearranged appointments and even to the grocery store and diner, but he'd rather Devlin was out of downtown. It would be safer for all concerned until the trial.

After glancing around for the last time, he said, "I suggest you get someone to trap the mouse. It wouldn't help your brother any if you got arrested for disturbing the peace, especially if you climb over your next rescuer wearing only bra and panties."

She squealed, this time not from fright but anger.

Just as he started to close the door a red stiletto shoe flew by his head and landed on the pavement. He laughed. No sooner than he slammed the door closed, he saw the shoe's mate hit the window.

Chapter Six

The next day, Molly felt like she'd been placed in a washing machine during the spin cycle, and probably looked it too as she sat in a booth and ordered breakfast. Between being awoken at three in the morning by her brother's loud singing and gracelessness as he made himself at home in her studio sleeper, and replaying the memories of what she'd done with J.T., she'd given up sleeping by six and walked over to Bill's Diner.

She couldn't believe how she'd acted. Once again, he probably believed she was some sex-starved brainless female. Why did she act like that with him and only him? The few other special men she'd cared about, she'd been in control, taking her time before allowing them access to her body. But with J.T., all her finesse went out the window. She was fourteen years old again, begging him for his attention. Why him? She didn't need a hero.

"Hi, Molly."

The deep voice brought her head up, masochistically hoping it was J.T. She sighed. Nope. Eddie McDonald's voice had deepened since she'd last seen him in high school.

The khaki uniform, that looked so good on the sheriff, hung on Eddie's skinny frame.

"How you doing, Eddie?" She took a sip of her orange juice. "So when did you join the sheriff's office?"

He slid onto the bench across from her. "I'm doing okay. I went through the academy about three years ago. Remember my cousin Brooke?"

She nodded, realizing he would be a good source to find out what made J.T. tick and why he kept turning her down.

"Well, she'd decided to go through the academy and wanted someone she knew to go with her. I've always looked out for her, you know, since she came to live with me and my parents. Anyway, I went and found out I liked it. You wouldn't believe the guns and equipment I get to use, especially since J.T. became sheriff. You know he used to be with the FBI and knows all about that type of stuff. Anyway, he has whipped the department into shape and has even gotten us recognition for being one of the most efficient small county forces in Alabama."

She recognized hero worship when she heard it and Eddie had a bad case. He would brag about his hero, telling her all the good things about J.T. and nothing bad. Not that she wanted to use any of the information to hurt anyone. She only wanted to understand the man.

"You want a cup of coffee and a cinnamon roll?" She waved at the waitress walking by, hoping if he was eating and drinking, he would think nothing about the questions she'd ask. Friends always talked while they drank a cup of coffee or ate a snack. Right?

"Yeah. That would be great." He smiled and leaned back giving her a look that told her he misunderstood the offer completely. But first things first. For the moment, she would encourage his conversation, and later discourage his interest. Somehow.

Once the waitress placed the rolls on the table, Molly pushed the plate nearer to the deputy. She tried to think of a way to keep Eddie talking about J.T.

"It sure was a shame what happened to J.T.'s dad," he said.

That was easy. Almost too easy.

Eddie stuffed a piece of roll in his mouth, icing dripping down his chin, making him look like the sweet kid from elementary she remembered.

She took a bite of her eggs and swallowed, trying to keep from looking so anxious. "From what I've heard, he and his brother had a hard time growing up with no mother and a dad that drank every penny he made."

"Then you didn't hear. Before his brother died, Brandon accused his dad of killing their mother and burying her out in the field behind the old rental they lived in on Rose Trail Road." He swiped at his chin and took another bite.

Rose Trail Road, situated on the poor side of town near the mill, was where everyone mostly minded their own business. If anyone had seen something strange, like a man burying a large black garbage bag, they would turn a blind eye and never admit they saw a thing.

"Well, did his dad confess when J.T. arrested him?" She hated to think how hard it would be on J.T. to handcuff his own dad.

He looked away and began to run his finger along the edge of his plate.

"Eddie?" she prompted.

His dark gaze returned to meet hers. "Three years ago, J.T. heard his dad was living in Woodlawn, a suburb in the eastern part of Birmingham, and went looking for him. He didn't find him. But after his brother's death, J.T. had sections of the field dug up behind his old house and cadaver dogs brought in to search around the neighborhood. Nothing turned up."

"That has to be hard on him. It sounds like his brother lied," she said more to herself than the deputy across from her.

Brandon had always given her the creeps, and to think, he'd been considered the good brother. From what she'd heard growing up, that only happened because J.T. took the blame for most of Brandon's pranks.

The deputy glanced at her and quickly looked away. What was going on? Why was he so nervous? He had more to say.

"Come on. Tell me what you're holding back." She smiled, hoping he would relax enough to tell her the rest.

He cleared his throat. "Were you aware that your dad and old Harry, J.T.'s dad, had dated your mother when they were teenagers?" Eyebrows raised, he waited for her reaction. "That's why they feuded for so many years," he added as if it clarified everything.

She sat back and stared at him. Talk about unexpected. No one had ever mentioned that.

"Sorry. I thought you knew," he said, taking a sip of his coffee.

Nodding several times, she gave herself a moment to recover. "Hey, stuff like that happens a lot. Anyway, everyone has a past, including my parents. Go ahead and tell me more."

She worked at keeping her mind on track instead of sliding back into time and understanding why her dad was so furious the night J.T. explained her misbehavior. Big Joe had rarely cared what she'd done before. Of course, a lot of things had changed since then, including her dad pushing her at J.T. to obtain her brother's release. Thankfully, he was out of jail now and her dad no longer mentioned the sheriff. It had been bad enough keeping J.T. off her mind without her dad adding to it.

"Your dad was the one who ran Harry out of town."

"Why did he wait so long?" she asked, a little surprised. How did Eddie know all of this and she didn't?

"I have no idea. Before he left, I saw Harry. He was stone-cold sober. In fact, from what I heard, he'd stopped drinking for more than a month. No one could remember him doing anything like that before."

Talk about drama. Why did her dad's name pop up in every—

"Hey, what are you doing? Giving information about your brother to the enemy again?" Raymond the Weasel stood next to the table glaring at Eddie.

Crap! She covered her heart and took a deep breath. He'd startled her. "What do you want, Weasel?" Molly hoped her dad's lawyer would walk away so Eddie would continue with his story.

"You and I need to talk about your brother."

"No matter what you and Dad believe, I'm not my brother's keeper. He did okay without me for over five years. He'll do fine now." If only she believed what she told Raymond.

Her attention drifted over to Eddie. His eyes shone bright with interest. Her first instinct was to shout her brother's innocence. Then she reconsidered. Maybe it would be best to leave with Raymond and see what he wanted to discuss. She didn't need him asking any questions about their conversation.

"Excuse me, Eddie."

When she got down to it, she loved her brother. Until he understood the answers he searched for were not found at the bottom of a whiskey bottle, she needed to stick around and help.

As soon as they emerged from the diner and turned the corner at the back of the building, Molly stopped and glared at Weasel. Like she thought, his beady little eyes had been staring at her jean-clad butt.

"What's so important that you had to interrupt my breakfast with a friend?" Hands on her hips, she dared him to let his gaze drop to her breasts. Her knee itched to slam his weasel-sized dick.

"Your daddy said you're to bring your truck and park it on Magnolia Farms behind the house. Then he can keep an eye on your brother. Once you do that, you're to make nice with the sheriff." His leer said what kind of nice he meant.

She narrowed her eyes. "Did Big Joe really say the last part or did you?"

"We discussed the danger of your brother shooting someone else and how it would be nice to have the sheriff on our side. Plus it sure would be helpful if the sheriff testified that your brother was an upstanding citizen. So far all our overtures to ensure that happens have been turned down." Weasel stepped nearer.

She felt her face flush. "First, as Devlin's lawyer, you should know he didn't shoot anyone. In fact, I hope to God you have a private detective looking for the real killer as we know our esteemed sheriff will not. Second, are you saying since you and Dad can't bribe him with money, you two plan to use me in finding a way to blackmail him?"

"Blackmail. No." He shook his head as he gave a greasy little grin. "The man doesn't visit prostitutes, married women, underage girls or boys. He's so squeaky clean it's sickening. He must lead a terribly dull life."

A shiver of disgust ran down her spine. She hated to imagine what Raymond thought was exciting.

"Then what do..." She noticed the leer on his face "No! There's no way. Even if I could persuade him to...you know...to go to bed with me, I can tell you right now, he won't be led around by his...you know." She couldn't believe she was having this conversation.

Face hot from embarrassment at having this discussion with...with Raymond the Weasel of all people, she covered her mouth with a hand.

He took another step closer and leaned down. "I can show you how it's done." As one of his hands brushed a breast, her knee landed between his legs. Later, she would describe his scream like a cat in heat.

Shortly after, she slammed the truck's cab door, cranked up the big rig, and stomped on the gas, shifting gears as she pulled away from behind the diner. The few miles to Magnolia Farms gave her enough time to organize her speech for her dad.

As soon as she reached the mansion and the back door banged shut behind her, she started her march through the kitchen.

"Hey, little girl, where are you going in such a huff?" Her mom closed the pantry door behind her and stepped into the kitchen.

"Dad did it again." Molly barely held onto her anger. She didn't want her mom to talk her into seeing her dad's side in the situation.

The older woman laughed. "Your dad does so much. I can guess what he did, but why don't you tell me?"

Taking a deep breath, she concentrated on keeping her

words rational and tone even. "He's pushing me at J.T. again. He wants me to sleep with the sheriff and convince him that Devlin's innocent. You and I both know Devlin didn't shoot anyone." Did she sound whiny?

"Honey, let's sit down." Her mom pulled out a chair and pointed at the one next to her. Once Molly was settled, her mom asked, "Did your dad say this to you?"

"No. But he sent Weasel to do his dirty work." Molly already felt the heat from her anger dissipating.

"Your dad and I love you and we'd never have you associate with someone you don't like." Her mom patted her hand. "Sweetie, we need to protect Devlin and if it's in our power, then we should do it."

Unmoving, Molly stared at her mom. Her chest ached from the knowledge her parents would sacrifice their daughter to protect their son. "So you want me to sleep with the sheriff too." She slid her hand out from under her mom's.

The older woman shook her head. "You misunderstand again."

"I don't think I misunderstood anything, Mom. I just can't believe you expect me to do this." Maybe she should jump in her truck and leave Sand City. Without even realizing she'd done so, she stood, knocking over her chair.

"Molly Lynn Hicks! You sit back down!" Her mom used her drill sergeant tone in her little-girl voice. How could anyone not respond? Plus she'd used the dreaded full name. Using her first name or her first and last name was bad enough, but all three meant a person was in the worst kind of trouble. Molly picked up her chair and sat. Her mom cocked one gray eyebrow. "Are you telling me that you're not interested in J.T. Rogan?"

Feeling hot and cold, Molly couldn't believe she was

having this conversation with her mom. "What happened to your opinion that I wasn't J.T.'s type?"

"I was wrong."

"Why?" Molly bit her lip and kept her eyes on the woman across from her. *Please, please say I'm woman enough for him.*

Her mom sighed. "I've seen the way he looks at you. When you were fourteen and so in love with the town's bad boy, I'd worried J.T. was planning to use you to annoy your dad."

Molly sighed. Why did her parents believe a boy could never be interested in her for just herself?

Leaning over, her mom grabbed her hands and continued. "Listen. When he returned and became sheriff, I was certain he would try to make our life miserable. But he never did. I believe he's a good man like his dad was before his mom disappeared. Now he's only trying to follow the law, but we need him to understand your brother is innocent, and the sheriff's office needs to be looking for the real killer. You can help us by convincing him how important it is to look at other suspects."

The pleading look in her mom's eyes had her wondering, was she being selfish by thinking only of her own pride? Or was she doing what they wanted because she had her parents' blessing in running after the only man she'd ever love? No matter how much of an asshole he could be, especially after the way he kissed her.

Molly stood. "I'll think about it." She leaned over and kissed her mom's cheek before heading out the door.

Life was so much simpler on the road, hauling stuff from one city to the next, stopping for food and gas along the way and watching for crazy drivers. She'd made lots of friends and rarely had to fight the loneliness that often plagued long-haul drivers.

Did she really have to think about it? She'd wanted J.T. since the day he'd saved her from the boys in the park. And it was cemented the day she'd heard he'd gotten tattoos as a graduation present from high school. At the time, no other teenage boy she'd known had more than one tattoo. Of course, for J.T., it helped to have a friend who was a tattoo artist. She always wanted to know how many he had and where. The day she'd been sitting in jail and he'd stood before her with only a sling covering his chest, the sexy sight had almost made it worth being there. Maybe circumstances would let her find out what every inch of his tattooed skin looked like.

Well, time to find J.T.

She skipped down the back steps and headed toward the farm's general service Jeep.

Chapter Seven

"Well, do you think she'll do it?" Big Joe walked into the kitchen and stood beside his wife. They watched as their daughter jumped into the old Jeep everyone on the farm used and flipped down the visor, catching the keys in her hand.

"She's loved that boy most of her life. Yeah. I think she will." She looped her arm through his and leaned against him. "But are we right to do this?"

"You know Harry would've been tickled." He held his breath for a moment when he realized how he'd slipped, hoping she hadn't caught his error. He squeezed her arm and kissed her on the cheek. "If it doesn't work out, she'll at least get him out of her system and move on. Then maybe she'll settle down and give us some grandbabies."

"I wish Harry would come back to Sand City and see them together," she murmured.

He closed his eyes. Harry wouldn't be coming back. Dead men don't come back to life.

Chapter Eight

Within a second of J.T. shifting into reverse, the passenger's door opened and Molly slid into the seat, throwing her backpack-style purse onto the floorboard.

"Damn, Molly, what do you think you're doing?" Crazy woman. He slammed on the brakes and turned to glare at her. "It's too early in the morning for me to deal with you."

"Gee, thanks." Her hair stuck out every which-a-way from her braid, giving her a sexy just-rolled-out-of-bed look he wished he'd been somehow involved in creating. "We need to talk."

"I'm on duty and about to make a call. It'll have to wait." He liked how her eyes flashed whenever she was mad or excited. The other morning in her sleeper, after he'd kissed her, a light show had been set off in those beautiful dark eyes.

"It can wait for a little while." She grinned and pulled the seatbelt across her mouthwatering chest, clicked and waited, staring straight ahead. "But I'm going with you to make sure you don't try to give me the slip."

The slip? She was a strange woman. He frowned. Why couldn't she find other people to pick on? He didn't need her kind of trouble.

She kept smiling as she peered through the windshield.

He shook his head. What the hell? His plans centered on visiting Franny Osborne and going over her newest complaint. So it was unlikely Molly would interfere. Maybe her presence would prevent Franny from trying to grab his butt. Nah. It was best she stayed in the vehicle. Of course, he wouldn't mind if Molly grabbed his butt.

Damn it. Internally flinching, he squeezed his eyes shut for a moment. Why would he ask for that kind of trouble? Big Joe would throw a fit. J.T. could only hope to survive with all his extremities attached, unless her daddy had something to gain from it. He took in her profile, liking the fresh girl-next-door looks she possessed. What a shame she was a Hicks.

"Times a wasting," she urged, brushing hair from her face with shaking fingers.

Molly was nervous? Maybe that was a clue to what she had up her sleeve. Even in jail, he'd never noticed her being afraid or worried. Mad, but never nervous.

"Okay. But keep quiet and then afterwards we'll talk." He eased out of the parking space and headed down the highway to the Osborne place.

"Sure thing."

He expected an argument, but she did what he'd asked.

After a few miles, he sneaked a quick look her way. Still grinning as she stared straight ahead. If he didn't know better, he'd say she was enjoying herself. Her carefree demeanor softened her face and reminded him of the shapely teenager he'd admired so long ago. Her sassy mouth and determination to get her own way were welcomed leftovers from that time.

He'd always stayed away from Molly Hicks and the other daughters of wealthy families in Sand County, but she'd been relentless. When she'd waylaid him behind the school gym after his graduation and kissed the hell out of him, his defenses had dropped. She'd stuck a hand into his pants and grabbed his cock. Such an expert, she'd stroked and squeezed, bringing him to the edge of climax. Then someone shouted. They'd promptly jumped apart. Too late. They had been seen, and within twenty-four hours, her daddy had dragged her away to a private girls' school. Two days later, Big Joe had the authorities run J.T. out of town.

He'd almost felt sorry for her back then. Sure, her daddy had been the richest man in Sand City, probably the whole county, but he could tell she wanted someone to love her. Why she latched on to him, he wasn't sure. Maybe it had something to do with his being the bad boy in town and defying her daddy.

As he turned into the Highland Crest neighborhood, he glanced over at Molly. She was staring at his wrist. His sleeve had moved up slightly, showing the tip of a dragon's claw, one of the many tattoos covering his arm beneath the shirt. On his eighteenth birthday, he'd gotten the first one, a Celtic symbol encircling his bicep. By the time he reached twenty he had one arm covered with all types of mystical signs and the large dragon. Before his twenty-first, he'd changed his major to criminal justice and decided more tattoos would never help his career and stopped.

Some of the good, older people of Sand City had a problem with his tattoos. They believed only criminals and carny people wore them. Hell, for that matter, some had a problem with *that Rogan boy* being sheriff. They expected the son of the town's drunk to royally screw up, or at the least slam back booze like his old man.

On thinking of his constituents, he remembered Franny Osborne was complaining again about teenagers holding wild parties in the empty Farley place. Eddie had visited with her last week and posted a couple of "No Trespassing" signs outside the old house but apparently more teenagers had broken in.

Franny had insisted the sheriff come to investigate. First, he needed to talk with her again.

J.T. turned into the wide circular drive and parked near the front door. Her Tudor-style home seemed out of place in the midst of a neighborhood of stately Victorian-style houses. That was Franny. She had a style of her own.

"Stay here. It shouldn't take long." Without looking Molly's way, he slammed the door and strode down the sidewalk. He heard the passenger's door close—he shook his head in frustration—Molly stepped up beside him on the front step.

"You must be hard of hearing," he remarked dryly as he knocked.

She merely grinned and waggled her eyebrows. Her show of meekness during the ride over and continued quietness worried him. This was not the Molly he knew. What was she up to?

"Come on in, Evil." Franny Osborne opened the door wider, smiling and waving them into her house. The woman was no more than five-one with dyed honey-blond hair and still had a pretty good figure for a seventy-eight-year-old.

"Please call me J.T., ma'am." Evil had been his nickname growing up as he'd been known for pulling pranks.

"And it's about time you called me Franny." Eyebrows

raised, her gaze moved to Molly. "Who's this beautiful amazon with you?"

"Molly Hicks." Molly held out her hand. Instead of shaking her hand, the woman clasped it and pulled her closer.

"Oh, yes. Big Joe and Lisa's daughter." The older woman held Molly's wrist tightly and leaned over her palm. "What a beautiful love line you have. It shows that you met your true love when you were awfully young." She released her hold. "You're so lucky to have so much time with him. I only had thirty years with my Harold before he died from a heart attack. We met when we were both in our forties. What an energetic lover he was. He died when we were going at it like two wild monkeys in—"

"Ms. Osborne, uh, Franny, you called complaining about the noise next door." J.T. felt his face heat up. Hell, that woman could make a whore blush.

"Yes. I heard shouting. This isn't like the other times when I heard loud music and screams." She reclined on her white sectional couch, moving a sleepy white miniature poodle next to her while another climbed in her lap. "You two have a seat." She indicated the other end of the long couch. As she waited, her fingers combed the dog's curly fur. The poodles watched them with beady black eyes. J.T. loved dogs, but there was something about the little creepy buggers.

"Screams? You never mentioned screams before." Everywhere he looked white upholstered furniture and carpet blinded him. Between the crystal chandeliers and gold accents, he felt as if he'd stepped into a little girl's jewelry box.

"I didn't? I could've sworn I told that cute deputy of yours. What's his name?"

"Eddie?" J.T. eased down on the end of a chaise lounge sporting cupids on the upholstery across from the older woman. Molly sat on the edge where Franny had pointed.

"Yes. That's the guy," said Franny. "And the other one. The female."

"Brooke?" He'd need to reread the report when he got back to the station.

"Yeah. That one too. I'm so sorry to hear about Mike. He was always so patient and had the sexiest walk I've ever seen on a man." Franny pressed her red manicured nails to her lips.

J.T. began to cough. He wasn't too sure how Mike would've felt about that. Then again, everyone expected Franny's outrageous comments. In her younger days, before moving to Sand City, she'd been a sex therapist. At least that was what she claimed.

"Did you see anything different this time?"

"I didn't see any souped-up cars or motorcycles, if that's what you mean." Franny turned her attention to Molly. "Are you helping the sheriff today?"

"No. I'm doing a ride-along," Molly smoothly said.

J.T. hid the flash of anger shooting through him. He didn't like how easily she lied. Yet he had to admit it was sort of the truth, if you omitted the official application. Less mess than explaining her presence. Considering he had no idea why she insisted on coming with him in the first place. Whatever she wanted to say to him could've waited for his return.

The older woman's eyes lit up with curiosity. "You drive that big truck across the country."

"Yes, ma'am." Molly glanced at J.T., probably wishing he'd save her from the older woman's nosiness. Yeah, sure. If she'd stayed in the SUV like he'd told her, she wouldn't be in such a predicament.

"You don't look like you're interested in women."

"Pardon?"

"Well, I assumed you're a lesbian since you drive a huge rig."

"Driving a truck has nothing to do with a woman being gay or not, Mrs. Osborne. It's only a male-dominated job that pays well." Molly glanced at J.T. again and blushed.

Franny looked at J.T. and then back at Molly. Her eyebrows rose. "Of course." Her grin grew as she absent-mindedly rubbed the back of a poodle. "You're still single, aren't you, J.T.?

Deciding now would be a good time to escape before Franny began matchmaking, he stood. "I'll go next door and check out things. They're probably gone now, but I'll make sure everything's okay. Maybe Mayor Quinn will finally arrange for the old house to be sold or torn down." Of course, the mayor would first check to see how she could benefit. Mayor Rachael Quinn looked out for herself first and the community who voted her in last.

"That would be a sad shame to destroy it. The house is over a hundred years old and one of the first mansions built in the area." Franny followed them to the door with the two dogs darting around her legs in excitement. "I was told a moonshiner built the place. I have to say if that was true, he was rather successful."

The older woman followed behind them, rattling on about the history of the neighborhood. She could drive a preacher to cussing with her chatter and salacious comments. Franny rarely kept her mind on one subject for long.

As soon as he stepped outside, he sighed. By the time he

reached his SUV, he realized the older woman had caught Molly by the arm. Whatever she was saying had brought a bright pink to Molly's cheeks.

He never imagined someone like Molly would blush so much. For goodness' sake, she had been shameless as a teenager, and who knew what she'd done while traveling alone throughout the U.S. for the past five years. Then again, Franny had made him blush too, and he was long past embarrassment for a decade or more.

When Molly climbed inside and closed the door, her face had regained its usual honey color.

"What did Franny have to say?" J.T. asked.

Chapter Nine

No way would she tell J.T. what the old woman said. Franny Osborne had a wicked mind. One that Molly found fascinating as she could imagine herself being the same way in the distant future.

"Just being her usual crazy self," she said in a bored tone.

Hopefully, he wouldn't ask for more information. She knew it would be days, if not months before she erased from her mind what the older woman said about J.T.

Shortly after they left Franny's, they turned into the next driveway. A towering mimosa stood sentry near the mailbox and sported a large "No Trespassing" sign on its trunk. The two houses possessed long driveways from the winding road, but as the properties were side by side, loud parties in one could still disturb the other.

J.T. parked in front of the old Victorian-style home and pulled out a key from his pocket. Marked in red was the name Farley on the white tag. He'd come prepared. Several families in and near Sand City would leave their keys with the sheriff's office in case something happened while away on vacation or waiting for an empty house to sell.

"Stay here while I check inside and I mean it this time. There could be some kids sleeping off a bender from partying all night. Who knows what I'll find? No one has lived in it for at least six years." J.T. left the engine on so the air conditioner could continue to run, keeping Molly cool in the spring heat.

She appreciated his thoughtfulness with the air. Though she'd rather follow, by the irritated look he shot her way, she figured she'd already pushed her luck. So she relaxed against the headrest and watched him stride toward the house. The sight of his long-legged walk with a manly shift of his duty belt and narrow hips replayed in her mind what Franny had whispered in her ear. "Mike wasn't the only one with a sexy walk." Franny had nodded toward J.T., strutting down her sidewalk to his SUV. "Uh-huh, sex toy walking."

Gaze still on the man, she leaned forward and tipped the front vent with one trembling finger toward her face, cooling her hot cheeks. Franny was so right. A fine sex toy for sure. She wished she could stash him near her bed.

Within minutes, J.T. came striding out of the front door, his face darker than the Warrior River during a storm. He jerked open the driver's door and—without a word to her— picked up the two-way radio's speaker-mic and began talking to Janet at the sheriff's station. Molly wasn't sure of half what he'd said as most was in some type of police lingo, but she'd pieced together that he'd found a body in the house.

"Who is it?" If she hadn't seen her brother passed out at her parents' house before leaving to find J.T., she'd be panicking.

"I've seen him somewhere before but I can't remember where or when. He hasn't been dead long, maybe an hour. Body is warm. Rigor mortis hasn't set in. As soon as everyone gets here, I'll have Eddie drive you home." He looked into her eyes. His dark gaze pulled at her, waiting for a reaction.

What had he expected? When she remained quiet, his forehead wrinkled. He'd anticipated her to argue? What kind of women had he associated with? Apparently, types who loved arguing with a fence post. Despite whatever he thought, she wasn't the kind. The man took his job seriously and death was as serious as it got. Besides, from what she'd seen and heard since returning to town he hadn't changed much since he was a teenager. Hardheaded as ever.

When he continued to stare, saying nothing, she couldn't stand it any longer. "What?"

"You're nothing like I remember."

"Is that good or bad?" She liked how his eyes heated whenever he looked at her so intently. Nothing else on his face gave away his thoughts, only his eyes.

"I'm not sure."

Was he like other men she dealt with? Believing only a man should drive an eighteen-wheeler. Not being feminine enough. To her, shopping was a chore. In and out of the stores with only what she needed was her custom. Haircuts and manicures were for special occasions. She wore minimal makeup, and blue jeans or khaki shorts were the norm. Yet she did love dangling earrings and strappy shoes with four-inch heels whenever she went on a date. The last one was vague. Six months ago? Maybe a little longer.

For goodness' sake, driving a truck turned off some men. Even if one was interested in her, she found she could be terribly picky. She certainly didn't want to sleep with every handsome face she met, though there had been only a few. And then there was J.T. She hated admitting she'd spent the last few years trying to forget him, but apparently she was a one-man woman.

The same man who had been run out of town because of her. The same man she'd shot.

That wasn't the way to go about showing a man she loved him.

Chapter Ten

Hours later, the sun was still barely up. Mid-April in Alabama didn't see the sun set until around seven o'clock. So Molly sat underneath a large oak tree, watching the EMTs load the body into the back of the ambulance. The dead man was beyond help, but his body was going to the hospital where the county's medical examiner performed autopsies.

During all the excitement, J.T. and Eddie had forgotten she was still there. She found all of the comings and goings too fascinating to bring their attention back to her.

As soon as the ambulance drove off, Eddie stepped out of the house and waved—he hadn't forgotten her, how sweet —before getting behind the steering wheel of his marked sedan and driving off with two state troopers following close behind. Another deputy followed the other personnel from the state. They hauled out the gathered evidence and drove away. Then she was alone with J.T. frowning at her—uh-oh —from where he stood next to his SUV. He'd moved his automobile by a stand of trees that blocked the view of the houses near by.

"Why in the hell are you still here?" he barked.

"I came with you. So I figured you can take me back to the station," she said in an even tone. He only thought he could intimidate her. She'd lived with a pro in the art for years. Besides, they hadn't talked about what she planned.

He stared at her a moment longer and then nodded. "Get in."

She stood and wiped dried grass and leaves from her butt as she slowly walked by him, grinning. His hand grabbed her arm and pulled her next to him. The back of his hand pressed against her breast. Awareness tingled from that one breast to her complete body. There was no way he couldn't know where he touched her. She wanted to purr and rub against that large, strong man.

"What do you want from me?" he asked, his voice rough with dark emotions.

A shiver went through her.

When his dark gaze lowered to her lips, she did what any sane woman in love would do, she whispered, "I want you."

His mouth took hers. Not a gentle, slow torturous kiss, but an open mouth, tongue playing, mind-blowing kiss. He nipped at her bottom lip and sank into her mouth again, tasting, exploring. She tilted her head, her response equal to his. She wanted more and rose to her tiptoes.

He pushed her against his vehicle's hood. She laughed as she felt his hips rest on hers. Joy shot through her as he showed her how much he wanted her in return. His hands covered her breasts, massaging and pinching the tips in a rhythm that matched their hips dancing against each other.

Unable to resist, she shifted and slipped her hand between them to cup the hard bulge in his pants and squeezed. So happy his body wanted hers as much as she wanted his, she sighed and stroked. Pure need clouded her mind.

A breeze tickled her breasts.

He'd pushed her T-shirt up and unclipped her bra. Wow, he was fast. He lifted her off the ground by her waist until his mouth reached one taut nipple. She had no care if anyone was watching. She bit her lip to keep from screaming as she clutched his shoulders. The mixed pleasure of his lips, teeth, and tongue, and the knowledge he lifted her as if she weighed nothing, brought a throbbing between her legs she hadn't experienced in a long, long time. His crazed attention confirmed J.T. truly desired her. She bit the side of her mouth to stop from shouting in happiness.

Was she about to explode without J.T. even touching her between her legs?

He shifted, placing her cloth-covered ass on the hot metal, keeping his mouth on a breast, sucking hard, while one hand deftly unsnapped, unzipped her jeans and then shoved them to her ankles. Without pause, he slipped his hand beneath her panties and jabbed two fingers into her slick folds.

They both moaned.

"You're so damn wet and tight," he growled as he shifted to press his thumb against the hard little knot.

Her body arched as he thrust his fingers into her heat. Her nails dug into his uniform-covered back, wishing he was shirtless, craving the feel of warm flesh to rub and kiss.

A couple more thrusts and a sharp pull of his mouth on her breast pushed her over the edge into a pulsating flow. Limp, she wrapped her arms around his neck. He licked the tender nipple as if in apology and then held her, breathing heavily, saying nothing.

That was okay. What was there to say? She was where she belonged. In his arms.

57

Loving The Small-Town Hero

That was okay. What was there to say? She was where she belonged. In his arms.

Chapter Eleven

Where was his brain?

J.T. gingerly shifted himself behind his zipper. Damn, he ached so badly. If only they were in a bed or a couch but hell no to the back seat of his SUV. He hungered to finish what he'd started. When she came apart in his arms, he awoke from his lust-induced haze. They were outside where anyone could drive up and catch them in an awkward moment.

He could claim after seeing death the automatic reaction was to seek life and comfort from any warm body. Was that what he sought from Molly and nothing more? Bullshit.

After the last several days, and in particular the last few hours, his mind and body were exhausted. Then to see her sitting patiently and so prettily with those freckles shining on her lovely face as she smiled up at him, it had been the last straw. His need for her snapped and he took what he so badly wanted. Well, not quite. Touching and tasting her was a close second to what he really wanted to do. Fuck her. Thrusting inside that hot, soft body and hearing her shout his name. Yeah, he was a Neanderthal.

That couldn't happen. For the moment, he would have to deal with her and the aftermath.

Would she expect more from him? Her flushed face and lopsided grin had him hating how it must be with them. He couldn't meet her expectations when it came to a relationship. What kind of husband would he make? Would the townspeople tolerate a Rogan with a Hicks? Would they believe he got and kept his job because he was fucking the richest man in the county's daughter? No matter that she had arrived months after the election. Did he really care?

Didn't matter. Presently, he needed to keep his distance until all of the craziness died down. What a sorry pick of words with all the people dying around him.

With a shake of his head, he released the woman in his arms and started to straighten his clothes. Molly probably sensed his mood, as she pulled up her jeans, reclipped her bra before tugging on her T-shirt, all in silence. Her somber face gave away little of what she was thinking.

Time to return their relationship to nothing more than friendly acquaintances, if that was possible.

Who was he kidding? Every time he was around the woman, his hands roamed over her, especially under her clothes.

His stomach rumbled. "Since you were stuck here and missed lunch, how about I buy us dinner at Bill's?"

Her smile grew all the way to her eyes, showing how pleased she was with his offer. "How about picking up our meal there and taking it to your place?" She reached out to touch his face.

He drew back his head. Hurt flashed across her face. His gut tightened. He hated upsetting her once again.

There were so many reasons why they didn't belong together. Not only was he in a stressful job with a high rate of divorce, suicide, and alcoholism, but he'd rather avoid stirring up Big Joe's anger. Why would she want to be with him anyway? What was she up to? He'd arrested her brother. He was the son of a murdering, alcoholic father. While with the FBI, he'd shot his own brother. Sure in self-defense, but what kind of person did that make him? What woman would want to be involved with a man who had a family like his?

"This was all a mistake. I got carried away and you were available...it would be best if we're not alone again after today." He clasped her arm and walked her around to the other side of his SUV. "Get in."

She jerked her arm out of his hand and climbed into the passenger's seat, slamming the door so hard it rocked the vehicle.

Good. He needed her mad at him. Then he'd keep his hands off her.

As soon as he slid behind the steering wheel and turned the ignition, he glanced her way. Thankfully, she appeared collected.

He turned his gaze ahead. He sped down the drive and turned onto the country road.

"J.T.," she said in a cool tone.

"Yeah?"

"You can drop me off at the station near my Jeep. I'll pass on the food." Her voice was low and even.

He glanced at her. Cheeks red, she obviously was trying to hold her temper.

"I thought you had something to tell me."

She shrugged. "Not really important now. Mainly, that Dad and Mom had hoped we would hook up."

He jerked the SUV to the side of the road and slammed on his brakes.

"What did you say?" He turned with one arm on the steering wheel and the other along the back of the seat.

"My parents believe if we became lovers you would take Devlin's side and start looking for the real killer." She started in a soft tone but with each word she became louder. "I figured it wouldn't work, however, I wanted you badly enough to go along with their plans. But I see that my first inclination was correct. You might lust for me, but you have no feelings for me at all. In fact, from what I've seen, you have no feelings for anyone. The FBI sucked it out of you. You're nothing but a government robot with a penis." She opened the door and stepped out before he could move. "So never mind. I'll walk." She shouted the last and then closed the door so hard he was surprised it remained on its hinges.

He shifted the SUV into drive and followed her down the road, keeping to the side, out of the traffic. Her braid whipped from side to side as she tramped down the shoulder of the road.

She was wrong. He felt a lot of things for her, but he knew he wasn't who she needed. She needed a man with a regular family background and a nine-to-five job. A man that would show her family how important she was in their lives and how she should be respected. He couldn't give her that.

Her family had already proved they didn't respect him or their own daughter.

But he sure did like her spunk. He liked how she stood up to her family and told him off when he acted like a prick.

He watched as she adjusted her small backpack purse on her shoulder and kept walking. Not much farther along they came to a green highway sign notifying them Sand City was two miles ahead. As each car passed by, the drivers and passengers stared. This was a bad idea. With his marked vehicle following her, they were only encouraging negative gossip. He shook his head and hit the gas, pulling in front of her, and braked with tires squealing. He jumped out and grabbed her around the waist, tossing her over his shoulder. Despite her screaming curses, kicking, and pounding his back, he threw her in the backseat and locked her in.

"J.T., you let me out now! You can't arrest me! I've done nothing wrong and you know it!" She kicked the cage for emphasis.

"Molly, calm down. I haven't arrested you, only detained you for a few minutes. I'm hungry and didn't want to wait until you walked into town to eat." He smiled into the rearview mirror. That got her dander up real good. "Friends can eat together."

"I should've shot you through your cold heart." She huffed and crossed her arms, looking out the side window. "Yeah, right. Friends," she muttered.

The couple of miles to town passed quietly and J.T. was happy for the reprieve. He should just drop her off at her Jeep and leave it alone. But he needed to talk to her about how her dad and mom treated her. Someone needed to intervene. It wasn't like he was their favorite person and certainly not hers at the time being. So he had nothing to lose.

Then why did he feel like an asshole? Maybe because he needed her mouth around his cock more than he wanted food.

Chapter Twelve

What in the world was she doing there with him?

Molly looked around Bill's Diner and waved at a couple of the regulars she'd gotten to know since returning to town. Didn't J.T. understand eating dinner with her in front of God and everyone was like announcing to the town they were dating? No amount of swearing they were *just friends* would convince anyone, especially the two old gossips sitting in their favorite booth near the front door. Betsy Twilldale and Sue Marie Blackwood were the bane of Molly's existence since she was in elementary school. Anytime she skipped school or hung out with the wrong kind of friends, they would always be around the corner to catch her and tell her mom. Those two women could show the NSA a thing or two about gathering intel. The last few weeks she'd avoided them like the plague, but there they were staring at her and J.T.

"Who are you looking for?" J.T. took a bite of the diner's famous meatloaf.

"No one really. But you couldn't pick a worse time to

come. Everyone and his brother are here. It's date night! They'll think we're on a date." She nudged pieces of onion to the side and took a bite of onion-less meatloaf.

He lifted his glass and his Adam's apple slid up and down his muscular neck as he took large quenching swallows. Curling her fingers, she resisted the urge to stroke that part of him. Everything about the man was sexy. If only she could strip him and run her hands all over his body. She bet he'd like it too. But then again it would almost be like petting a tiger, dangerous and exhilarating at the same time.

He set his glass down. "Quit being paranoid. Those same gossips know your dad kicked me out of Sand City because of you."

"That's even worse," she said a bit too loudly, and then lowered her voice. "They'll start thinking we're some kind of Romeo and Juliet. I can tell you, I won't be taking any poison for you."

"He took the true poison. She stabbed herself."

A tough guy who knew Shakespeare?

No. It didn't matter what he knew about the old love stories. "You know what I mean. You're not worth dying for." She jabbed at the meat and mashed potatoes and stuffed her face. Deep inside, she didn't mean it, but he made her so angry. All he had to do was know a little Shakespeare and she got all mushy inside.

J.T. shook his head and chuckled.

Feeling ashamed of her outburst and wanting to change the subject, she cleared her throat. "When are you going to hear about the body?"

"Probably not for another week. Usually takes four to six weeks." They finished eating in silence until he shoved the plate to the side. "We've got company," he warned.

Molly looked up and there stood Sue Marie and Betsy.

The women were grinning big enough to burst their buttons. Obviously, they thought they had some new gossip.

"Mary and Luke said if I saw you today, Sheriff, to remind you about Jacob's birthday party tomorrow." Sue Marie turned to Molly and grinned, her round face shining. "And you come with him. You'll like Luke's wife. And I don't just say that because she's my step-daughter-in-law."

"Well, I would but—"

J.T. cut her off. "We'll be there."

"Humph! You better. I'm making the birthday cake, chocolate with buttercream icing. My mother's secret recipe." Betsy looked down her nose, and as she turned Molly caught the wink she gave J.T.

What in the world was the town coming to? How had J.T. gotten the two old biddies eating out of his hands? Too scary. Then again, those hands felt so good. She knew that for a fact. She squirmed in her seat remembering what they'd done in front of the Farley's house.

She pulled her attention back to the women as they walked off. "Why did you do that? For a man who only wants to be friends, you're making it hard for others to believe that." What was his game?

"Luke and Mary have been trying to fix me up with someone for the past year and I figured you owe me." He leaned back in the booth and placed one arm across the back as he stared at her, daring her to argue.

What else could she do? So she took the bait.

"Why?" She crossed her arms. The stance wasn't so much a warning about how stubborn she felt but more to hide the telltale sign of how the mere sight of his tattoos showing at the end of his sleeve cranked her engine.

"Well, there was that felony I didn't charge you with

when I let you out of jail." His crooked grin was completely sinful as he pointed to his shoulder.

"Yeah. You got me there. But I wonder how long I'll have to pay for that." She bit back her grin. How could she stay mad at someone so darn sexy? Plus, in a way, he was asking her out on a date. A date with sinfully naughty J.T. Rogan. Sure, sure, he was now a law officer, but deep inside he was still a bad boy.

"Probably as long as you live."

"That's what I was afraid of." She laughed with him. They sat staring at each other with what Molly figured was a stupid grin on her face and then about the time J.T. opened his mouth to say something, his cell phone rang.

"Yeah?" He listened for a few seconds. "I'm at Bill's Diner. It shouldn't take me but ten minutes to get there. Make sure he waits for me." He slipped the phone into his pocket and turned to her. "I've got to go. You behave. I'll pick you up tomorrow around eleven-thirty."

A moment of panic washed over her. "Pick up?" she asked to the empty side of the booth. He'd already reached the front door and in seconds was outside, racing across the parking lot to his SUV. "Crap! Now I've got to find a ride back to my Jeep." With a long sigh, she stared at the empty plate across from her and then her eyes widened. "The sorry son of..." she mumbled the last.

He'd stuck her with the check.

Chapter Thirteen

By one that Sunday morning, J.T. was bug-eyed tired. Special Agent in Charge Roy Reese had gone over all the evidence they'd pulled together about the dead body found in the Farley house.

It turned out, when Eddie had sent the details about the unidentified human remains to the National Crime Information Center, the FBI was already on the lookout for their missing special agent, Keith Hart. He'd disappeared about two weeks ago in the general area and their presumed fears were confirmed. There was no doubt he'd been murdered—too hard to commit suicide with a bullet to the back of the head and his hands and feet tied to a chair.

"I still want to know what your man was doing in my town." J.T. knew good and well he wouldn't receive any answers. During his time working with the FBI, they'd kept most of the key information from the local yokels. As the shoe was on the other foot—he being the yokel—he resented the hell out of their closed mouths.

"You know if I could, I would tell you everything. But there's a lot more going on than your office can handle. You keep us informed and we'll do the dirty work." Special Agent Reese closed up his laptop and shoved it into his briefcase.

In other words, J.T. should catch the chicken thieves but he needed to keep out of the FBI's way. He rolled his shoulders as he stood, not liking how it felt to be on the other side.

"I understand that you're trying to protect whatever Agent Hart was working on, but there's a possibility my deputy's death and his are connected." It didn't hurt to remind the man leaving his office how much of a stake the sheriff's office had in wanting the cases solved.

Roy hesitated at the front door. His wide shoulders slumped as if he was about to say something he'd rather not. Being a large man, he easily intimidated suspects by standing over them and glaring, but at the same time he handled victims' families with the same kind of ease. His sad puppy eyes and the small space between his front top teeth brought an odd comfort to those that needed it the most.

J.T. had always respected his former boss and hated there had to be a distance now.

"You know, J.T., if I could I would spill my guts to you, but it doesn't work that way. I'll tell you what I can as soon as we're certain about the suspect in Agent Hart's death." He opened the door and stopped again, looking over his shoulder. "Besides, don't you already have a suspect in Deputy Lindsey's death?"

"Yeah. Just some things don't add up."

Roy nodded and stared out the door. "They say death and taxes are the only certainties in life. Only thing is, people who say that don't work in law enforcement." Then he shut the door behind him.

What in the hell did he mean by that?

Too tired to think on it, J.T. pushed himself out of his chair and started locking up. He needed a few hours of sleep before picking up Molly tomorrow. He needed all his strength when it came to dealing with her. When he said she owed him and the date would be a partial payment, he'd almost laughed out loud. She'd looked so cute sitting in the booth with her mouth open and eyes wide.

Then it hit him.

Damn it. He left Molly stranded at the diner and forgot to tell her to put their dinner on his tab.

Boy, oh boy, tomorrow afternoon was going to be interesting. He chuckled as he headed home.

Chapter Fourteen

"Com'on, Sis, quit shaking the truck."

Molly pulled out another outfit and looked at Devlin in the upper bunk. Considering how drunk her brother was when his buddies dropped him off earlier, she was surprised when he made it up the short ladder without breaking his neck. She had no idea why he decided to sleep in the top bunk this time. She sure didn't want to know.

"You know this is my truck and you can go into the house anytime you want. There's a large suite of rooms waiting for you." She shook her head and pulled on her sixth, or was it seventh, top. The peach blouse brought out the gold in her tan and the highlights in her hair. Okay. She could live with it.

Some moments, she wished she was model thin but then she might as well wish for J.T. to fall madly in love with her. She'd have better luck in starving herself. Like never. Besides, after she'd hit twenty-five, she came to the conclusion whoever she dated had to like her as she was or they could hit the road.

Her brother leaned over the side of the bunk, one arm hanging down. "Where ya going?"

She looked up. Like he'd been told all his life, he was a handsome devil, and that he was, for sure. He'd gotten their mother's emerald-green eyes that sparkled with mischief most of the time. And though neither parent had natural blond-tipped hair, their mom claimed her father had been blond-headed until the day he lost it to radiation treatment for lung cancer. So with her dad's height and trim build and their grandfather's hair, Devlin was destined to be the so-called golden boy of the family.

Molly shook her head. Her brother had no idea how lucky he was and instead of lapping up parental approval, over the last year he did everything he could to make people regret caring for him. Yet he continued to receive their parents' love and support without fail. Go figure. Truth be told, she hadn't given up on him either. How could she? He was her brother.

"To a birthday party with the sheriff."

He winked at her and gave a lopsided grin. Oh, goodness, she did love him. He'd always be her sweet little brother, taking up for her with their parents, making sure she was treated as fairly as possible. Like the time her parents decided for her to wait until she was eighteen to receive her first car. They claimed they could get a better price if they bought two Mustangs at the same time. The months leading up to her sixteenth birthday, she kept telling herself it wasn't important, that she was fortunate to even have a car at eighteen. Two more years were no big deal. But Devlin wouldn't hear of it and appealed to their parents, by saying Molly could take him to ball practices, pick him up at school, and how Mom wouldn't have to be without a car. It had worked.

He was telling the truth and she gladly did all of those things. Yeah, he had her wrapped around his little finger too.

"Don't do anything Mom and Dad told you to. Have some fun and enjoy it." He closed his eyes as he chuckled.

Yeah, not everyone had a younger brother like Devlin. For a guy to have it so together when he was a teenager, she couldn't help but wonder what had happened to change him while she was gone.

She grabbed the dangling hand. "Dev, why won't you tell me what's wrong? You know we can talk about anything."

He jerked his hand away and rolled to the other side, giving her his back.

The same answer she'd received the last dozen times she'd asked. Tapping her finger against her chin, she decided more drastic measures were needed. First, he needed to return to the loving care of their parents.

"If you're gay, I'm sure Mom would be understanding and talk to Dad about it." She bit her lip to keep from grinning.

He sat up and hit his head against the ceiling. His cursing continued as he rubbed his head and worked his way down the short ladder. "If you wanted me out of your truck so bad, you should've said so."

Before he opened the door, she said, "You never answered me."

"I can promise you, Sis, one thing I've learned while you were gone is I don't have to answer anything my asinine family asks!" He slammed the door behind him.

Interesting reaction.

Hey, if making her brother mad had gotten him to do

what she wanted, maybe it would work on other men. Grabbing her purse, she headed out the door. First, she needed to shop for a new outfit, and then later, she'd see about trying her new tactic on J.T.

Chapter Fifteen

After a morning of shopping for new jeans, Molly reclined on the porch swing in front of her parents' house. With one foot she kept the swing moving as her other foot rested on an armrest. A steady breeze pushed flies away and helped in keeping her comfortable. A big, black GMC truck with barely legal tinted windows made its way down the long driveway and stopped in the half-circle near the verandah. When J.T. hopped out of the truck, she chuckled.

He sauntered up the three steps and stood grinning. "Well, it's mighty nice to know you're feeling good today. What's tickling your fancy?"

Instead of his uniform, he wore jeans with the perfect spots whitened by wear. His shirt was a white button-up with the top three buttons undone and the sleeves folded back, baring his gorgeous brawny forearms, especially the one with all the tattoos. How much would he freak if she licked them?

"Oh, I guess it's kinda perfect to see you drive an oversized truck. You know, to go with your oversized ego," she said with a smirk.

With a couple of steps toward her, he stopped the forward movement of the wooden swing with one hand.

Her insolent smile remained unchanged as he leaned over until his nose nearly touched hers.

"Should I remind you about the other part of me that's oversized?"

Her eyes widened and her mouth hung open. His teasing was so unexpected.

No wilting flower, she snapped closed her mouth and cocked an eyebrow. "As to that, I've never had the pleasure of actually seeing it, but I remember how it felt. Maybe I should check and see if it has grown since then."

Later, she would feel ashamed of herself for her lack of decorum by bringing up *that* time, no less making a move toward his groin. Before as her hand made contact, he released the swing and swatted it away. He straightened and moved out of range.

She laughed and then the dark glare he shot her quickly brought her amusement to a stop. "Hey, I'm sorry—"

"Sugarplum, who's that out there with you?" Her mom walked out of the house, letting the screen door creep closed behind her.

"It's me, Mrs. Hicks. J.T.," he said, before Molly could open her mouth.

He still stood in front of the swing, looking over his shoulder. When he didn't turn his body around as he continued his pleasantries with her mom, curiosity got the better of Molly. With a quick glance down, she understood. Her little brazen play with words had stimulated him more than he'd wanted. For the bulge to remain so large, either he had a full raging hard-on before her mom had interrupted or she was right and he'd grown, something else matching his oversized ego. Yeah, maybe he had a very good reason to possess such self-confidence.

"It sure is hot out here." Molly pulled on the hem of her blouse and began shaking the material in the hope cooler air would circulate beneath it. Just thinking how he reacted to her teasing caused her body to steam.

"Molly!"

She turned to her mom, wide-eyed, wondering if she had time to grab a tall glass of iced tea. "Yes, ma'am?"

"Stop that!" Lisa Hicks looked pointedly at her flapping blouse and Molly quickly let go. "I taught you better manners." Her mom shook her head and returned her attention to J.T. "You two have a good time and let Mary know we appreciated the basket of apples she sent over. And tell little Jacob happy birthday from us."

The older woman shook her finger in warning at Molly before returning to the interior of the house.

When J.T. continued to stand in front of her without a word, Molly couldn't help it. Really, she couldn't hold back. She looked again and the massive swelling was gone and only a normal sized one was underneath his zipper. *Oh, crap, what am I thinking? I've got to look him in the face again.* One eye closed, grimacing, she looked up.

The glower was so much worse than the glare he'd given her earlier. She was tempted to say their bodies' reactions were normal, and she appreciated the male body more than most women. Instead, she preferred playing dumb. At least, that was her story and she was sticking to it.

"What?" She refused to allow him to bully her again.

"Let's go."

That was all? No sarcastic remark?

Happy to move on to less inappropriate subjects and

thoughts, she grabbed her purse and followed him to the truck. No need to push. Who knew what he would do next? Maybe he was a little prudish and didn't like how her gaze lingered on personal places. Not that they had such a relationship with the exception of that one time at the Farley house.

Within fifteen minutes they were on a dirt driveway and pulling in front of the Blackwood farm, parking behind a sleek BMW Roadster. She'd forgotten Mary had bought Uncle Herbert Hicks's old farm. The place looked a lot better as Old Herbert hadn't been one for flowers and paint, and it looked as if the new owners put a lot of love and elbow grease into the place.

"Here carry this in for me." J.T. handed her a gaily wrapped present with cowboys astride horses galloping across the paper.

"Sure. So now you'll owe me for three things."

"Huh?"

Pressing the present to her body with one arm, she raised three fingers and folded them down as she counted. "One, you left me without a ride from the diner." She ignored his groan. "Two, you stuck me with paying for your dinner when I didn't have enough money on me and panicked until Bill said he kept a tab for you. By the way, I figured you could pay for my meal too, so it's included."

He chuckled. She narrowed her eyes until he stopped.

"Well, what's the third thing?" He walked to the back of his truck and lowered the tailgate.

"Three, you're making me carry your gift, leaving your hands free. What kind of gentleman is that?"

With a couple of grunts, J.T. pulled a large, blue ice chest from the cargo area and headed toward the front door. "I guess you only have two things," he said as he walked by her. "But we're still not even from you shooting me and, out of my kindness, me letting you go."

She caught up with him and placed the present on top of the chest. "Yeah. I guess you're right." Laughing, Molly ran ahead to the front porch and knocked on the door.

"Hey!" he protested. Before he could say more, the door opened and a sophisticated woman, wearing clothes that looked more suited for the big city than back-of-nowhere Sand City, stood watching them.

"Hi, J.T." Mary Blackwood was nothing like Molly expected troublemaker Luke would marry. The woman stood back, waving them into the house. She had a gracefulness to her Molly envied. She'd heard Mary had been a professional dancer. That made sense. Molly had always been a klutz and was grateful her mom had never sent her to dancing lessons. Who needed embarrassment like that?

"Mary, I hope you don't mind, but I brought Molly along." He kissed Mary on the cheek as he lugged in the ice chest with the present sliding on top.

At the same time, Molly tried to figure a way to apologize for J.T.'s rudeness in not asking if it was okay for her to show up at the last minute. Why hadn't he warned her he'd invited her without receiving an okay from the hostess?

"Sorry. I'm Molly Hicks." She stuck out her hand and almost brought it back. Did women shake hands? What a stupid thought. She blamed the indecision on hanging around men and forgetting how to act around girly-girls like Mary. Without hesitation, Mary shook her hand—she had a nice firm grip—and grinned. Molly felt relieved. She thought about hugging her but she'd never felt comfortable hugging strangers. Or would that be wrong too?

A little boy with large, dark eyes ran into the room and grabbed Mary's legs to peek around at Molly.

"This must be the birthday boy." She smiled. With mahogany hair and dark blue eyes, the child was the spitting image of his dad, Luke.

"Jacob, say hello to Ms. Hicks." Mary nudged the toddler from behind her legs. The little boy shook his head and ran back toward the party. "Sorry about that. He's at the age he's not sure what to say or do around adults."

"Don't worry. I'm at the age that I'm not sure what to say or do around kids, so I understand perfectly," Molly teased. They laughed as the woman touched her arm and indicated the direction toward the party at the back of the house.

"So I finally meet a Hicks," Mary said.

"Pardon?" Molly asked.

"I'm sorry. There're just so many businesses around here owned by Hicks and I've never met one. Even Herbert Hicks...any relation?"

"Yeah. Great uncle."

"My condolences on his death. I bought the property from his estate representative after his funeral." Mary led the way into the back of the house where a large kitchen opened into a family room.

"My great-granddad had twenty-two children." Molly nodded as Mary's eyes grew big at the number. "He had thirteen by his first wife, who died in childbirth—no surprise, considering—and nine by his second. I never understood when the man had time to plant a crop or preach a sermon." Molly chuckled at the choking sound Mary made from holding back her laughter. "I was told he was a bit of a ladies' man even though he was a preacher, and he took seriously the part of 'be fruitful and multiply.' But I do have to say his children must've loved him as most stayed nearby and bought land."

As soon as Molly walked into the family room, she came across more people she knew. Eddie and his cousin, Brooke, sat in matching recliners arguing over the remote for the big-screen TV, while outside a sliding glass door, Mary's husband, Luke, hovered over a commercial-sized grill. He talked with J.T. on a wide deck. Another couple stood off to the side in the large room, laughing. The woman held a baby wrapped in pink with the man hovering over her. Though the fair-haired man looked familiar, she'd never met the woman.

"Hey, Molly, come here and meet my wife and little girl."

Then she remembered. Bubba Hagley, former sheriff of Sand County and, in fact, he was the quarterback she'd paid to take her to the prom. If she remembered correctly, it helped him pay for his tuition to the police academy as the county was too poor to pay his way.

She hoped they didn't ask her to hold the baby. The little creatures always cried with her and heaven forbid if she dropped one. So far she'd been lucky, but she avoided them whenever she could.

As she moved a little closer, the baby's round eyes drew her in, and Molly found herself reaching out to the pink confection.

Chapter Sixteen

J.T. chuckled as he watched Molly on the other side of the sliding glass doors. She held the baby with stiff arms away from her body. From the look of it, she never or rarely held an infant. She tilted her head in puzzlement as if the child was an alien from space. Then a screech emitted from the bundle, and in a panic, Molly quickly handed the child back to the mom.

"She's a looker, isn't she?" Luke nudged J.T.'s arm with a cold soda bottle.

"Thanks." J.T. grabbed the bottle and twisted off the top before taking a long swallow. "Yeah, and she's trouble." Trouble in so many ways. He watched as Molly laughed and turned to accept the glass of tea Mary held out to her.

"No trouble really at that age. Just change her diaper, give her a bottle, and she's ready to go," Luke said with a solemn face.

With a shake of his head, J.T. grimaced. "Very funny." He knew good and well Luke had been talking about Molly.

"You two dating?" A billow of smoke floated from the grill as Luke opened the top and began flipping hamburgers.

"Hell no!" He shook his head. When Molly frowned and looked his way, he realized how loud he'd rejected the question. And he was staring at Molly again. J.T. turned and caught Luke's mocking grin. "What's so funny?"

"You. You got it bad."

No need for him to pretend he didn't know what his friend meant. His interest in Molly would probably find him dead from another gunshot wound if he didn't watch it. He placed the cool bottle against his forehead.

"The girl is crazy, probably stalker material crazy." Why, with all the women he had chasing him, did he want to slow down for her?

Another peek into the house and he spotted Molly immediately. Her thin blouse showed a shadow of a black bra. Small points stabbed the material. Probably proof of an excellent air conditioner. He swiped his brow and rubbed the bottle across his cheek. How freaking hot was it out here? Maybe he needed to step inside for a little while and let the air conditioning cool him off.

"Oh, yeah? So she returned to town when you returned. Wait! You've been back years, a lot longer than the few weeks she's been back. So that's not right. Oh, I know. She wanted to be with you so bad, she shot you. One way to see you every day, though the distance from the cell to your office could be a little bothersome, what with her not having the keys and all." Luke chuckled and flipped a couple more burgers.

The big grin on his friend's face had to go. "Yeah, you would know the distance," J.T. said as he reminded Luke of his criminal foray as a teenager and prison stay.

"Oh-ho! Look who's talking? I heard about the times you were brought in for drunk and disorderly as a teen."

"Yep. We were all young and dumb." He took another swallow of soda.

J.T. patted his best friend on the back. Luke never acted stupid like some other guys and insisted he drink a beer with him. Life had taught J.T. drinking wouldn't solve his problems or even mask them, only create new ones. Besides, he'd decided after he made it into college he didn't want to turn out like his old man.

With another look through the glass into the family room, J.T. noted everyone stood or smiled as a woman walked in.

"Why in the hell is Rachael Quinn here?" He set the soda down and headed toward the sliding doors.

His hope to have one uneventful day since Mike's death was shot to hell and back. The mayor of Sand City hadn't made many friends in the city-run departments since she'd taken office three months ago and the sheriff's department had been her favorite whipping boy.

J.T. stopped inside the kitchen and crossed his arms. When Rachael turned around, she smiled and her gaze traveled up and down his body. Yeah. That was another reason why he didn't like her. She was a piranha on the make and had decided she wanted the sheriff in her bed. She was twelve years older but had a body of a twenty-year-old. Nevertheless, J.T. worked hard to stay out of her clutches. Had he thought piranha? Make that black widow spider. If he had sex with her, afterwards, he was certain she would bite his head off and eat it.

"Hello there, John." She placed one hand on her hip as the other played with a dangling earring. "Sorry I was so late." Her yellow sundress with matching sandals looked alluring with her salon-treated blonde hair.

Most everyone called him J.T., but the mayor insisted on

using his legal name. Only once had she included his middle name, but she'd quickly learned if she wanted to stay on his good side, she better stick with John or his initials.

"I'm surprised to see you at Jacob's birthday party. I thought you didn't care for kids, being nonvoters and all."

He caught out of the corner of his eye Luke shaking his head.

J.T. was well aware he was pushing it, but his friend had no idea the stunts the woman had pulled. Any person could excuse a fourteen-year-old Molly—as he hadn't been much older—yet a forty-two-year-old knew better than to reach into his pants uninvited.

Her smile didn't falter as she walked toward him. "Ah, but their parents can."

Before Rachael reached him, Molly stepped in front of her. "Hi, I'm Molly Hicks." She stuck her hand out.

Oh, hell. What was Molly up to? He grabbed for Molly.

Chapter Seventeen

What was she doing? It wasn't like he belonged to her. When J.T. grabbed her hand, Molly used it to her advantage by holding on and pulling his arm around her waist. To keep his balance he had to let his body rest along her back. She looked behind her, her forehead even with his mouth. Hoping he guessed what she wanted, he did. He brushed his lips above her eyebrows.

"Hello, Molly. My, haven't you grown?" The woman couldn't be more than five-two and she had to tilt her head to look into Molly's face.

"Have I met you before, ma'am?" Molly really couldn't help adding the ma'am. She knew it would burn the woman's scrawny butt. Yes, she was aware the thought was beneath her, but the jealousy monster would do it to a person.

The blonde straightened her shoulders and looked at Molly as if she'd underestimated her. "Yes, you have. I'm Rachael Quinn. I met you at your daddy's Fourth of July barbecue, the year you graduated high school."

The woman made it sound like it was last summer. Hinting at Molly being too young? For goodness' sake. "A great party. Of course, that was *ten* years ago." There. Twenty-eight was plenty old enough to do what any woman dreamed about doing with J.T.

"Sorry about Mike, John. I did hear you got the guy who did it," Rachael said, ignoring Molly.

Too late, bitch.

Molly lifted her eyebrows in amusement. The woman obviously wouldn't win on the age issue so she decided to change strategy.

"We arrested the suspect and he's out on bond now." The arm around Molly squeezed her in warning.

The woman's eyes narrowed as if she understood J.T.'s movement.

"Who was it? The person telling me couldn't remember his name." Her innocent face didn't fool Molly.

"Devlin Hicks," he said in a tone flat enough to convey reluctance.

J.T.'s arm was about to cut off Molly's circulation. She pulled the hair on one arm until he loosened his hold.

"Oh, poor Big Joe. That's such a burden to bear when your children don't live up to their potential," Rachael said with a glance at Molly.

"You—" Molly's epithet for what she thought about Rachael's sarcastic offer of sympathy was muffled by J.T.'s hand over her mouth and his other arm beneath her breasts, holding her to his big body. No matter how she wrestled, he refused to let go so she could place her hands around the bitch's neck. His tight hold barely allowed her to breathe, no less tell the creature what she thought of her.

The woman had the audacity to laugh.

Molly screeched behind his hand. J.T. lifted her tighter

to his chest, his arm pressing against her rib cage. "If you'll excuse us," he said between grunts as Molly's elbows jabbed him in the ribs and her heels slammed against his shins.

Within seconds, he carried her outside, past numbers of trucks and SUVs and a white Lexus sedan parked next to his truck. He uncovered her mouth. It gave him the opportunity to wrap another arm around her. No way could she move, not with one at her waist and the other pushing up her breasts, her back squeezed to his broad chest.

"Let me go," she whispered. She stiffened her body, refusing to allow it to mold against his. Plus she didn't want to create a bigger scene than she had already.

J.T. released her and quickly stepped back. Smart man. She wanted to knee him hard, so he'd be singing soprano for a week.

"Molly?" His concerned tone matched the worry in his eyes.

She inhaled deeply several times to help her calm down. She turned to face him, hoping she looked sane, and waited for him get whatever he had to say off his chest. "Rachael Quinn is the mayor of Sand City and no matter how much she deserves an ass-kicking, that's the last thing your brother needs at this time. She's rather popular with the general citizens and her sister is an investigator for the county's district attorney. With those connections, I would think through any retaliation. She could make your family pay big time."

He stood beneath a large oak tree. Rather appropriate as he was just as strong, considering there weren't many men who could hold her back from hurting someone insulting her family.

As her temper cooled, she realized no matter what the woman said, J.T. was right. But her jealousy had stoked her temper. Molly had no right to act the jealous girlfriend. She needed to go back in and apologize. She hoped she hadn't ruined J.T.'s friends' party.

She covered her hot cheeks. Lord, what did they think of her? It was their kid's birthday party. Tears welled in her eyes. She turned away and brushed the moistness away, pretending interest in the house.

"Molly." His deep voice sounded close by.

She felt his warmth before his hand turned her around and folded her in his comforting embrace, one cheek against the crisp—soon to be wet and smeared with makeup—shirt. All of the stress from her brother's arrest to dealing with her parents and fighting with the man she still had feelings for came crashing down on her. She began sobbing. Though she tried to stop a couple of times, he murmured something sympathetic and she started again. When she regained a little of her composure and wiped tears from her face, she tried to pull away, but he held on to her. A slight nudge from him brought her head to his shoulder, tucked beneath his chin, and he began swaying to the slow music drifting from the back of the house.

He felt so good.

Time drifted by as they continued to sway to the music, rubbing various hard and soft parts against each other for a few minutes until she pulled away enough to look into J.T.'s face. He smelled good too. Not cologne, but plain soap. So sexy. She liked how he already had a hint of a five o'clock shadow. Her gaze traced his thin lips.

They stopped dancing. The birds quit singing and the trees ceased bobbing in the breeze. As if in slow motion, his head dipped down and their lips met then slightly parted, tongues delicately touching. She wanted to lift to her tiptoes to press her mouth harder against his but large hands held her shoulders, keeping her flat-footed on the ground. He apparently wanted to take his time exploring her mouth.

She wanted it to go on forever.

J.T. moved from her lips and kissed the tip of her nose. "Let's go back inside and eat."

"Maybe I should call Mom or Dad to send someone to pick me up. I don't want to ruin little Jacob's party. Well, no more than I have already." She moved out of his arms, nearer to his truck where she'd left her purse with a cell phone inside.

"Quinn's gone."

Molly searched the long drive and noticed the white Lexus she'd seen earlier had left. In fact, the drive had become a bit congested since J.T. had brought her outside.

"Are you sure they won't be mad?" What would they think of her? She ran her fingers through her hair, beneath her eyes, and then pulled at her blouse. Thankfully, she'd gone light on her makeup.

"You look fine. Come with me." J.T. held out his hand.

A couple of swipes at her jeans with her palms insured they wouldn't be sweaty. Her hand enclosed his, even making her hand look feminine.

"I probably shouldn't, but for some reason, I'll go where you lead." She gave him a shaky smile.

Wasn't that the awful truth?

Chapter Eighteen

Later that evening, after taking Molly home, J.T. returned to Luke's house and walked to the rear, taking cautious steps around Big Wheels and other riding toys to reach the party sitting on the brightly lit back deck.

"I hadn't really expected you to return. How's Molly?" Luke handed a soda to J.T.

"She's okay. She told me to tell everyone thanks for being so nice to her after she'd made an ass of herself, but the phone call was from her brother. He bought a round of drinks at the Sandbox and didn't have the cash to pay. Since he's not a popular fellow, Casey wouldn't let him put it on a tab. She's going to pay Devlin's bill and take him home." J.T. leaned against the deck's railing.

"Makes you wonder how he got along without her for so many years," Luke said.

"The way I understand it, he used to call Raymond." J.T. waved to Mary as she stood in the family room talking with Susan, Bubba's wife.

"Weasel?" Luke asked.

"Yep." J.T. twisted the soda top off and took a swallow.

"I wouldn't wish him on my worst enemy." Luke shook his head.

J.T. chuckled. "Well, Devlin's sister's here now. Maybe she can straighten him out."

"You and I both know when it comes to drinking, he can only help himself." Hooking it with his foot, Luke pulled out a white plastic chair and nodded toward it.

"You're singing to the choir." J.T. took the offered seat and raised his bottle in salute to Eddie as the young deputy walked out of the house.

"Hey, boss, everything okay?" Eddie pulled a chair near to where they sat.

"Fine," J.T. answered and turned up the soda for another long swallow.

The men were silent, and a few minutes later Bubba along with Luke's dad, Reverend Ezekiel Blackwood, were all seated, staring at the stars twinkling above.

Eddie shifted in his chair. "Mike sure would've liked the party this afternoon."

"Yeah. He would've brought his guitar. He sure could play the blues," Luke said. "I guess we'll never know who his secret girlfriend was."

"Huh? What do you mean secret girlfriend?" J.T. leaned forward.

"A couple times after he got off work, I would spot him at the drugstore, all spiffed up. He wouldn't tell me a thing, but he was always buying condoms. Mike must've been seeing some married thing."

"The ladies always liked Mike." Eddie nodded and took a sip of his beer as tears welled up in his eyes. Everyone pretended not to see and remained quiet while they thought about their lost friend. Eddie and Mike had been tight friends.

"Eddie, did Mike ever say anything to you about any certain lady he liked to visit the most?" J.T. didn't remember seeing Mike play favorites. He flirted equally with every woman, young and old.

"Nope. Not a word," Eddie croaked.

Everyone shifted in their seats, feeling uncomfortable dealing with all of the emotion. The deputy was young and Mike was the first person he'd ever known to die.

"I can play 'Smoke On The Water' on a guitar," Bubba offered, probably hoping to lift the mood.

J.T. laughed. "Every fifth grader can play that."

"Mike played some beautiful gospels too." Reverend Blackwood cleared his throat before adding, "J.T., do you think Devlin had something to do with killing that fellow at the Farley place?"

The FBI had asked J.T. to keep quiet about the victim being a special agent. So J.T. couldn't say much. "I don't know. All I do know is whoever killed Mike will pay."

"You don't think it's Devlin?" Brooke said as she walked out of the house onto the deck.

"That's for the D.A.'s office to decide. But I'm keeping my eyes and ears open for any new evidence." J.T. stood, no longer in the mood to socialize.

Brooke nodded and then said to the fellows, "Hey, Mary said to come and get the last of the ice cream and cake. She needs to put it up before Jacob gets sick from eating too much."

J.T. quickly made his excuses and left, heading toward his house, wondering who Mike's secret girlfriend could be and whose husband was being made a cuckold. An enraged husband or boyfriend finding out about an affair would certainly put them in a murderous mood.

Thoughts of Molly with another man flashed red through his mind. He shook his head and climbed into his truck. Nothing good was served with imagining that.

His foot was heavy on the gas all the way down the road.

Chapter Nineteen

"Hey, Dev?" Molly kicked the bunk above her. Too funny that she and Dev had nice rooms in the mansion waiting for them, but they'd rather stay in her studio sleeper.

"Hmm?" Her brother rolled to the edge and dropped his hand over the side, waving at her as his face stayed in the pillow.

"I made a fool of myself earlier today." She cringed, closing her eyes and then promptly opened them when the memories popped into her brain even with eyelids closed.

"It's in the Hicks blood, luv," he murmured and then rustling of sheets drifted from above her. "Did anyone get hurt?" He leaned over to stare at her, hair sticking up and eyes red rimmed.

"No."

"Then I wouldn't worry." He jumped down from the bunk, straightening his clothes.

He rarely slept in pajama pants anymore and she refused to let him sleep in the nude or just his underwear while sleeping in her truck's sleeper. Yuck.

"Don't you want to know what I did?"

Her brother stood nearby, hands resting on his knees, not looking her way. "Nah. I have a feeling you've already beaten yourself up over it several times. You need to let it go or come with me and get drunk. Sometimes the liquor helps you forget for a little while anyway."

"I'll pass. And no more buying everyone a drink. Don't expect me to pay again." She grabbed his arm before he could move away. "Dev, why won't you tell me what's wrong? You know you really shouldn't drink while out on bail. If you must, don't get into fights."

When he looked at her, his beautiful emerald eyes glassy with sorrow, her heart felt like it would implode from the pain gripping it as she waited for an answer. She wished she could help him. If only he would let her.

"Sis, I would love to, but this is something I need to work through on my own." Then he was out the truck's passenger door.

Could it be he was guilty? Was guilt from shooting the deputy eating at him? She prayed not. She couldn't help him as long as he refused to open up. J.T. wouldn't open up either. Did all the men in her life expect her to keep banging her head against the wall?

Her father demanded she use whatever it was between her and J.T. to encourage the sheriff in protecting Devlin. While J.T. wanted her, yet didn't. Talk about feeling her head bouncing off that proverbial wall. Then there was her brother, lovable and focused and sober when she left home for the road just a few years ago, and now he was almost unrecognizable. What happened?

She pulled a pillow to her chest and looked up through the skylight in the middle of the ceiling. The stars were beautiful. She wished she were a thousand miles away from all the trouble and craziness in Sand City. But she couldn't desert her brother. And if she hadn't come back, she'd have never experienced dancing with J.T. beneath an oak tree during a spring afternoon.

That was worth a whole truckload of troubles.

Oh, goodness, she hoped she wouldn't regret thinking that.

Chapter Twenty

What was he doing? He rubbed the back of his neck. Working and trying to keep his mind off Molly? He shook his head. Time to try harder.

He shifted in the driver's seat of his marked SUV and stared at the old Farley house. He'd hoped something would click and tell him what had happened in the back bedroom. Even looking past the gingerbread trim and gables and examining every window covered by blinds or curtains, it still gave off an air of being closed up and empty, not revealing anything.

It was his day off, if there was such of thing for a sheriff. But this was definitely a time for overtime. Two deaths in days of each other were two too many for the little county seat. With one exception of his brother being killed, the last person to die of unnatural causes in Sand City was Jeff Mason about ten years ago. His wife had purposely and fatally run over him with the tractor after she'd found out he'd gambled their farm away at a casino in Mississippi. Truth be told, losing her family homestead was bad enough, but she also found out he'd taken out a million dollar life insurance policy on her and had planned to spend it on his girlfriend.

And how did she find out about the policy? Five minutes before he'd died, he tried to shoot her with his hunting bow but missed. When she'd jerked the bow out of his hands, he took off across the corn field, yelling about the policy and his pregnant girlfriend, believing that explained it all. He never was very bright. Using his bow, she shot an arrow into his leg, slowing him down. Then she jumped into the tractor and did the deed. Later in court she'd pleaded self-defense. It would've worked too except she ran over him twice and then got off the tractor and shot three arrows in his groin. Sometimes it doesn't pay to be too thorough.

J.T. shook his head as he looked at the old Farley place again. Maybe he needed to take his own advice and go back home. What if he found out Molly's brother was involved in the special agent's death? So far there wasn't a connection, but anything was possible in this crazy world. Devlin could be involved in drugs, porn, or smuggling in cheap liquor.

Bootlegging was still alive and well in Alabama. The hard liquor was controlled by the state and sold through the Alcoholic Beverage Control Board's retail outlets, more commonly called ABC stores. Some counties were considered moist counties. That was when one or more cities allowed the sale of liquor, but the county surrounding the cities did not. Sand City was in a moist county. J.T. had busted a couple of bootleggers and a few moonshiners since coming into office.

The yellow tape Eddie had stretched across the door was still in place. J.T. broke the tape and used his key to enter. He started with the basement, ignoring the musty smell of a long closed-up house with a tinge of death. About forty minutes later, he'd started on the second floor when he heard a faint voice on the main level. Was the person talking on a cell phone or to someone in the room?

He walked as close to the wall as possible, keeping the stairs from creaking and alerting whoever was in the house to his whereabouts. They would know he was on the premises as he'd parked in the driveway. He wanted to see what they were up to before his SUV was spotted. As he reached the last landing, he saw a small figure dressed in black, head bent, hurrying down the stairway straight at him. He grabbed the person's shoulders before being mowed down. Franny Osborne, wide-eyed, with a white poodle clasped to her chest, stared up at him.

"What are you doing in here?" J.T. asked, confused by her appearance, and released his hold.

The thin woman shook her head, her face washed of color. The dog whimpered. She probably had squeezed the poodle in her fright. "Lord of Mercy, you scared the bejesus out of me."

"You know this is a crime scene, and you're breaking the law by circumventing the tape outside. I could take you in." He wouldn't but needed to make a point.

"She's with me." Deputy Brooke McDonald stepped out of a back hallway. "I was helping her find Snowball."

When had his deputies started a search-and-rescue program for dogs? J.T. led Franny outside with Brooke following and they watched the older woman make her way along a small path back to her house. She'd turned down his offer of a ride, saying she needed the exercise. Before turning his attention to his deputy, he glanced up at the front of the mansion. One side of a curtain on the second floor was pulled back. Had someone done that when they had searched the house earlier? He hadn't noticed it while sitting in his SUV.

"Well?" J.T. eyed Brooke, squinting in the midday sun. He folded his arms, waiting for her to explain.

"Sorry, boss. We couldn't get you on your cell. I was on my way to find you when she waved down my car." Brooke pushed a wisp of hair from her face.

J.T. looked down at his belt and noticed the phone was missing. Then he remembered talking with their dispatcher before he reached the Farley place. He must've left it in the SUV's cupholder, a habit he intended on breaking.

"First, let me ask you, did you go to the second floor's last room on the right?" he asked.

"No. Mrs. Osborne had hollered she'd found Snowball in one of the upstairs bathrooms on the left, facing the back yard. Why?" She eyed him with curiosity, probably in the hope of finding out some juicy tidbit to tell around the station.

"No reason. Where's your cruiser?"

"Parked in front of her house."

That made sense. A few trees blocked the view of Osborne's drive from where they stood.

"Okay, now tell me what happened to cause you to come looking for me?" He uncrossed his arms as he stared at the windows of the old mansion and prayed another body hadn't been found. If so, he'd have to explain to his deputies about the importance of human life over canine.

"Devlin Hicks is back in jail."

He dropped his gaze to Brooke and let loose a string of curse words that had Brooke's eyes widening in appreciation. She was known for her own inventive swearing.

"What did he do this time?" he asked between gritted teeth.

"Drunk and disorderly. He was over at the Landings Salvage Yard."

"Mark built another moonshine still?"

"It appears so."

J.T. lifted an eyebrow, waiting to hear his well-trained deputies were following up and destroying the illegal still. In Alabama, the state controlled the liquor licenses and expected taxes to be paid on any alcohol sold. In turn, a person couldn't produce alcohol, even for personal use.

"Eddie's hunting for it now. Mark's got a lot of land with stacks of cars and junk piled sky-high that he can hide it behind." Brooke's shoulders straightened. "Rachael was at the station when I left. Said she had something to talk with Devlin about. Figured you'd want to know that too."

"Okay. Let me lock up and I'll be there in a few minutes." J.T. didn't see a need to chew out Brooke for letting the mayor in to see a prisoner without his permission. Knowing Rachael, she probably pranced in like she had a right and dared his deputies to even try to stop her. If she'd been a man, J.T. would've decked her many times for her entitled attitude. But she was a woman and the mayor.

Besides, he needed to hurry and return later to the Farley house and check the second floor to see why the curtain in the corner room moved in an empty house, and how Franny's dog found a way into the same locked house.

"Hey," he called out to the deputy. "How did the dog get in the house?"

Brooke turned and shrugged. "I have no idea. Since it doesn't have opposable thumbs, I say someone let it in."

"How did you and Franny get inside?"

"The backdoor was unlocked. No damage to the frame."

He nodded and waved her on. Damn. Who else had a key?

Chapter Twenty-One

Molly paced in front of the sheriff's desk. She'd rushed over to the jail as soon as Devlin made his one phone call to her and then she'd called Weasel. The lowlife was in Birmingham and couldn't get back to Sand City for a couple more hours. The deputies wouldn't let her in the cell block to talk to her brother. What did they think she would do? Bake a cake with a file inside?

"I thought you were supposed to look after your brother." J.T. stalked into his office, slamming the door shut.

She warily eyed the door for a moment. Few would dare interrupt the sheriff with the door closed. When she looked up, his dark gaze stayed on her face as he stopped mere inches away and tossed a cell phone on his desk. He smirked and moved even closer. A flush heated her cheeks as his smirk changed to a grin and he came closer. Could he make it any more obvious how much he liked having her in debt to him?

"He's a grown man and I can do only so much." As she inhaled his wonderful scent of soap and man—he must've stopped and washed up before coming into his office—she leaned her chest against his, her breasts brushing buttons and a badge. A few seconds passed before she realized she was holding her breath.

She exhaled, sliding her hands up his broad chest and then around his neck. She hadn't planned to touch him. She hadn't planned to follow through with the seduction, even though her parents had given her permission. Like she needed their permission.

He grabbed her arms and pulled them from his neck, allowing her body to remain against his. "No matter what you and your father believe, I can't release Devlin." His deep, soft voice shot waves of heat through her body.

She struggled, trying to step away and regain control of her libido. Why had she thought she'd be successful in luring him into her bed? The man continued to flash conflicting signals, that was why.

With little effort he held her tight, clasping her wrists behind her back in one hand, pressing her body harder against his. Her emotions were mixed in how she felt about his macho maneuvers. She liked how he was taking control of her body, but then again she didn't like how he thought it was okay to take control of her body. See. Confusing.

"Let me go." She turned her face into his neck, her cheeks burning.

"I want you to understand one thing before I let you go." Using her wrists, he moved her away enough to look into her eyes. "You and I are going to fuck. Certainly not here and not now. Probably not today. But soon. And it'll have nothing to do with what your daddy wants or the status of your brother."

To hear him being so blunt, well, it took her breath

away. If not for his hold, she would surely melt onto the floor.

He released her wrists and covered her mouth with his. She gasped as he forced his tongue in to tangle with hers. The kiss numbed her brain. About to faint from lack of air, she grabbed the sides of his face and pulled away and took a deep breath. Her gaze met his as her palms roamed over his prickly face hair. Then she stretched to her tiptoes to cover his mouth, hungry for more as she sucked on his lower lip and then licked his delectable upper one. She liked how he playfully nipped at her. She slid her tongue over his lips and dipped inside.

He growled—so deliciously male—and pulled away again. Before she knew what he planned, he tweaked her nose and then pushed her into a chair near his desk.

She stared up at him, blinking in confusion. What was up with that? Anger began to build. What was he thinking, ending such a hot kiss like that? The other day he kissed her on the end of her nose and now with a twist of her nose? Sure, a gentle twist, but what the hell? The man made her crossed-eyed by turning his emotions on and off in a split second. How did he do it?

Frozen in the chair, she took a couple calming breaths as her gaze followed his fine self around the desk to his chair. Before sitting, he adjusted his pants and himself. She coughed in an effort to hold back a giggle. Good. The kiss bothered him too.

"We've got to talk about your brother," he said after clearing his throat.

That was one way to keep her in reality. "What about my brother?"

She blinked again. Was she getting a tic?

"He needs professional counseling." J.T. crossed his

arms and leaned back in his chair. His silence and the shifting of his jaw hinted he was unsure how to tell her something.

"Spit it out."

"I've been in a similar situation. It's hard to admit when someone you love is an alcoholic. You feel like you're to blame in some way. That's how I felt with my dad for years."

Molly couldn't believe he was being so open with her. His dad had been the town drunk and often was teased by some of the mean kids in town and likely J.T. and his brother were treated the same way. The brothers were known to fight with anyone. A person could only take so much teasing before fighting back.

"How could you blame yourself?" She slipped to the edge of the hard seat, crossing her arms on his desk. "He was the parent, the adult. It wasn't like your mom was around to help." The urge to walk around the desk and hug him was so strong. Her chest tightened with so many emotions she couldn't name. He sure didn't want her sympathy.

His face closed up and darkened as if he'd wanted to say more. Instead he shook his head.

"We're talking about your brother. Devlin needs professional help. Here's a card for a rehab facility in Birmingham. It's expensive but it's not like your family can't afford it."

What? It was the first time J.T. had ever thrown her family's wealth in her face. She would let it slide for the time being. Maybe she was being oversensitive as their conversation was personal and a touchy subject for both.

"Rehab, huh?" She was stalling, trying to slow the conversation down. Never in her life had a kiss thrown her off kilter to the point she couldn't think clearly. And his personal comments about his past and her brother? Was he trying to tell her something? She hated feeling stupid.

"If you want him out of jail this time, that'll be the terms. Otherwise, he'll stay until his court appearance, and there's not an opening for several months."

"Months?"

No way could her brother survive locked up that long. He had always been a free spirit.

She sighed. "Okay. Let me talk to him and I'll get him to agree." Or she would bust his kneecaps. Between his drinking and the murder charge hanging over his head, his prospects of a long life weren't looking good.

J.T. stared at her for a few seconds as if he wanted to say something more. Instead he nodded toward the holding cells.

"Come on. I'll let you have fifteen minutes." He opened the door and she followed his lead.

Though concerned for her brother, she couldn't help but stare at J.T.'s butt—looking that good in plain khaki should be against the law. She shook her head and squared her shoulders. It was time to concentrate on the best way to approach her stubborn brother. Hopefully, she could convince him in the short time the sheriff offered that counseling, preferably in a rehab, was the best decision.

When J.T. unlocked the door leading to the now familiar block of cells, she heard Rachael's voice. "If you'll do what I say, I'll get you out." The woman reached between the bars and patted Devlin on the chest, letting her hand slide down toward his jeans.

"Mayor, we need to discuss this in my office." Arm and palm stretched out indicating the way to his office, J.T. waited for the mayor to comply.

Molly wanted the woman to take her hand off her brother. Would she then try touching J.T.? It was a bit of a dilemma. No. If the woman dared to touch either man, it would be over her dead, mutilated body.

Fisting her hands, she barely restrained herself from reaching out and shaking the little twit. This pulling and pushing between her brother's welfare and her desire to keep J.T. for herself was wearing thin.

"Of course. I have something I need to talk with you about too." Rachael finally removed her hand from Devlin. As the blonde walked by J.T., she caressed the sheriff's face. He glared and jerked back.

Molly bit her lip to keep from laughing. At least he wasn't falling for the cougar's tricks so she was saved from stomping the woman into the floor.

The older woman didn't even glance in her direction. Apparently, she believed if you couldn't do anything for her, you didn't exist. J.T. shook his finger at Molly as if to warn her to behave. She shrugged and crossed her arms, brows raised. He frowned and followed the mayor.

Once the door closed behind those two, Molly turned to her wayward brother.

"Are you an idiot? What in the world were you thinking?" she asked with no little amount of derision. She loved him, but time for some hard truths.

She wasn't buying the sheepish look from her brother. He couldn't care less what anyone thought.

He sighed and shrugged. "I heard Mark had a new still. Besides it's your fault that I sunk that low. You'd convinced the package stores and the Sandbox Bar not to sell me alcohol." He walked to the back of the cell and flopped on the cot, covering his eyes with an arm.

"I don't have that kind of power. You know it was probably Dad. He can get people to do anything." Yeah, Molly was well aware how miserable their dad could make life.

"You're right. Look at you." Devlin turned on his side, his eyes betraying the pity he felt for her. "He's got you doing his dirty work by chasing me down and pulling my carcass out of jail. Again. And let's not forget how he first ran J.T. and then you out of town."

"I'm not here to rehash the past. The sheriff has offered you a deal to get out of jail." She leaned against the bars, holding the cool iron with both hands.

"I'm listening." His red-rimmed eyes watched her with such a mix of hope and sorrow, she almost broke down in tears.

"If you go to this rehab for however long to get you back on your feet, he'll let you remain out on bail, but under house arrest. Otherwise, you stay here." She handed the card to him.

"Do you want me out of your hair that bad?" He pushed to his feet and shuffled over to her. With a trembling hand, he took the white rectangle and glared at it.

"Now, little brother, I would gladly stay on your ass to keep you straight, but you need more than just a keeper to get you back on track." She could tell he wanted to fight the offer, but one thing was for sure, her brother was smart, although he hadn't proven it lately. He knew this was it. He either went to rehab or stayed in jail until the trial.

"Okay. Your sheriff has me by the balls."

"Dev, you know he didn't have to sway the judge to offer. And he's not *my* anything." She reached through the bars, wanting to comfort him.

He moved away before she touched his face. Stretching out his lanky body on the cot, he stared at the ceiling. "You still got it bad for him, don't you?"

She pulled her hand back. Denying it would only be lying to herself and everyone. "Yeah. For all the good it does." She looked away for a second to regain her composure.

"You just be careful. No matter how that woman was playing with me, she really was waiting for J.T. to show up."

Failing at her act of not giving a damn, she raised an eyebrow. "What did she offer you?"

"A long weekend in her bed for my release."

"She actually said that?" Molly took a step back.

"Now, Sis, she's a little slicker than that." Her brother rolled, giving her his back. "Go. Protect your man and let him know I'll take his offer. The sooner, the better."

Molly closed her eyes for a couple of seconds in relief. She wanted to say more but had to be satisfied he'd agreed so easily. Almost too easily. The nagging headache she had on and off five years ago had returned. Only a few weeks with her family and their shenanigans brought on a migraine when she needed it the least. She'd always suspected the frequent migraines she'd had as a kid were tied to her family and this confirmed it. To think of it, the last one had been last New Year's when she'd met her parents in Lake Tahoe for the weekend.

Leaning against the wall outside the holding cell block she rubbed her forehead, trying to ease the pain long enough to reach her truck and the prescription inside the small fridge.

"Hey, are you okay?" Eddie peered into her face, his forehead wrinkled in concern.

"Just a headache." One that could make her throw up and become easily distracted.

She hated to admit any weakness. Her family was never known for their compassion in sicknesses. They believed if a sick person wasn't bleeding or had a broken bone, they were wimps. She'd even gone to school with the mumps because her mom had sworn she was faking it.

"Are you okay?" The deputy cupped her elbow and led her to one of the chairs lining the hallway outside the dispatcher's office.

"Yes...no. Give me a moment." She eased into the chair, certain her head would shatter if she moved too quickly.

"The way you were stumbling along and holding your head, I would say it's a migraine. Do you feel like your head will explode? Mike used to get them whenever he ate chocolate." Eddie blushed, looking away and shuffling his feet.

"You miss Mike, don't you?"

"Yep. He was a good friend. Actually my very best friend."

"More than your cousin, Brooke."

"That's different. She's family."

When she noticed the tears in Eddie's eyes, she politely turned away. After a few moments to give the deputy time to recover, she asked, "Do you mind letting J.T. know Devlin agreed to rehab?"

She really hated leaving J.T. in Rachael's grasping little hands, but it would be embarrassing if she threw up. Of course, the thought of throwing up on the woman's turquoise-colored silk suit was enough to bring a grin—somewhat of a weak one—to her face.

He cleared his throat. "Sure," he said in a deeper than normal voice. "Do you want me to call Big Joe or Weasel?"

"Heavens no!" She grabbed the sides of her head. Whoa, that hurt. "I'll be okay. Usually I have about an hour before the worst hits. It'll only take half of that for me to reach my truck."

Chapter Twenty-Two

Molly woke to a cold cloth being placed on her forehead. Her eyelids weighed as much as a heavy-duty tarp on a fully loaded flatbed trailer. All she could do was moan in pleasure from the coolness. The medicine had kicked in and knocked her out, but her forehead was sore from the aftermath. Her mom must be in the truck checking on her.

"Do you need another pill or something?"

Huh? That voice was too deep. She finally opened one eye and looked into the gorgeous face of Sam Savage, her friend, business partner, and sometimes co-driver.

"Whatcha doooing?" Still feeling goofy from the drug, she slurred her words.

"Been missing you, doll."

She smirked. "Yeah. Tell me 'nother."

"Atlanta can be a bore after a month of partying. So I thought I would check on you and see if you're ready to hit the road again." He sat on the edge of the bunk and stretched out his feet alongside her. "Dispatch said they've got a load going to Washington, state of, and wanted me to go along. It's for the government and would be a good haul. I told him I couldn't run without checking on you."

"Could've called." She took a deep breath, her stomach finally staying down.

"Sure. But I wanted to see the little town you grew up in and I don't leave for another week." Sam clasped his hands behind his head. His arms were the width of the tread on her truck's spare tire. She knew he worked out daily and because of him they never had trouble at any of the truck stops.

They'd met the first year she'd been on the road. She'd pulled into a truck stop near Dallas and a couple of assholes decided to pick on her about her truck's huge studio sleeper. He stepped in and, by his size alone, scared them off. She asked if he was interested in teaming up for longer hauls. After some discussions of shares and what each would expect of the other, he'd agreed. At the time, his rig was an older model needing an overhaul and teaming with her helped him make the money required while it was in the shop.

He now owned six brand new Kenworths, but still teamed with her, hiring drivers to run his small fleet. They made a good team. She drove during the day and he took the night run. She handled the paperwork and he managed any roughnecks they came across.

"Have to wait until I'm better. Maybe tomorrow night." Closing her eyes, she turned over on her stomach.

"Okay. Sleep. I'll make sure no one bothers you," he whispered.

Sam patted her back and then moved to her head, yanking off his shirt and then pulling her into his arms, her cheek resting on his broad chest. She grinned. The bottom bunk was his usual spot as he hated heights.

Chapter Twenty-Three

J.T. walked toward the eighteen-wheeler sitting near the six-car garage but his gaze was on the car parked on the far side. The new black Charger with a Georgia tag was something to admire. Mrs. Hicks had directed him to the backyard, saying a friend of Molly's was visiting. When he asked about her daughter's migraine she'd acted surprised but then said Molly's friend was probably helping. He shook his head. The way Molly's family treated her, he was glad to know someone in her life would help while she was sick.

The hum of the generator said she was indeed inside as her brother had left for rehab at the crack of dawn this morning. He'd planned to take her out for breakfast. So taking two ladies out for a meal wouldn't hurt his budget.

He knocked on the door and waited. A minute or so passed. Nothing. He knocked harder. Again. Nothing. All kinds of scenarios flashed through his mind. Two lone females in a truck several yards away from the main house, anything could happen. At least, that was his reasoning. He lifted the handle and the door opened. That decided it. The damn door wasn't locked.

He'd enter, check to see if everything was okay and, if they were asleep, he would turn around and leave. As he stepped into the cab, small lights lining the edge of the floor lit up. The space-age-y feeling had him nodding his head in appreciation.

The dim lighting helped as he moved into the sleeper with the habitual one hand on his holster. A soft glow near the bottom bunk was enough for J.T. to make out two bodies lying on each other. He stared for a few seconds. Was he seeing it wrong? He blinked. A long braid, identifying Molly, snaked across a broad manly chest.

J.T.'s throat tightened and his lungs momentarily stopped taking in air. He fingered the safety latch on his gun. Images of cramming the barrel into the guy's face zipped through his mind. With a shake of his head, J.T. scrubbed his chin and glanced toward the cab. He could make it out of there before he did something stupid. It was none of his business if Molly had a boyfriend. He was glad she did. Then he could relax, quit thinking about her.

When had he started lying to himself? He wanted her. She traveled around and probably had boyfriends all over the country. He couldn't expect her to wait around for him to make up his mind about taking her to bed.

A deep sigh came from the bunk. The man tightened his hold on Molly and shifted her higher on his chest. Who was this guy? How long had she known him? His jaw ached from gritting his teeth. He didn't like any of this at all.

With only a creaking sound of his leather duty belt, he sat down on a small bench near where a table folded into the wall. Yeah. He wanted Molly. He looked toward the cab again. Either he ran or stayed to see what she had to say. She'd been running after him as much as he'd been running the hell from her. It was time for everyone to stop running. He wanted answers. No one ever called him a coward.

Chapter Twenty-Four

"Molly." Sam's voice had a touch of panic to it. "Molly, we've got company."

Struggling with her weak limbs, she lifted her head from Sam's magnificent naked chest—the man usually wore only briefs in bed—and squinted at the tall drink of water called J.T. Rogan. His cowboy hat rested on his knee and his elbows on the low shelf behind him, his long legs blocking any escape. His cold stare chased a chill across her bare arms. The old-fashioned nightgown she wore wasn't more than a cotton shift, long enough to cover the important parts, but the neckline scooped a little deeper than she felt comfortable with considering how his stare dipped down and back to her face.

Molly grinned. Obviously, he liked her full figure. His eyes gave it away. When he continued his badass stare, she realized with her body plastered to Sam's in bed, it didn't look good. She sat up and knocked her head on the top bunk. Her head was sore enough from the earlier migraine. Was she asking for another one? Rubbing the spot, a bump was already forming. She scrambled off the bunk and stood swaying in front of J.T.

Thank goodness the pain medicine was still in her system.

One dark eyebrow lifted as his gaze returned to the man behind her. She looked over her shoulder to see what he thought was so interesting. Shirtless, Sam still wore his jeans and socks. That had to prove to J.T. nothing was going on. When she turned back, she placed hands on hips and glared back.

"What are you doing breaking into my sleeper?" Back straight and head up, she refused to feel guilty. Sam was a friend and nothing more.

"I was concerned. Eddie told me about your migraine." His dark eyes slowly returned his attention to her.

"I'm better." Oh, Lord, he was concerned? The man was too hard to read. Then again, he appeared angry with her more often than anything else.

"Who's your friend?" He was giving Sam the evil eye again.

"Sam Savage," her friend said as he leaned forward and held out his hand. "I'm sometimes Molly's co-driver."

J.T.'s gaze dropped to the offered hand and then he stood. Sam scooted Molly to the side and stood too.

She realized the two men were about the same height. Sam had some extra bulk on him, while J.T.'s shoulders were just as wide. They were fine-looking manly specimens.

"I better get going." J.T. picked up his hat from the floor and headed to the front of the truck.

Before Molly could fuss again about J.T.'s unexpected visit, he'd walked through the cab and stepped out the door. Confused, she opened her mouth to apologize for J.T.'s behavior.

Sam shook his head. "Go. Tell him."

"It's none of his business."

"I don't care. Besides, you love the Neanderthal," he muttered, his voice muffled by the shirt he was pulling over his head.

In seconds, she was out the door and running across the backyard, not caring that anyone could see her in a nightgown or that she was barefoot.

Geez. J.T.'s long legs quickly covered ground but she did the same. Within seconds of the sheriff climbing into his SUV, Molly grabbed his arm and held on tight.

"It's not what it looked like." Her voice sounded airy as she panted, trying to regain her breath.

"Molly, that line is so old it's not funny."

"I'm not being funny. Only Sam is. That is...he's gay." The look on J.T.'s face wasn't what she expected. He appeared angrier.

"Is that what you told your boyfriend? That I'm gay?"

"Hell no!" She lowered her voice. "I would be lying. You wouldn't have kissed me like that if you were." His expression said he didn't believe her. "You think I'm lying to keep you from being mad." She released his arm and stepped back. "You egoistic asshole," she spit out. "I don't lie. I might fudge on the truth to protect family, but never would I straight-out lie." She took another step away. "Go. Leave. See if I care." How could he think that of her?

She gave him her back and started back to the sleeper. The tears streaming down her face had nothing to do with realizing J.T. could lust after her but would never trust or love her. She'd already come to terms with the love part. She was upset because the man she loved thought she was a liar. No way could they have a relationship without trust.

Chapter Twenty-Five

J.T. watched Molly stomp barefoot across the wet grass. The rising sun outlined her long legs all the way to her well-shaped thighs. He rubbed a hand over his flattop and then put his hat back on, the front brim shading his eyes. About halfway to her truck, she stumped her toe and tripped, landing in the dirt.

Before he even realized what he was doing, he was bending over her and lifting her into his arms.

"Put me down," she said, hiding her face against his shirt. He shook his head more in disbelief than in disagreement. The way her fingers dug into his neck and back, she didn't want down. Damn, she felt good in his arms. All soft and silky smooth.

He shifted her higher as he walked toward his SUV. She smelled flowery and fresh, the way a woman should smell. As he moved closer to the passenger door, he held her tighter. What was he thinking? That was it. He was thinking with the wrong head. All he knew was he wanted this woman and hated imagining any man, sexually or not, lying next to her. Somehow he opened the door and slipped her into the front passenger seat.

For only a split second he'd considered locking her in the back, but changed his mind as he was certain it would make her madder. Good thing she couldn't see the grin on his face as he walked to the other side or she would be throwing another hissy fit for sure. After he slid behind the steering wheel and cranked the vehicle, he turned it around in the large driveway.

"What do you think you're doing? I'm not dressed to go anywhere." Though she didn't reach for the door handle, the glare he caught out of the corner of his eye warned him she'd recovered from her fall and was seriously considering jumping.

"Put on your seat belt." He was pleased to see she did as he ordered without argument. The woman had some common sense.

"J.T., this is kidnapping." The calm tone she used almost brought the grin back to his face.

With another quick look, he noticed her taut nipples underneath the thin cotton gown. As if she knew where his eyes had been, she crossed her arms and watched the road. He turned a knob on the SUV's HVAC system to a warmer setting.

Every breath the woman took, every move she made pulled at an invisible string connected to his groin. He hoped nothing or no one stopped him along the way. There was no way he could function normally with a raging hard-on. He needed his mind on something else for the next fifteen minutes until he reached his home.

"How's your toe?" he asked.

"It's throbbing but no blood. I'll be okay."

"So not broken." A moment passed without a word from

her. Then she muttered beneath her breath. He looked her way. "What?"

"Where are you taking me?" Her calm tone assured J.T. he wasn't making a mistake. His unceremonious treatment of her hadn't scared her. That was one thing certain about Molly he'd noticed since her return. She almost acted like a man. All logic and controlled emotions most of the time. But thankfully she didn't look anything like a man.

Another glance her way. Nope. She looked all woman.

"J.T.?" Her voice was a little higher pitch.

"I've decided you and I need some alone time."

Hell, he wasn't even sure what this would prove but maybe they could satisfy their curiosity about the other and go on with their lives. This was lust and nothing else. It had to be as he had nothing beyond his body and a few hours of pleasure to offer a woman who was used to having it all.

Fighting the tightness in his groin, he pulled his attention back to the road. He almost missed his turn. Moments later, they arrived at his house and not a second later they were in his garage. Alone. No brothers or co-drivers. No deputies or lawyers.

"What now?" she asked.

Yeah, smart boy, what now? Jump the girl's bones?

He took off his hat and slung it into the backseat as he released his seat belt. He turned in the seat and placed one hand on the dashboard and the other on her headrest, his knuckles whitened. She looked all wide-eyed and innocent staring back at him. Maybe he needed to explain.

"I want to taste the back of your knees. I want to hear you moan my name. I want to feel every silky inch of you beneath that damn virginal white nightgown you've got on," he said in a husky voice. One thing was certain: right now, his libido couldn't take it any longer. "I want to suck on your nipples until you scream from climaxing so many times."

He'd never seen Molly's face so pale. Oh hell. Was he wrong? Had he pushed her away and he was too late? Had he screwed up? Did she no longer want him?

Chapter Twenty-Six

Molly had finally gotten what she'd always wanted. J.T. Rogan lusting for her in return.

All she could think about was, what if she disappointed him? What if she was a terrible lover? None of her former boyfriends had said, "You're a lousy lay." But then again she had so few, what with her schedule and pickiness. She had a total of three. Who would've ever thought she would lament the lack of lovers just before she finally had a chance with J.T.?

Looking into those dark hungry eyes, she decided even if she was lousy, it would be worth the humiliation to have him one time.

She pressed the button on her seatbelt and dove across the console into his lap. He grunted but squeezed her tight as they kissed. The seat moved back—he must have pulled the lever on the side—giving her plenty of room. Oh, he still tasted so good. His tongue filled her mouth and she wanted more. Her hands clasped his head as she deepened the kiss. One broad hand massaged her breast. She moaned against his lips.

The horn blared, echoing in the garage. Hot-faced, Molly moved her elbow from the steering wheel.

"Let's go inside." He grinned and kissed the tip of her nose. "There's plenty of room for us to do whatever we want. That's why we're here."

Wanting to look into his face, trying to believe this was truly happening, she leaned back, once again pressing the horn. Cheeks hot, she shook her head as his sexy chuckle chimed in with hers.

"Yeah, I guess we're less likely to draw attention from the neighbors," she said. Unable to stop touching him, she brushed a fingertip across his lips. They looked so stern and damn sexy.

"Unless you're a screamer," J.T. teased.

"Maybe." She smiled big and tilted her head as she shrugged.

Once again, in a show of strength, he pressed her tight to his chest and stepped out of the SUV. Muscles expanded and contracted as he shifted her in his arms. Mercy, the man was strong. He could pick her up a hundred times and she would never stop being amazed.

"You know I can walk," she said with what she was certain was a stupid grin on her face.

"Wouldn't want your feet to get cold or stump your toe again." His voice deepened.

Images of how he could keep her warm raced through her mind.

He carried her into the house. She only glimpsed the different rooms: a kitchen with shiny appliances, a small breakfast nook that looked out over the spacious backyard, and a long hallway leading to...yes...a huge master bedroom.

He owned a king-size bed—unsurprisingly—covered in a white chenille bedspread—surprisingly old-fashioned and feminine. The other sticks of furniture faded in the background as he moved closer to the large expanse of white. Instead of throwing her on the mattress as she expected, he dropped her legs and let her slide down his hard body until her feet hit the floor covered with a hooked rug.

Her eyes lifted to his. The heat flaring in his dark eyes was enough to send her up in flames. She was hot and cold all at the same time. This was where she'd wanted to be since she was fourteen and first fell in love with J.T. and acted stupid behind the gym. She never imagined the journey the two would go on to reach this point.

Why wasn't she jerking his clothes off?

Scared silly, that was why.

"Are you okay?" He brushed her cheek with his thumb.

"I...we...uh..."

J.T.'s deep-throated chuckle filled the room. "I never thought to hear Molly Hicks lost for words."

She stiffened. His laughter wasn't the reaction she wanted from him. Oh, no. Her eyes welled up with tears. What is going on? She was becoming a wuss. Looping her arms around his neck, she pressed her body against his. Her face in the crook of his neck. Just a few minutes was all she asked for. His strong arms and heated skin pushed all thoughts of inadequacies from her brain.

"Molly?" J.T. pulled back, his hands clasping her shoulders as he stared into her eyes. "Slow down, baby. We've got all day. I'm off-duty, well, as much as I can be."

She took a deep breath. "Do me a favor."

"Okay." His guarded expression said he was sure he'd regret his acquiescence.

"Would you strip first?" Her face felt sunburned.

For goodness' sake, she'd chased off half-naked male and female prostitutes in truck stop parking lots without blinking an eye. When J.T. stood, towering over her, and smiled with a glint of mischief in his eyes, she hid her hands behind her, fighting the urge to tear his clothes off.

"Sure. As long as I get a show too." Without waiting for an answer, after a tug at the laces, he kicked off his boots and at the same time threw his tie onto a nearby chair. A little bit of white showed in the vee of his loosened shirt. He undid a couple of buttons and then, showing his impatience, drew off the shirt and undershirt in one clean pull.

Oh, my. Every inch of the skin he revealed was toned, begging for her lips and tongue to trace each dip and swell. His chest, nicely taut without the swollen look of a body-builder, promised to be a great place for her hands to roam. The tattoos she'd been fascinated with for so long swirled over one shoulder and down his muscular arm, stopping at his wrist. A dragon like the one St. George had killed covered most of the area with Celtic symbols covering the balance. She'd never seen a man so beautifully dangerous.

She cleared her throat and took a step back. "Uh, do you work out?" The back of her knees hit the bed and she sat with the grace of a cow.

"Some." His hands reached for his belt and hesitated.

With what had to be considerable superhuman strength she pulled her gaze from his tattoos and looked into his face. The need burning in his eyes inflamed hers.

"You're not backing out on me, are ya?" she asked. At the same time, a little voice in her head taunted, *you only wished. Then he wouldn't know what a scaredy-cat you are.*

"Here's your answer." He wasted no time in unbuckling his duty belt, pulling out the gun, checking the safety and placing it into the top drawer of the nightstand. Then he unhooked and unzipped his pants, duty belt still threaded in the loops, and with one quick push, pants and briefs fell to his feet.

Oh, my goodness, he was gorgeous. Unabashed and solemn, he waited for her reaction as her eyes took in every hard inch. Truth be told, she really hadn't expected him to go through with it. But she was so happy he had. When he stepped out of the pile of clothes and stalked toward the bed, she knew she was in bad trouble.

His beautiful cock was hard and shifted across his stomach with each step. Tight balls nestled between muscular thighs. The Adonis belt defined and tempted her to run a finger along the ridge running from hip to hip.

He towered over her. With a gentleness she could not resist, he pushed her shoulders back to the mattress until he stretched above her, arms straight holding up his torso, only their legs touching. There was something wicked and wonderful about her wearing a gown while he wore noth-ing. All that manly flesh waiting for her to touch. Her hand drifted over the colorful designs on his brawny arm.

Was she dreaming? She was in bed with J.T. Rogan and he was naked. Marvelously naked. Her gaze drifted down his torso until she reached what she craved. Without a second thought, her hand grasped and began to pump. So hard. He became larger with her touch. She smiled, taking pleasure from his reaction. She loved the feel of silk over hot steel.

"Molly." He eased to the side, placing his hand over hers, stopping her caresses. She tilted her head. What did he plan next? "The old-fashioned virginal look is hot, but it's your turn."

As if in a dream, she reluctantly released his cock. Without a second thought, she sat up and pulled the gown over her head and dropped it. The gown cascaded to the floor in a pool of whiteness.

"I don't normally wear a gown, but when I have a headache, my usual T-shirt and shorts bother me. The loose, lightweight material doesn't irritate me."

When she looked at him still stretched out on the bed, her breath caught. She wanted to pinch herself. There he was naked and on his side, one hand holding up his head as he watched her. Broad chest, small hips, thick thighs, and the most beautiful part of him hard and resting on the bedspread alongside his body. He was a wet dream and fantasy rolled into one big, sexy man.

Her feelings for him may have started out as a teen crush, someone she admired for his uniqueness in a vanilla town, a bad boy in need of saving. The few times they met in passing, he'd often teased and pulled her braids. Whatever she felt had grown as he changed from bad boy to good man with a dangerous streak. She liked it. A lot.

"It's sexy, but you look even better without it." His rough and heavy voice filled with emotions.

His hands slid up her sides to stop beneath her breasts. The pressure of those warm hands brought her back to the here and now.

"You're beautiful." His large hand cupped one breast as his lips met the taut mound.

She inhaled long and deeply and arched into his touch. He covered her. His knee parted her legs. Her nipples hardened as the hair on his chest brushed their tips. His lips traveled up her neck. Taking her mouth with his, her moans muffled when he thrust his middle finger deep between her legs.

He growled approval. "Yeah. You want it as much as I do."

His upper torso shifted as he withdrew his finger, circling her clit on the way out.

"Come back," she protested.

Her hands clamped on his arm, but she was quickly distracted. She traced the inky design on his shoulder, fascinated by the tattoo. As he moved to reach something to the side, she sighed. His skin slid against hers and felt so good. Vaguely, she heard a drawer open and close and then a tearing sound before he righted above her, his hot gaze meeting hers.

"Condom," he said in a guttural tone filled with need, offering his assurance he would protect her.

He slipped the thin latex over the tip and expertly rolled it down. She loved watching. There was something erotic about the whole process.

"Next time let me do it," she whispered. When she finally lifted her gaze to his, she caught a flare of heat in their depths.

"Next time, heh? Woman, you take my breath away." His salacious grin caused her heart to skip a beat.

Obviously, he liked the idea of a next time too. Then he kissed her as if he wanted to devour her, and she sucked on his tongue, hoping to drive him wilder. The thought of the big guy losing control because of her was...intoxicating.

His knees spread her thighs and then he thrust his cock deep and satisfying. She moaned, loving how he filled her. As he pulled back to thrust again, a ringing came from the floor.

"Shit!" J.T. groaned.

No. This couldn't be happening. "Ignore it." She clasped his face, bringing his eyes to meet hers. "I need you. I need this." She wiggled her hips and thrust up, encouraging him to continue.

"I wish I could." He took a deep breath and began to move back. Refusing to let go, she wrapped her legs around his waist and stayed attached. He shook his head. "Come on, Molly. I've got to answer it."

"You said you're off duty." She despised the sound of that ringing, wishing and praying it would stop or it would be a wrong number. No matter. She wanted to strangle whoever it was. Better than anyone, she knew life wasn't fair, but she wanted this with him. Did he really expect her to give up so easily?

"This is a small town. I'm off-duty as long as that cell phone doesn't ring. Whoever it is, better have another dead body at the other end."

She refused to cry. She refused to be a wuss again. "Well, big boy, you'll just have to multitask!" Somehow she pulled a lopsided grin together. No way would she let him know how desperate she was for him to finish what he started.

He growled. "Don't you think this isn't killing me too?" His eyes narrowed.

She widened her grin. Let him think what he wanted. Without thinking of the consequences, she leaned over and bit a tiny male nipple.

He sucked in a breath and then lifted her, moving over to the edge of the bed. Feeling his muscles shift and expand sent shivers across her chest straight to between her thighs. He obviously enjoyed it too, as he was still hard inside her. With one long arm he reached his pants and looked over her shoulder to pull the phone out and open it.

"What?" he barked.

A woman's voice blasted into the room. Molly recognized Janet the dispatcher, but whatever she was saying to J.T. wasn't clear.

"No. She's here with me. Tell her friend, she's okay and will be back home later this afternoon." He listened a moment more, his neck reddened. "That's none of your damn business." With a little violence, he jabbed the dot to disconnect and then tossed the phone on the nightstand.

When he looked at her, she knew nothing more would happen even though he remained firm. The solemnness of his face warned her he was already regretting his actions, his caresses. Being with her.

She slumped against him. What was the use?

He gently placed her on the bed as he pulled out and stepped away. She scrambled for the sheet and squeezed the cloth over her breasts. Taking her time, she hid her legs beneath the covers, her face heating in embarrassment. There she was again, feeling like the fourteen-year-old rejected by the man of her dreams.

She watched as he jerked on a pair of jeans, not bothering with underwear, and cautiously tucked himself in as he'd softened enough to take off the condom. Leaving his jeans unhooked and the zipper pulled to midway, he rubbed his chest as he stared at her with a thoughtful expression on his face.

She hated what that look meant. He wanted to claim he'd gotten carried away? Or some other stupid crap. Why couldn't he be like so many other guys and just want a quick, easy lay? That had a simple answer. Because he was a good guy. And she wanted more.

"What was it about the call that made you want to stop?" she asked.

At the same time he said, "This is all wrong and we have to talk."

He held his hand up when she started to protest. "Wait.

I'll explain, but first, that was your friend. He was worried and had called the station to see if I had taken you in."

She nodded. "I should've borrowed your cell phone and called him before we got here." A nagging feeling said she would need her friend and his broad shoulder to cry on once again. "Answer my question before you explain."

When he looked at her in confusion, she asked again, "What was it about Janet calling that made you stop? My friend looking for me doesn't mean we're romantically or physically involved or he's interested in me, not like I am in you."

Hands on his hips, he looked at the floor for a moment. Well, this was certainly not a good sign. Why did he have to be so honorable and noble? Then again, maybe she should beg, plead with him to screw her brains out. She couldn't do it. No matter how much she loved him, she still had a little pride.

"That's just it, Molly. Why me?" He eased onto the foot of the bed.

"As in, why I'm interested in you?" she asked.

His nod and narrowed eyes brought a flush to her face.

Her gaze drifted over his bare chest, flat stomach, long legs, and returned to the semi-hard shape showing beneath the zipper. When he shifted his position on the mattress, her face heated.

Why couldn't she keep her eyes or hands off his cock? Oh, well. Her mom had always said she'd never possessed a lick of modesty. Never being one to embarrass so easily, yet she'd blushed numerous times with J.T. in the last hour. Anyway, she wanted to act like a lady around J.T. That was what he wanted, right? That was the kind of woman he probably dated. Not a truck driver. Not someone like her.

"I'm waiting." His firm, no-nonsense command raised the small hairs on her neck. She didn't need another daddy.

"The hell I know! Maybe in the beginning it was like any teenage girl's crush on a bad boy. But you're not the bad boy anymore. Though I know I still see him underneath that cowboy hat occasionally. Maybe it has something to do with admiration. You started from nothing and made something of yourself and your life. You're not intimidated by my dad. You're your own man. I don't know." Frustrated with trying to express her feelings without saying "I love you" shook her temper like a bottle of soda in the back of a Jeep speeding down a cobblestone road. "For that matter, why do any two people become interested in each other? Maybe it's all to do with chemistry and hormones. Why must there be a reason?"

They stared at each other for a few minutes. Her chest rose and fell as she tried to regain her composure.

"This can't be more than two consenting, single adults giving in to mutual attraction. I have nothing more to offer. I don't need the trouble dating you will bring. The last problem I need is Big Joe breathing down my neck, wanting to know my intentions to his daughter. I don't care what you believe he meant by giving you permission to sleep with me. Most likely it was just an excuse to come after me with a shotgun. So no talking to him or anybody about our time together. Our time will be spent in bed and nothing more. No discussing your brother and any of the county's business. Do you understand?"

For a man known for being closed mouth, he sure had a lot to say. Yet this wasn't what she wanted to hear. Dreams of marrying and living the rest of her life with him were going up in smoke. Not that she'd realized until now, but she had picket fence and two-point-three-kids dreams about him. So it was time to pull on her big girl panties and leave.

His offer was for a few good times in the sack with no strings attached. What happened to that bit of pride from a little while ago?

Well, it went up in smoke along with her dreams of a dark-eyed sheriff being in love with her. Maybe a small part of that dream could come true. Being able to touch him, having his body between her legs and rubbing against hers. How could she turn it down when he offered it on a china plate? She wanted to feel J.T. in her arms as he thrust into her body. She deserved at least one time with him. No longer would she kid herself. Most likely one afternoon in his bed would have to last her a lifetime as she doubted he'd want more. The other men in her life never returned for an encore performance.

Oh, my goodness. She *was* a lousy lay. Her cheeks heated with the realization. Her palms itched to cover her face, but she refused to acknowledge her embarrassment.

He hadn't taken his eyes off her, waiting for her answer.

She lifted her chin. "Okay," she said. "I understand."

Before she could immerse herself in a pity party, he jerked the sheet away and crawled over her body until her back pressed against the mattress. Nose to nose, he stared into her eyes. His broad shoulders blocked the light and she soaked in his heat, his dominance.

"Then let me give you some ground rules. One, when I call, you're to meet me where I say and when I say. Second, you show up prepared to be thoroughly..."

The rest of the rules were lost in a haze of sensual overload and delight. The rules meant he wanted to see her more than once. Hey, rules were made to be broken and somehow she would find a way to keep from blurting out how much she loved him. Anything to keep him in her bed and coming back for more. Maybe that was why none of the other men returned. Her heart belonged to J.T. all these years and no one else. They had to sense that.

His hands massaged and stroked her with a skill she'd never experienced. She followed his lead, and she found he enjoyed his nipples and the small of his back scraped with her fingernails. Impatient to reach what she really wanted, she dipped her hands into his pants, taking a moment to squeeze his tight buttocks before shoving his pants down his legs and slinging them across the room.

Her hand wrapped around him and met his as he worked a new condom down his length. She wasn't sure if she was helpful or more in the way as she followed his fingers unrolling the thin latex.

As soon as he finished, he cupped her between the legs and slipped a finger into her slick folds. Her back arched off the bed and she whimpered, wanting more. She moaned when he took away his hand, shifted his body, and plunged into her heat. He felt wonderful, so thick and hot lunging into her. Each rise and fall of his hips brought her closer to what she'd failed to experience with her other lovers. A feeling of being taken and possessed by a real man. He grabbed the back of her knees and lifted her legs to thrust into her with a strength she reveled in. Later she would have bruises on her thighs, but they would remind her of the time she spent with the man she loved.

She screamed his name as her body tensed and flowed with the low moan he released while he made a final slow thrust.

Closing her eyes, she let the feeling of happiness seep into every inch of her limp body. A small niggling worry tried to worm its way into her contentment, but she mentally slammed the door shut.

She was woman enough for him. Repeating that mantra would keep her strong and show him she was made for him. Her fascination with J.T.'s body would help her keep him occupied and his attention on her.

From the way he sighed, she suspected he was a satisfied man and she was the woman to keep him gratified in every way.

Watch out, Mr. Rogan, whirlwind Molly is about to change your life.

Chapter Twenty-Seven

He was the scum of the earth.

Slumped in a chair, J.T. watched Molly as she slept in his bed. Holding back the satisfaction he received from the sight would be insane. He'd never been the caveman type to pull his woman by the hair into his lair and have his way with her. Actually, she was the first woman he'd ever treated this way. Always before, he'd wined and dined them and they would quickly fall into his bed. Hell, sometimes it only took wine. Occasionally, one would try to play hard to get. He'd just walk away. He didn't play dating games.

Except Molly's cards were on the table. Poker was a game he enjoyed and understood. A person could bluff, but the cards never lied. Undeterred, she refused to listen to her father. Smart woman. And damn, she'd worn him out. The woman had skills. Aggressive one moment and submissive as hell in the next. Would he ever get enough of her? That was a dilemma for sure.

Though Molly still had a crush on him, he had planned never to take advantage of it. But when he walked into her sleeper and caught her in bed with another man, gay friend or not, his anger took away all reason.

He wanted her. No other man had ever made her scream with an orgasm. At least that was what she'd told him as they snuggled together before she fell asleep. Snuggle? He actually snuggled. What was it about her that had him acting unlike himself?

But now...

That was the problem. What was he to do now? He swiped a hand across his face and rubbed his chest. Hell, she was Big Joe's daughter. Though the man didn't treat her right, he wouldn't like to know J.T. Rogan had fucked her bowlegged.

His cock grew harder as he watched her sleep. Closing his eyes, he inhaled and exhaled several times to regain his composure.

A sweet sigh released by Molly brought his gaze to her. Even in sleep she was so cute. She rolled onto her back. The thin sheet shaped to her breasts as twin nubs topped the mounds. Damn, cute and so fucking sexy. She'd gotten what she always wanted. Him in bed. What was next? They had history, what with her inappropriate action behind the gym and their subsequent exile from Sand City. And then there was their fathers' mutual past.

His dad had often talked about how he and Big Joe had been great friends until they fell in love with the same woman. Their true love. Rarely had it registered with Harry Rogan when he said such things how much it had bothered a young boy who loved his missing mother. Then again, J.T. had imagined, his mother had finally grown tired of hearing the accolades of another woman along with Harry's drinking and heavy fists. Far less would push a woman out the door into another man's arms.

He knew the truth now. Though they hadn't found his mom's body, he felt in his gut his brother had not lied before he took his last breath. Dad had killed and buried her somewhere. And no matter how much he tried, J.T. couldn't find his dad or her body.

Damn, why was he dwelling on that? The past was the past. He shook his head and stood. No matter what Molly expected, he wasn't marriage material but he could at least show her how a real woman was treated. And oh, yeah, she had grown up to be all woman.

"Hey, baby, have you rested enough?" He shoved the sheet from her and cupped her petal soft breasts with their jutting nipples. He liked how his large hands couldn't cover the full mounds. What could he say? He was all man.

Chapter Twenty-Eight

"Hey, girlfriend, good to see the lawman decided to uncuff you from his bed."

"Shh! People will hear you." She looked around her booth in the diner before glaring at Sam. "For your information, he's a good guy and doesn't do kinky stuff."

"Sorry to hear that." Her friend scooted into the seat across from her. His eyes sparkled with mischief.

"Quit." She blushed and began laughing. Only Sam wasn't teasing. He enjoyed several of the specialty clubs in Atlanta that catered to those looking for more than vanilla sex. Too embarrassed to admit to her best friend that last night she'd experienced her first orgasm with another person and no batteries needed.

After they ordered their lunches, Sam's smile disappeared. "Listen. I apologize for interrupting your afternoon, but next time you run off with a man, let me know so I won't worry." His concern rung in his dry tone. "Okay, sweetie?"

"Okay." Her nose wrinkled. "I'm sorry too. I really didn't

mean to leave you like that." She fiddled with the utensils rolled up in a napkin. "Wow, he got jealous when he found us in bed together," she whispered, peeking up at Sam.

"Did you tell him?"

"Yeah. But he didn't believe me."

"Too funny." Sam leaned back and grinned.

"You're enjoying this too much." She resisted the urge to kick his shin.

"Any man or woman would be proud to have a woman like you on their arm. It's about time someone appreciated you. So when are you moving in? Or did he ask you to marry him?"

She looked toward the kitchen. "I wonder how long it takes to make a burger around here."

"Molly, what aren't you telling me?" Sam reached across the table and placed his hand over hers, stopping her from shredding the napkin.

"Nothing." Trying to act blasé, she moved her hand from his and placed her fist beneath her chin. She smiled, maybe a little lopsided but she didn't want anyone's pity.

"Don't give me that. You know me. I'll nag the crap out of you until you tell me what's going on." He studied her while the waitress placed his salad in front of him and then hamburger and fries in front of her. As soon as the woman left, he prompted, "Well? I see you're eating comfort food. So spill."

Sighing, Molly shook her head. "Please let it go. You know that someone can want to...to be with you and not... you know."

After J.T. had left the bed, what he'd been telling her had finally sunk into her stubborn brain. He wanted her body but nothing else, and she was crazy enough—crazy being the operative word—to go along with anything he wanted.

"Damn! I thought he was smarter than that," Sam said. "And you know having a 'relationship' is not a bad word."

"Please. Let's just enjoy our lunch then I'll take you around and let you see what a real small southern town looks like." She detested seeing the pity in his eyes. It was all J.T.'s fault. If it wasn't for how he made her tremble with a simple caress, she'd shoot him again and not miss this time.

"How's it going, Molly?"

She'd been concentrating so hard on ignoring Sam's compassionate stance, she'd been clueless to her surroundings and that Eddie had walked up.

"Okay, I guess." Holding her sandwich near to her mouth—luckily, she hadn't taken a bite yet or she'd be choking, she blinked up at Eddie. He stood beside the table, his eyes glued on Sam. Was he waiting for introductions? All right. "Sam Savage meet Deputy Eddie McDonald."

The two men stared at each other for a long pause before they shook hands. Eddie frowned. She released her breath. What was the matter with Eddie? They were friends and he treated her as nothing more. Was it a guy thing? He'd always been the friendly sort. Men. Couldn't they meet each other without measuring who had the biggest?

"How did you meet Molly?" Eddie asked, suspicion giving the question an edge.

She slid over, making room for the deputy. As he settled in and ordered a cola, she chowed down on her burger.

After about forty-five minutes she realized Eddie and Sam had talked nonstop. Just like two hound dogs, sniffing and growling, but now acting all friendly like. For two men to be total opposites, they had found a mutual love of hunting. When they started on deer hunting in Alabama versus Colorado, she knew it was time to leave. Besides, her dad had left her a voicemail and wanted to see her.

"Hey, fellows, nice to hear about all the laws involved in shooting helpless animals, but I need to go." She grabbed her purse. Eddie moved for her to slip out of the booth and then he returned to his spot without hesitation.

As she stepped outside and headed toward the Jeep, a hand grabbed her arm and jerked her into an alley. J.T.'s angry face barely registered before his mouth covered hers. Her startled squeak changed to a delighted moan. The rough kiss didn't hamper her libido, instead heated it up, and she wrapped her arms around his neck. After several minutes of mind-blowing kisses, he leaned back to stare into her eyes, his hips still pressing hers.

"Where are you going?" he asked.

"My goodness, Sheriff, you do have a way with interrogation," she teased, wiggling her hips. The hardness behind his zipper brought a smile to her lips.

She ran a hand along the side of his face, noticing he wasn't wearing his hat. She wished he had it on. How hard would it be to kiss him beneath the brim? He looked extra sexy when he wore it tilted, hiding his eyes in the shadows.

He grabbed her hand, moving it from his face. "Molly." His tone said his patience was coming to an end.

She rolled her eyes. Like he had any. "First, I'm going to my sleeper to freshen up, change clothes, and maybe take a nap, and then Dad wants to see me. Why?"

His hand still held hers. Would he like to do something more strenuous? She squeezed his hand. She liked the feel of his big, rough hand touching and engulfing hers. Considering what they had done yesterday and throughout the night, they should be beyond handholding, but this was J.T.

Besides, she never had the chance to hold his hand for holding sake. It was nice.

"What about?" he asked.

His question threw her. "Wait. That's not how it goes. You ask a question and I answer. Then I ask a question and you answer. It's your turn to answer. Why?"

He pulled his hand out of hers and looked toward the street. "If he's found out about our time together yesterday, I don't want him to manipulate you further. Though I'm not sure what he could do with Devlin's already in rehab. Your dad may decide to tell you to stay away from me or find another reason to use me through you. I think I need to play along."

His last sentence didn't make sense. Something in that little dialogue was a lie. The unreadable expression on his face warned her before he looked away. Her brother had the same blankness on his face when he thought up excuses to drink. All lies.

Now the question was why? She sounded like a four-year-old asking why over and over. But, hey, there was only one way for her to find out. Ask. As she opened her mouth, his cell phone rang. She hated that blasted thing.

All J.T. said the whole time on the phone was "Yeah" and "Thanks for the info," and then he hung up. "What time are you meeting with your dad?"

"At five, why?" See, like a four-year-old.

"I'll meet you at four-fifty-five outside your sleeper." He started to walk away.

"J.T.!" Did he really think he could get away that easily?

He stopped and looked over his shoulder, dark brows raised.

"Why?" Her voice echoed against the buildings' walls.

He shook his head as he headed out of the alley.

"Hateful man," she muttered.

"I heard that!" he said as he kept walking.

"Good!" She really wished she could stop grinning. The man was tightlipped, arrogant, and infuriating. Yet he had the most beautiful ass. Yep. Sex toy walking.

Chapter Twenty-Nine

J.T. shifted in the seat of his SUV. Just staring at the truck and knowing Molly was inside made him hard as the muzzle of his gun. Never in a million years would he imagine he'd become obsessed by a Hicks. From the time he was able to understand the drunken ravings of his old man, he knew all Hicks thought they were too good for Rogans.

Molly stepped out of the truck, dressed in dark blue jeans and form-fitting top. Nothing flashy, but he liked how she filled out her blouse and how her long legs felt around his waist. He struggled to take his gaze off such a soul-searing view. The swing of her hips tempted him to forget everything and grab her and take her back to his place and reenact their day together.

Dammit. He needed to keep his mind on what he was about to do. Chances were he wouldn't be enjoying the heat between those legs for a long time if not forever after his conversation with her dad.

Chapter Thirty

Molly stood beside the cab of her truck as J.T. strode toward her. His uniform, crisp and fresh, stretched across broad shoulders and slim hips. Remembering their time together, she realized being with him was like eating a tub of chocolate without a spoon. You knew it would be messy and might kill you, but you still dove in head first, hoping it wasn't over too quickly. And, crap, he was worth every second or, in the case of yesterday, every hour.

"You really don't have to do this. Dad probably wants to talk to me about Devlin's rehab or his plans for my brother when he returns home."

She liked the way he slowed his stride to match hers. But why did he insist on coming with her? No chance he'd forgotten her parents had given their blessing on her bedding him. She only hoped her dad hadn't gotten word about her and J.T.'s time together.

Of course, J.T. could be telling her the truth. He could be worried about her. Other than her brother, she couldn't remember anyone taking up for her, wanting to protect her. This was nice.

She hooked her arm in his and leaned against his side, smiling up at him. He frowned at her. Holding back a silly giggle that wanted out, she kept walking toward the side door.

The kitchen smelled of garlic bread and olive oil. Her parents ate early on Saturday evenings and usually watched a movie on the big screen in the den upstairs. The butler and all-round caretaker usually could be found in his suite off the kitchen area and would know where to find her father. She could hear the roar of the stock cars coming from that direction.

"Willy! Is Daddy in the den?" Molly called.

"He said to let you know he's waiting upstairs. Your mama had to go to the store to pick up popcorn and should be back any second. I told them they'd ate the last of it over a week ago, but do they remember? Nooo. Hardheaded young'uns." The older gentleman's voice came closer as he shuffled through a doorway on the left, rubbing his left hip.

"Thanks. Sorry to bother you during your race."

"No problem. My boy ain't in the lead lap." The man eyed the sheriff. "You here on official business?"

She shook her head and turned to J.T., expecting him to laugh. The cold look on his face stopped any thought of amusement. Uncomfortable with his attitude, she tried to ease her hand from his arm. His hand covered hers, stopping her escape.

He stared at the older man and then as if he'd remembered she was there, dropped his gaze to her for a split second before returning his attention to Willy.

"Which way?" J.T. waited for Willy's answer.

No! This couldn't be happening. She'd been wrong. He

didn't act like he was there to protect her from her dad. How stupid could she be? When had anyone truly thought she needed saving? Even her own parents had thrown her to the wolves to shield their beloved son from the big bad sheriff. He obviously had a motive to catch her dad off guard.

What in the hell was yesterday? Just a way to soften her up? Why? She would never learn.

In a daze, she followed J.T., numb with the realization he'd been using her. When they reached a turn in the stairs, she dug her nails into his arm.

He grabbed her hand and loosened her grip.

"Why did you make me believe you were doing this for me? What do you have planned? What has my dad done to you?"

He released her and then pressed her against the wall. His voice low as he dipped his head, he said in a rush, "I'll explain everything later, but I need to talk with your dad before someone warns him."

J.T.'s nose almost touched hers. Her chest rose and fell in rhythm with his. Anger and hurt straightened her spine, helping her glare back. She wanted to believe there was a logical explanation. But the stranger staring at her with a mixture of fury and pity was not what she wanted. She seriously thought about hitting him in his self-righteous, sexy mouth. She didn't want his pity.

A push on his chest gave her enough room to start up the stairs.

"Hello, Daddy." She stomped across the room to where he lounged in a recliner. Her dad folded the newspaper he'd been reading and pushed down the footrest. She leaned over to hug his neck. "Watch out," she whispered.

Family first was what her dad had always preached. She was beginning to understand the importance.

The sinking sun in the large paned window beside him brought out all his wrinkles and caused his white hair to nearly glow as he stood. Though his face looked every one of his sixty years, he still had the stance of a twenty-five-year-old ready to fight.

"Rogan." Her dad nodded at the younger man, not offering a hand.

Odd. This was the first time she'd ever remembered her dad calling J.T. anything other than sheriff or J.T.

"Did you get my message?" J.T. rested his hands on his duty belt. He made no move to shake hands.

"Yep. Been kinda busy." When her dad crossed his arms over his chest, she knew he was preparing for a fight. One of the drawbacks of living with the man for roughly eighteen years plus a few summers was that she'd learned his habits.

"We received a most interesting package in the mail today," J.T. said.

Confused by the interplay and her mixed feelings for the two men she loved, she remained still, waiting, listening to what was not being said. Their attention centered on each other as her mother entered the room.

"Why do I have a feeling that J.T. and Molly are not here to watch movies with us?" Her mom stood to the side, arms crossed beneath her breasts.

"No, Mom. J.T.'s here to either accuse or question Daddy." Molly glared at the sheriff. Her stomach churned with the thought of how little their sleeping together had meant to J.T. Those hours had meant the world to her.

Her mom's eyes narrowed. "Now, Sheriff, this isn't the time or place to conduct police business. Why don't Joe come down to the station tomorrow and you two can talk about whatever you want?"

"That's just it. Big Joe refused to come down to the

station and one of my deputies said Willy wouldn't let him in to talk with Big Joe. He kept swearing Big Joe had left for Nashville and wouldn't be back until next week. That's why I'm here," J.T. said in a tone colored with anger.

Her mom turned toward her dad with well-drawn eyebrows raised. "Joe, is that true?"

"Sugar, you know what a busy man I am." He grinned with one corner of his mouth higher than the other. "Willy probably misunderstood something I said."

"Don't 'Sugar' me, Mr. Joseph Devlin Hicks, Sr. We're law-abiding folks and you're to show up or at least call the sheriff when he asks." Her mom placed her hands on broad hips.

Molly waited to see how her father would react to her mom's ultimatum.

"If that's what you want." His unexpected answer was a shock.

Molly wasn't sure what to make of the glint in her dad's eyes. When she turned to look at her mom, the same glint showed in her eyes. What in the world were they up to?

"Big Joe, why don't you ask your daughter and wife to leave the room?" J.T. stood his ground.

"Anything you have to say can be said in front of me and Mom too." No way would Molly let the two men push them out.

"You heard my daughter. But think long and hard. Do you want to involve them in any of your misconceptions?" Her dad grinned, but when she turned to look at J.T.'s face, she knew her dad had miscalculated.

"What do you know about the death of Paige Elliott Rogan?" the sheriff asked.

"What?" Molly stepped toward J.T. When he'd said death, she expected the name of the deputy or the man in the Farley mansion. Never J.T.'s mother's name, a woman who disappeared twenty years ago. "You need to find your dad and not hassle mine."

"Molly, hush." Her dad returned to his recliner. "Paige disappeared a long time ago. Why do you think I'll know anything?" Her mom moved to the recliner next to her dad's.

"This morning the package we received showed pictures of you and my dad outside the Sandbox. Casey told me the picture was taken before he bought the bar as the lettering on Sandbox's sign is now in blue and in the picture it had been red."

"Everyone knows your dad and I were close friends." Her dad reached over and squeezed her mom's hand without taking his gaze from J.T.'s.

"The picture was taken the same day my mom disappeared. The date is written on the back in my dad's handwriting." J.T. remained standing, motionless.

"That doesn't prove anything. Your dad was plastered more days than not. He could easily have written the wrong date." Her dad pressed a button on the side of his recliner, leaning back, still holding her mom's hand. "Let's say Harry and I are out drinking that night, what difference does that make?"

"The missing person report filed on my mom had you telling the deputy investigating her disappearance that you were out of town. And from the records I pulled, my dad's driver license had been pulled for DUI. I was told that at the time his car had been towed in for nonpayment. So you most likely drove him home. Considering how you two were such *good friends*, there's a reasonable chance when he needed help in hiding my mom's body, he called you."

"Stop! This witch hunt you're waging against my dad

has to stop." Molly couldn't believe the cold, analytical man standing across the room was the same one who kissed a path down her spine. "I think you need to leave."

J.T. coldly stared at her dad for a moment longer. "I'll expect you down at the station at eight in the morning."

"He'll be there," her mom said as she squeezed her husband's hand.

With a brief look at Molly, J.T. walked out the door.

When she heard his footsteps on the stairs, Molly turned to her parents. The guilty look on their faces told her so much. J.T. was right. Her parents would continue to manipulate her at every turn. They also knew something about J.T.'s dad's disappearance and his mother's death.

"I have no idea what game you two are playing"—she pointed at each of them—"but I want to be left out of it." She shook her head and marched out of the room, her chin quivering.

Chapter Thirty-One

Big Joe released his wife's hand and shook his numb fingers. No need to look at her. Squeezing his fingers until she'd cut off the circulation every time the sheriff asked a question was a dead giveaway of how she felt. When he finally glanced her way, the scarlet on her cheeks confirmed she'd been holding back and waiting for their daughter and her guest to leave before firing at him with full barrels.

"Joseph Devlin Hicks, Sr., what were you thinking?"

Damn. That was the second time in less than twenty minutes she'd used his complete name. It would take some fast talking and lots of honey-dos to calm her down. He'd likely be building her that greenhouse she'd been going on about for the past few months.

"Now, Sugarplum, if that girl of ours had done what I asked and kept the sheriff busy just a little while longer, he wouldn't be worrying about some stupid, old picture." He leaned over and tried to grab her hand.

"You can keep your hands to yourself and don't go blaming Molly. She looked awfully disappointed in you and that boy. The girl's as smart as me and knows when there's something rotten in the pumpkin patch." She narrowed her eyes. "When was the last time you talked to Harry?"

"I'm not sure. About six months ago." He hated lying to her.

She was right about being smart. The woman graduated valedictorian two years after he'd left Sand City High with barely a C-average. She'd also been on the dean's list at Birmingham's Samford University. He'd gone to a local two-year tech college and did okay.

"I haven't been married to you for thirty-plus years without knowing when you're hiding something. So I'm putting you on notice. You better tell me what you're hiding, or when I do find out on my own, you can only hope I'll let you back in my bed before we reach our golden anniversary." She placed her hands on her hips and glowered.

He flinched. She sure knew how to hurt a guy.

Joe cleared his throat, sat up, feet on the floor, and perched on the edge of the recliner.

"Okay. But you better lean back and get comfortable. It all started when Harry called at two *that* morning crying..."

Chapter Thirty-Two

J.T. sat once again in his SUV, staring at Molly's cab and studio sleeper. Only two weeks had passed since the disastrous night he'd questioned her dad, but it felt more like centuries since he'd slid into her warmth and held her in his arms.

He'd really screwed up.

Questioning her dad in front of her was the stupidest thing he'd ever done. His reasons at the time had seemed so important. The picture had been the first clue that his brother's dying words could be true. Whoever had sent the picture probably knew more, and J.T. needed to talk with him or her. He'd made copies and sent the original picture off for an expert to lift the fingerprints, but they'd only found his dad's and Big Joe's. When he and his deputies passed around copies, the old timers recognized the two men but had nothing more to add.

He was at a dead end. Between his mother's death and the two recent murders, he had squat. Rubbing his eyes, trying to relieve the grainy feeling, he closed them for a few moments.

The pounding at his ear jerked him awake. Blinking to help his eyes adjust to the light shining near his face, he leaned back against the headrest and turned the key a little so the window could roll down.

"Come inside." Molly stepped back for him to open the door as she held a flashlight in one hand and an umbrella over her head with the other.

He rolled his window up and slipped out of the SUV, smoothly taking the umbrella from her as they ran to the truck. Within seconds they were inside. She kicked her wet jogging shoes off and tossed her leather jacket, missing the hook, and drops of cold rain dotted his uniform.

As he suspected, her friend was nowhere in sight. Good. He was thankful she'd invited him in. Until he'd dozed off, his subconscious had been conjuring up ways to come inside. That was, without begging for forgiveness. Damn, he'd missed her.

With a wave of her hand, he sat near the folded built-in dinette table and looked around, seeing if anything had changed from the last time he'd been there. The dimmed lights and the sound of a hard rain pounding against the metal roof gave the sleeper's interior a snug feeling. When his gaze landed on the bottom bunk, he noticed the mussed up sheets. Gritting his teeth, he glared at her. He wanted to jerk the damn linens off and spank her ass for...what? Because he hated imagining any man holding her instead of him.

"What do you want?" She narrowed her eyes and crossed her arms under her breasts while waiting for his answer.

Where the fuck was her bra?

Immediately his boiling blood changed from anger to lust. Her taut nipples begged him to bite and suck the tips.

His fingers flexed, desperate to touch, to hear her moan with need. Swallowing once to regain composure over his body, he looked above her head, staring unfocused at the upper bunk.

She released a humph. "Sam's not here. He went to Birmingham with Eddie and Brooke, and won't be back until tomorrow."

Like he cared where Sam was. He groaned. Yeah, he did. The man needed to keep his hands away from her. Hell, he needed to do the same. She might know if and how her parents were involved in the disappearance of his mother.

His gaze traveled over her again. The hell with it.

He stood and wrapped one arm around her waist as he pushed up her blouse and bent over to cover one sweet nipple with his mouth, sucking and laving as he dipped a hand beneath the waistband of her flimsy shorts. Her sighs encouraged him to cup and delve one finger into her moist folds. Needing more, he wanted the taste of her on his lips. He made quick work of her blouse and shorts, throwing them in the corner of the bunk, and with a gentle shove she landed sprawled on the mattress. Her chocolate eyes appeared big and bottomless in the faint light. He kneeled between her legs.

"Oh, my," she whimpered as he stroked his fingers into her softness before replacing them with his tongue. Pure hot nectar on his tongue. When he found the small knot of nerves, hard as a marble, waiting for his attention, he decided he needed to hear her scream his name.

Sucking on the center brought her body arching off the bed. He lightly pinched the ridged flesh and she groaned, digging her nails into the sheets. Pleased by her reaction, he grinned, making sure she felt his lips lift. A hard thrust of his fingers and a long sharp suck brought the scream he anticipated.

Yeah, he relished the way she squealed his name.

Chapter Thirty-Three

Molly traced the Celtic design on his arm with the tip of her finger. Chill bumps popped up on his skin when her finger reached the sensitive area beneath his arm.

"You're ticklish?" She wiggled closer to J.T., resting her head on his chest, her bare legs stretched out alongside his. Hard-muscled man with a strong heartbeat beneath her cheek reassured her this was real.

"Uh-huh." Though his eyes were closed, the grin on his face told her he enjoyed her attention.

When her eyes leisurely moved down his chiseled, naked body, she realized another part of him was also enjoying the attention.

Unable to resist—what red-blooded woman could?—she sat up and began nudging her fingertips along his side, pressing hard as he began jerking away from her.

"What do you think you're doing?" He met her tickling with some of his own moves and before she knew it, he held her hands above her head as he stared down at her, his dark eyes flashing in amusement. As they looked into each other's eyes, his wide grin slowly faded. "I'm sorry, Molly."

For a second she thought he meant about his tickling and holding her down, and then she realized he referred to the other night and her dad. She wanted to forget how much his betrayal had disappointed her. That was her way: if she couldn't run from it, she'd ignore it. But she'd loved J.T. for too long to run from him again or give up so easily.

"You using me like that....it hurt." She'd hoped he would be the only person in the world not to use her. Too many others had never considered her feelings when they had their own agenda. Having a wealthy dad with a lot of power in town had its drawbacks. Unable to meet his eyes, she looked to the side and noticed her blouse hanging on the flat-screen television. Heat spread across her face.

"I know," J.T. whispered as his fingers traced her jaw. "At the time, I thought I was right to do it. I thought you wouldn't care."

That brought her eyes back to his. "You weren't. And why would you think I wouldn't care?"

He rolled off her, his palms cupped beneath his head, staring at the bunk above. "It was a misjudgment on my part. My dad's never been any kind of dad as long as I can remember. I thought with the way yours treated you...well, hell, I don't know. That you would understand."

His forehead wrinkled as he clenched his fists. Whatever he recalled appeared to be painful. She scooted closer and wrapped an arm across his chest, giving him a hug. His sigh brought an echo of her own. Strange as it may seem, she did understand, but it didn't mean she liked it.

She grinned when his broad hand carefully smoothed her hair. His way of saying once again he was sorry, wanting to comfort her too. The heaviness weighing down her heart lifted. So what if it wasn't the perfect relationship, he'd proven he wanted her in his bed again. Happier than even the first time they'd made love, she drifted off to sleep in the arms of her dream man.

"Damn it, Molly! Wake up!"

She shot up as jeans landed on her head. Why was he throwing clothes at her?

"What's the matter?" She glared at J.T. as he stood over her with only his pants on, zipper and duty belt open and his shirt in one hand.

He stepped to the side and waved toward the cab. "The truck's on fire!"

That was when she saw the flames waving at her from beneath the windshield, filling the cab. Smoke churned along the ceiling, slowly moving into the studio sleeper. With little time to spare, she jabbed her legs into the pants and yanked on her blouse.

"Where's your fire extinguisher?"

She yanked at a small panel in the wall and looked inside the compartment. Nothing! "It's supposed to be here!"

He grabbed a couple of towels and soaked them in the sink nearby. He draped a dripping towel over her head. "Here, keep this near your nose and mouth. Is there another way out of here?"

"Yeah. Help me pull the carpet up." She scurried to shove a chair to the side.

With the carpet out of the way, a small hatch was revealed. Once they opened it, they wouldn't have much time as the fresh air would feed the flames. She eyed the size of the door and then looked up at J.T.

"I believe I can get through, but you're a big guy and those shoulders..." She had no need to finish the sentence.

Good thing he had small hips, and yet his duty belt would barely fit.

"Go ahead and don't worry about me. I'll find a way." He nodded and stood to the side, giving her enough room to wiggle down into the opening.

She slid to the ground, receiving only a few scrapes and bumps along the way and landed in the dirt between the truck's large double wheels. On her elbows and knees, she scrambled from beneath the truck and waited for J.T. to emerge. Precious seconds ticked by and yet he didn't appear.

"Molly, are you okay?" Willy touched her arm, drawing her attention from the fire.

"Yes, I'm okay. But I'm worried about J.T. He's still in there." She began to pace, eyes wide in fear as the glow in the glass became brighter. She muttered beneath her breath, "We've got to get him out. I knew that hatch was too small. What was I thinking? Stupid to stay in the sleeper." She wanted to cry but was afraid if she did she wouldn't stop. Waving her arms around like a mad woman, she stepped toward Willy. He winced as if she was going to hit him. Poor man. He'd never seen her this crazy. She dropped her hands to clasp her hair, anything to stop herself from pushing the man to make him move faster. "Go, go. Call the fire department."

"Good thing I needed a drink of water. I saw it from the kitchen window and called. They are on their way." He patted her back. "It was so good to see you crawl out before I got out here. But from the look of that fire, I don't think the sheriff's going to make it," Willy said in a sympathetic tone. "I would use this, but I don't think it'll be much help." He lifted a small fire extinguisher normally kept in the kitchen.

She grabbed the red canister from Willie.

"No. He's too stubborn to die in there. I have to do something." She was determined to find a way to save him. No way would she leave him in there to burn.

"Let me. Stay back." Willy reached for her arm, but she jerked away and had just taken a step when the windows blew out of the cab, glass showering the two as they landed on the ground.

Oh, God. Oh, God. *No.* She refused to believe he was dead. He couldn't be. He was strong and smart and oh, God, she loved him. She didn't deserve him, but please, she would go back to church, give more to charities, whatever it took to bring him back to her. As the seconds ticked by and nothing more exploded, she moved her arms and lifted her head.

Juggling the extinguisher in her arms, she regained her feet.

The glow from inside the cab warned her that the fire had spread into the sleeper studio. No one could survive such an inferno. Her vision blurred as tears streamed down her face.

Then she saw movement. Something dark stirred beneath the truck. First a head and then shoulders. J.T. crawled out from between the wheels. In a split second, she dropped the extinguisher and reached his large body to wrap her arms around the most handsome man in the world.

"Thank you, Sweet Jesus." She'd almost lost him.

He groaned as she squeezed him tight.

"Are you hurt? Where?" Without waiting for an answer, she turned to Willy. "Call an ambulance!" She began running her hands over J.T.'s bare back and chest, looking for burns and gashes.

"I'm okay. The blast pushed me the rest of the way out

of that damn little opening and I hit my head. I believe my shoulder's dislocated." He pulled her under his other arm, leaning slightly on her. "I still feel a little woozy."

That was when she noticed how he held his elbow, keeping weight off his shoulder. More soot than blood covered him from head to toe. He made her think of the pictures she'd seen of coal miners coming off their shift.

Her mom and dad came out the side door.

"Oh, no. Molly are you all right. Are you hurt? What happened?" Her mother ran to her side while wringing her hands.

"I'll tell you in a few minutes. First, let's get J.T. away from the fire."

"Looks like to me the boy is the only one hurt." Her dad placed an arm around J.T.'s waist, being careful not to jar his bad shoulder, as he helped with moving him toward the pool area near the house.

About the same time J.T. sat down in one of the patio chairs, they heard the sirens. Red lights flashing, the fire truck pulled into the back and men in reflective striped jackets and pants scrambled around the yard, hooking up the hose to water down buildings. There was no way to save the sleeper studio and cab. They mainly wanted to protect the garage and house surrounding it.

Less than five minutes later, the ambulance pulled up. Though J.T. refused to go to the hospital—men!—he allowed the EMT to check his head—a butterfly bandage was enough. The EMT wasn't allowed to reset his shoulder or inject it with pain medicine. What the hell?

That didn't stop her dad, with J.T.'s fervent permission, to fix the shoulder. The big badass sheriff merely grunted when her dad helped move J.T.'s shoulder back in place. She did notice a band of sweat glistening on his forehead.

Her mother did her maternal part and handed a glass of water and a couple of white tablets for J.T. to take.

Being the usual skeptical law officer, he asked, "Ibuprofen?"

"Of course," her mom answered.

Later, again with her dad's help, they made their way into the house and limped into her old bedroom.

"You know, you're hell on my body," J.T. said as his eyes boldly looked her over.

"Shh." She nodded her head toward her parents. Not that her parents didn't know at this point they were intimate, but she'd rather their private humor remain...well, private.

"Sugar, come down when you get him settled and tell me how all of this craziness happened." Her mom squeezed her in a hug and brushed Molly's hair out of her eyes.

"Leave her alone. We'll find out when she's ready. Let's get downstairs. I need to talk with the fire marshal." Her dad turned to J.T. "Do I need to tell him anything certain?"

"Just to be sure to let me know what he finds. We weren't burning any candles. " J.T. shifted on the mattress.

Her parents finally left the room.

Stretched out on the queen-size bed, J.T. barely fit. For the first time, she was thankful her mom had redecorated the room not long after she'd left home. No embarrassing stuffed animals or posters of movie stars clinging to the walls.

"Come over here and get me out of these." He tugged at the waist of his khaki pants.

She couldn't help it, but she lifted one eyebrow and grinned.

"Dammit, woman, if I wasn't hurting so bad, I would certainly take you up on the offer, but the ibuprofen your mom gave me has knocked me on my ass and my head's spinning."

"I doubt that's the legal term," she muttered.

"What?" His eyes were half open and in seconds he was out.

She stripped his pants off, throwing them into the corner to wash later, and then cleaned him up.

"I didn't have anything to do with the fire," she said to his sleeping form as she sat on the edge of the bed, trying not to jostle his shoulder. After adjusting the pillow beneath his head, she traced his manly brows. Her hands refused to quit touching him. Her fingers caressed the dark bristles making an appearance on his cheeks, traveled down his neck, and over his uninjured bare shoulder, imagining what came close to ending him...well, her stomach rolled with the thought.

They were waiting to hear what the fire marshal had to say. Molly had no idea how the rig caught fire. She'd always been careful with storing the cleaning supplies and keeping up the maintenance of the sleeper and cab.

What a relief to know no one died, especially J.T. She looked at the man who had saved her life. His forehead creased as he gritted his teeth in his sleep. The pain medication, strong enough to knock him out, maybe was not enough to take all of the pain away.

A knock on the door brought her to her feet. Willy opened the door and peeked in.

"Miss Molly, I thought these would come in handy for the sheriff's shoulder. It would have a lot of swelling." Willy handed her a plastic bag of frozen peas.

"Thank you. You're right." She nodded and returned to the bed. J.T. stirred for a moment and was still once again.

She placed the cold bag on his shoulder. He jerked but

didn't wake. With a deep sigh, she leaned back, letting her gaze travel across his massive chest. A little bit of hair sprinkled down the center of his torso. The cotton sheet stopped her perusal, so she checked out the tattoos as they moved with his muscles, drawing her hand to touch them.

He groaned and shrugged, knocking the makeshift compress off his shoulder.

With gentle movements, she adjusted the bag in place. He hissed. She flinched with sympathy.

"Sorry," she whispered.

"It's fine. Just damn cold." He cracked opened his eyes.

"Sorry, but it's not good to let them sit in one spot too long."

The man was amazing. Between the still-healing bullet wound and now his replaced dislocated shoulder, he looked beaten up but only complained about the cold from the frozen peas.

He covered her hand with his and moved over. "Come and lie down with me." He nodded to the side with his good shoulder and arm.

How could she resist such temptation? She placed a knee on the bed.

"No. Take off your clothes. It's only fair."

She laughed. "Sorry. My mom or dad might come in here any minute. There's no way I'd let them see me like that."

"Lock the door." The heated look he gave her brought a flush to her face.

Eyeing him she was sure with a lustful look of her own, she hesitated only a moment more before running across the room and turning the lock. Without another thought, she stepped out of her jeans and tossed the blouse into the corner.

"You know the drugs Mom gave you might interfere with your performance, not counting how sore you must be." She grinned, knowing how most men would take that as a challenge. The warmth of his bare skin pressing against hers was wonderful. Hanging around her appeared to endanger his life more than necessary.

"I disagree." He grabbed her hand.

"You're not grimacing with every move. I'm glad the pain medicine finally kicked in." Her grin spread wider as he wrapped her fingers around his proof. "Oh, I do believe you're right, Sheriff Rogan."

"Don't forget that either." He pulled her down to his lips, and sucked a nipple into his mouth.

"Yes, sir." And she scooted down, taking the sheet with her. He released her nipple with a pop. Then she showed him what else she remembered.

Her mouth encircled the tip as she drew him in. Her tongue danced around the edge and followed her path down his hard length. Where her mouth couldn't reach, she clasped his cock and squeezed. His hips came up and thrust. She choked and pulled away.

"Damn, you're good." His voice sounded gruff but his gaze was soft and needy.

She lifted her eyebrows and returned for another try. Taking in his cock a little farther, she sucked hard as her tongue ran along the raised, throbbing vein.

He clasped her head and pulled her away and then brought her down fast on his length. She didn't choke this time.

"Breathe through your nose and swallow."

Without a second thought, she did as he told her. Why not? Most likely he was the expert. Her lips twitched as the stiff hair tickled.

"Such a good girl. That's enough." He released her. "Straddle my lap. Sit on me."

She scrabbled over, excited to finally have his beautiful cock there again. She needed the closeness, the knowledge he wanted it too. With his good arm, he lifted her up as if she weighed a feather, and brought her down slowly every incredible hard inch and then bounced her a few times. Mercy, the man was about to blow her mind. She planted her hands on the mattress by his sides and rode him hard. He grunted and began to thrust up, skin slapping skin. She moaned. Her orgasm flowed over her and he quickly followed.

She landed flat on him, her ear pressed to his chest, his heartbeat matching her speeding one. Dizzy, she felt like the earth was moving. No. It was only his chest lifting and lowering with each breath. She could stay this way forever.

"Yeah. Such a good woman." Then he grabbed her hair and tilted her head back and brought her mouth to his.

Chapter Thirty-Four

After the fire three weeks ago, the fire marshal had found the fire anchor point beneath the steering wheel but had no idea what started it. They'd hauled off the burnt shell of Molly's cab sleeper to investigate further and report their findings. They sent a section of the dashboard to a lab in Georgia and waited for the results. So far the fire was not considered arson.

J.T. suspected something was terribly wrong. Only he wasn't sure if the fire had been set because of him or Molly. For Molly, it could be some ex-boyfriend with a grudge. For himself, someone he'd put away. After following every lead and questioning every connection, he was tired of beating his head against the wall.

He shifted his irritating sling as he read the week's reports for any new or missed clues. Waiting around for someone to confess or screw up, between the murders and the fire, would certainly drive him insane.

"Hey, boss." Eddie poked his head into J.T.'s office. "The mayor said she's going to be here in about fifteen minutes, wanted to know if you're in."

"That's just what I needed. Tell her I'll call her when I have something concrete."

"She already hung up. She wasn't asking, just checking to make sure you don't leave, and she told me not warn you she's on the way." The deputy grinned.

J.T. chuckled as he grabbed his keys off the desk and pocketed them. "You're a good man." He slapped the deputy on the shoulder as he left his office. "When she shows up, tell her I had a call of domestic disturbance at the Hicks."

"You did?" Eddie followed him through the communications center, which was no more than several desks in a large room with the dispatcher nearest the front door.

Eddie was a good guy, but some days J.T worried about the kid. "No." He looked at him from beneath his brows.

"Oh, yeah. Okay. I'll tell her." The deputy laughed, shaking his head, realizing J.T. was planning to visit Molly.

As J.T. walked out the door, Brooke was coming in. "Hey, where're you going in a hurry?" She pushed her hair out of her eyes and a large diamond ring flashed on her right hand in the late morning sun.

"Got somewhere to be." He continued walking toward his unmarked SUV, wondering who was buying her such extravagant gifts. She wasn't dating anyone he knew of and she sure couldn't afford that big rock on deputy pay. Probably fake.

She called out to him.

He looked back, squinting in the sun.

"Before I forget, Franny said if I happened to see you, for you to swing by the diner around noon. She's got something to tell you." Brooke stood at the door, one hand on her duty belt.

"She didn't tell you what it was?" he asked. It had been

a while since she complained about noise at the Farley place.

"You know how she is. Always wanting attention. She claims it was something she remembered from *that night* is all she'd tell me." Brooke rolled her eyes.

J.T. could guess how Franny's vagueness bothered Brooke. The deputy thought she had to know everything going on in Sand City. Two of the biggest gossips, Sue Marie Blackwood and Betsy Twilldale, had nothing on Brooke McDonald.

He tolerated the different townspeople who loved to share gossip with him. Occasionally, it came in handy in solving a crime or defusing a situation. But inside his department, the last thing he needed was a deputy blabbing confidential internal information. She'd been written up several times by the previous sheriff and a couple of times by him. Between gossiping and staying on the phone with personal business, she was the worst deputy the county had and it had nothing to do with her being a female. During his stint in the FBI, he'd worked with plenty of female special agents. They proved to be twice as competent and hard-working and knew how to keep their mouth shut even more so than their male counterparts. If not for Eddie, a hard worker and respectful of others' secrets, she'd be long gone. At this point, J.T. just didn't need the headache and paperwork required to fire her.

What he needed was to see Molly. Since he'd snuck out of her bed earlier in the morning, he fought with himself on how to proceed with their relationship. Going through a life-and-death situation and sleeping in her bedroom under her parents' roof—which required him tiptoeing in and out of the massive house—qualified whatever they had as more than a fling. He swallowed. He admitted being connected with the Hicks was scary enough, but with a woman he couldn't stop thinking about scared the shit out of him. He'd never felt this way before about another person.

Nothing else would do. He needed to see her again, touch her and hear her voice. Fuck, he had it bad.

He glanced at his watch and grimaced. He rubbed his shoulder and slipped off the sling. The EMTs had told him if the pain continued, the tendons could be damaged, and he would need surgery. Good thing the soreness of his shoulder only bothered him when he moved a certain way. So no surgery.

It was twenty minutes before twelve and the drive out to Magnolia Farms—and Molly—would take too long. Hell, he'd never had a problem keeping his personal and work lives separate. He was losing his mind. Focusing on what he needed to do, he headed toward Bill's Diner and his appointment with Franny. He wondered what she'd remembered.

After pulling over in front of the diner, he lifted his cell phone and called Molly. He dropped his head back on the padded headrest, staring at the roof of the SUV. Yeah, he had it bad. Why couldn't he remember how pushy and frustrating she could be? Instead, the visions of her hair spread out on her pillow and the sexy little grin on her face drove him to distraction.

She should be awake. Considering how he'd been surprised with his stamina and her willingness to try new positions, all in the name of protecting his shoulder, it was no wonder he couldn't keep her off his mind.

Molly's phone rang and rang with no answer. Was she avoiding him or was it simply she couldn't hear it? He shook his head. Now he sounded like some love-sick teenager. As he keyed in the first three digits of the Hicks's main number someone knocked on his driver's window.

He turned his head. Damn. Rachael.

She stepped back as he opened the door. "You're a hard man to get a hold of, Sheriff." The petite woman batted her eyelashes while he ignored her double-entendre.

"What's got the mayor's office all wound up?" Always when he mentioned her elective office, the reminder slowed down her come-ons.

"I wouldn't have to hunt you down if you stayed in one place long enough for me to visit." She placed her hand on his arm. "Did I hear correctly? The night Molly's pickup truck caught fire, you were with her and almost became toast?" Was her concern for real? Or part of her mayor act? "I was at a conference that week, and Fire Chief Randall just informed me of that particular fact."

Pickup truck? He grimaced. If Molly had heard her big rig called a pickup truck, once again he'd be pulling her off the woman. Besides, he doubted the mayor was so concerned about his hide. It was more likely she didn't like competition from Molly. Rachael believed the sheriff's office was her own hunting ground. More importantly, if something had happened to him, she could handpick her own sheriff for his replacement until the next elections.

He moved his arm from her grip. "That was weeks ago and it was her eighteen-wheeler's studio sleeper. No evidence has been uncovered to indicate if it was set deliberately." He really wished the woman would leave him alone and let him do his job.

She patted his cheek. He grabbed her hand, taking it away from his face. Still grinning, she eased her hand out of his grasp.

"You might want to check and see if that brother of hers

escaped out of rehab and set the fire. The whole family is nuts. You would be safer away from such a strange female." Then she sauntered off.

He shook his head. Odd to hear her call others nuts or strange. The woman was nutty as a fruitcake. Chances were the mayor set the fire rather than Devlin endangering his own sister. J.T. had been around women similar to the mayor more than he cared to remember. Her desire was for all men to fawn over her, and heaven forbid if they showed any interest in another woman. He watched as she stopped in front of Nana's Hair Salon. Then Raymond the Weasel stepped onto the sidewalk, exchanged a few words, and hugged the mayor. Rachael hooked her arm in his and they continued on down the sidewalk.

Prime examples of strange bedfellows. J.T. shook his head in disgust. He'd worry about what she was up to with the greasy lawyer later. At the rate he was going, he'd have all the women in town mad at him.

Chapter Thirty-Five

Molly stepped into the diner to see J.T. sitting alone in the corner booth. She almost turned around, but Sam grabbed her shoulders and pointed her to the man who would probably call her a liar. Anyway, she had nothing to say to a man who sneaks out of her bed—not once, but several times—before the sun could peek over the horizon. Okay. Granted it had to be hard on him to sneak in and out of her parents' house, but her bedroom was something like half a city block from her parents' bedroom. Besides, they were adults.

"Are you sure we have to tell him?" She leaned back into his hands as he continued to push her toward the sheriff. "They probably have a don't ask, don't tell policy."

"You're thinking military from years, years ago." Sam released her and gave her a gentle shove. "From what I heard at the gym, they believe Mike's lover was a married woman. They're looking for the wrong person. You got to tell J.T. It'll help your brother. Besides the deputy won't tell, so you have to. You know how important the information could be."

He was right. But she really dreaded telling J.T. What if he believed she was making it up to blame someone else?

They stopped next to the booth. Forehead wrinkled, J.T. looked at her and then Sam and back to her.

"Hey, Sam, haven't seen you in a while." J.T's gaze remained on her as he placed his napkin on the table and crossed his arms. Instead of greeting her, he eyed her as if he'd rather eat her up.

A delicious shiver ran up her spine.

"Yeah, went into Birmingham to visit friends and ended up in Nashville for a few days," Sam said. "Love Sand City, but it's limited on entertainment."

Sam pressed his finger between her shoulder blades and shoved her closer to the sheriff. She shrugged off his touch and then shot him a glare over her shoulder before returning her attention to J.T.

"Uh, I've got something important to tell you." She rubbed her palms down the sides of her blouse and jeans. Why was she so nervous? She and J.T. shared a bed most nights. They even talked after having sex. She just didn't want to lose what they had going on.

"Oh, hell, Molly, have a seat. You too, Sam." J.T. stood and pushed Molly along the side of the booth he'd occupied and followed behind her.

"Hey, quit manhandling me," she half-protested. What was up with these guys pushing her around? She always forgot how strong J.T. was. Yet there was something sexy about how he moved her around without any effort and still be so gentle. Not many men could do that. Well, besides Sam.

As if he were reading her mind, Sam, still standing, grinned. "Thanks, but I can't stay. I've got an appointment with a driver in Trussville." The dirty rat was abandoning ship. "I'll see you tomorrow." Before she could object, he waved and walked away.

When she turned her attention to J.T., his narrowed stare had her straightening her spine. She hadn't done anything wrong. He was the asshole who disappeared this morning.

"Why didn't you wake me?" She hadn't meant to ask that. Where was her determination to prove she could be just as blasé about their relationship as he was?

He moved closer on the bench seat until she was pressed between the wall and his big frame. "I didn't wake you because if I had, I'd never have made it to work on time. Since the fire, I've been late more often than I care to count." He leaned down until his lips brushed her cheek. "It took all my will power not to taste you again this morning."

Thankfully, he said all that in a near whisper. Though the other customers could probably guess at what he was saying by the redness of her face and the nearness of his big body. She was near to breathless from his words alone, not counting the numerous memories of his tongue traveling down her body to the center of her pussy.

"Take me to your house and I'll let you taste me all you want." The way the pupils in his eyes flared, she could tell he liked the idea. She knew she did. Of course, the added bonus was ignoring what she needed to tell him.

His thumb swiped over her lips before he moved back a little. "Wish we had time, but Franny was to meet me here about thirty minutes ago."

"Did you call her?"

"Yeah. Didn't answer." He fingered the material of her silky blouse. When the back of his hand grazed the skin near her shoulder, she took a few quick breaths, hoping her heartbeat would slow. "I was about to go and check on her when you and Sam walked in," he said.

"Okay. Let's go," she said as she worked on regaining control of her libido.

"I don't remember asking you." His intense stare didn't change her mind.

"Franny likes me. What would it hurt if I tag along?" She grinned and leaned toward him for a kiss.

He leaned away. "Then come on," he said in a gruff tone.

With a firm hold of her arm, he pulled her from the booth and headed toward the door, not releasing his grip.

"Hey, I could've gotten out of the seat under my own power, and really, you're squeezing my arm in two."

He quickly released her. She was getting tired of his caveman routine. Despite it being sexy as hell. Just because they slept together, he was acting as if she was his to push around. *His*. If only, but he'd have to work on the push around part.

He set her free and opened the diner's door, blocking half of the opening with his body. She shimmied by and deliberately grazed her breasts against his torso. His dark eyes smoldered. Certain he watched, she swayed her hips as she sauntered toward his SUV. He needed to be punished.

As soon as they buckled up, J.T. shifted the vehicle into reverse and then slapped it into drive. He grunted.

"How's your shoulder?" she asked.

"Fine."

What had she expected? He believed he was too macho to complain. Maybe he'd let her check on it later that night. On nights he came over, they were too hungry for each other for her to stop and look at it. At the moment, the dark half-moons beneath his eyes and creases bracketing his mouth painted a tired man. Last night, she'd found him standing at her bedroom window staring out into the night. The murders and the fire bothered him more than he let on.

"Did they ever report on the cause of ignition?" she asked.

She worried as much as he did, but as no one hated her enough to want her dead, it had to be some criminal from J.T.'s past. All she could do was keep her eyes open. Meanwhile, he needed some tender loving care. She planned to baby him tonight. She bet he'd never been pampered before.

"So far the lab hasn't answered. They should know something more before the week's out." He kept his eyes on the road. "Things like this take time."

Was he hiding something? He was so hard to read while on the job. With a sigh, she settled back in the seat and waited.

In no time, they were at Franny's home. One of her little dogs stood near the door, scratching beneath the knob.

"Hello, little one, are you wanting inside?" Molly picked up the friendly pooch and turned to J.T. "Is Franny the type to forget?"

"No. The dogs are like children to her. Something must be wrong." He tried the knob and the door opened. "Please stay here this time until I tell you it's okay."

When she was about to argue, they heard a scream.

J.T. slammed the door against the inside wall and ran into the house with his gun drawn, muzzle down. "Franny!"

They found her sprawled on the floor in the kitchen near the back entrance, door wide open. J.T. ran outside and came back seconds later, shaking his head. He leaned down and checked her pulse.

"She's alive," he said softly.

Thank goodness. A thin stream of blood ran down her

forehead and along one cheek. The bump on her head was the size of a small boulder.

Molly dialed 911. She kept her gaze on J.T. as he patted the older woman's hand, waking her as gently as possible.

"Where is he?" she asked as soon as she opened her eyes. Franny tried to push up, but reached for her head with a groan and eased back on the floor. J.T. protectively hovered over her.

"Who?" He looked around the room.

Molly pressed the phone to her ear, answering questions as she looked around too.

No other cars were parked outside, and they hadn't seen anyone leaving the backyard, though someone could easily hide in the thick woods behind the house.

Molly shrugged when J.T. glanced her way. She handed Franny a clean dish towel.

"Your brother," Franny said as she pressed the bump with the cloth.

Obviously the blow was worse than they thought. Molly frowned as she told the dispatcher to hurry.

"He's dead." J.T. shook his head.

"That's what he wants you to believe." Her little poodle wiggled next to her as if he sensed her pain and confusion. "He thinks I didn't see him. When he slammed my head into the door frame, I saw him for a split second in the reflection of the glass."

Molly looked at the backdoor with the large, glass center. On the edge, at about the height of Franny's head, was what appeared to be a little skin and hair. She was surprised the glass hadn't broken with the impact of her head to the frame. The doctors would have to determine if her skull was cracked.

"How can you be sure it was Brandon? A bump like

that could make you see birds and stars along with several other imaginary things." J.T. stood and looked at the spot Molly had noticed.

"I'm old but I'm not stupid. I know what I saw and I saw your brother. It wasn't the first time." The older woman shifted on the floor, trying to find a more comfortable spot.

"Quit moving before the ambulance gets here." He kneeled next to her. "What do you mean?"

"The day you found that fellow dead at the Farley house, I spotted Brandon staring out of the second-floor window." When Franny moved the towel from her head and grimaced, Molly was happy to see the bleeding on her head had stopped. Though she did worry the older woman had truly lost it. Seeing dead people? Maybe this wasn't the first time she'd hit her head.

Molly turned to see his response to Franny's tall tale. From his scowl to the shake of his head, he didn't believe Franny either. They stayed with her until the EMTs took her away in the back of the ambulance. With no time wasted, they were heading over to the old Farley place and driving down the long driveway.

"I still say the woman's crazy. Everyone says she's crazy." When J.T. ignored her, she added, "Even nice old ladies can be crazy." From his expression, he was deter-mined to check out the old house. "I thought the Feds had gone over it thoroughly. If your brother was still alive and staying in that house, they would've found him."

The wild look on his face scared her as he slammed on the brakes in front of the Farley mansion and shifted the SUV in park. "What do you know about the FBI being there?" He looked at her as if she'd revealed a state secret.

"Hello. I was there. Remember?" What was up with

him? He'd been acting on edge ever since she'd met him at the diner.

Oh, no, that reminded her. She hadn't gotten around to telling him about Sam's discovery. This wasn't a good time to tell him, but considering she needed to get his mind off his brother and Franny's crazy accusations, she might as well sideswipe him with the news.

He nodded and stared at the upper-story windows, while one hand rested on the back of her seat and the other along the driver's window ledge as if he was settling in for a long wait.

"J.T., I've got something to tell you." Unsure how to say it, she decided on fast, like peeling off a Band-Aid. "Eddie's gay and he's Mike's lover...uh, was his lover." She'd expected a "What?" or something, not the silence and intense stare she received. Had he known already?

When he continued to study her, she shifted in her seat and waited. He obviously needed a few seconds to soak it in.

"What makes you so certain? You do understand if this gets out, it could cause trouble for Eddie, maybe cost him his job? You know how small towns are." His soft tone didn't hide the menace in his words.

"Surely you wouldn't take action against Eddie for holding back this information," she said, a little confused.

She hadn't wanted to get Eddie in trouble, but J.T. needed to know. It could change the direction of the case and take the heat off her brother. She hated throwing Eddie under the bus, but he should've already told J.T.

"No," J.T. said. "He's held back information and did not come forward and admit he's the lover we've been searching for. He could be charged with obstructing justice."

J.T.'s hand stroked her shoulder and began drawing designs on her skin exposed by the off-shoulder blouse. Shivers raced along her arms, beaded her nipples in remembrance of what those big hands could do. His mind appeared to be elsewhere. He probably didn't even realize he was touching her.

He looked up. "Where did you get this information?"

"Sam. He and Eddie hit it off. Whenever Sam's in town, they meet at the gym each morning. Sam's been showing him how to build up his upper body muscles." She hesitated, letting it sink in. When J.T. tilted his head and raised his eyebrows, she knew she'd better hurry with the point. "Anyway, this morning, they were swapping stories about lost loved ones and Eddie burst out crying. Then he tells Sam about the relationship he had with Mike for the last couple of years."

"How do you know this was something we needed to know?" he asked absently, his fingers beginning a new journey across her clavicle before dropping to her chest. He caressed the sensitive skin leading to her cleavage. She leaned toward him, wanting more of his touch, her concentration slowly slipping away.

"The town's been talking about Mike's mystery lover," she said breathlessly as her hand covered his to stop the delicious torture.

Sure, the other day they'd almost made love outside, but today he was keeping his mouth busy by talking and not by licking the parts of her craving his touch. Somehow she needed to snap out of it, positive she was doomed to show her bare ass to the neighbors if she didn't think of something quick. She placed her hand on his chest.

"Brooke," he muttered as he leaned across the console to take her mouth.

Wait. What? Blinking rapidly, as if waking from a daydream, she pressed her fingers to his lips.

"Did you just call me by another woman's name?" That was like cold water to the face. He'd better have a good explanation.

"Hell, no. That's who's been talking. Brooke can't keep her trap closed." He sat back and shook his head, rubbing his eyes as if he'd been in a trance. Kind of the way she felt too. "I need to talk to Eddie and find out what in the hell's going on. I can't see him killing Mike but you never know. And Brooke has a lot to explain."

"You've got to admit, it helped to bring an important answer to light." She reached out and brushed her fingertips across his lips.

His hand shot across the space between them and jerked her into his lap while the other hand yanked on the lever next to the seat, dropping the back. She found herself sprawled over him with his tongue darting into her mouth and encouraging her to taste him in return.

He lifted her blouse and slipped her bra down, revealing one breast to suck and lick the hard nub. "Your breasts are a work of art." He moaned and then took the tip of the other one in his mouth.

She inhaled so deeply, she couldn't regain her breath. The man had the magic touch. Before she passed out, he pulled her bra and clothes back into place and then squeezed her tight as he hid his face in her newly covered cleavage.

"I'm sorry, Molly. I should treat you better. You don't deserve to be manhandled." As though he couldn't resist, he dropped one hand to her butt and pushed her center against his hardness. "I want you, but Lord knows you deserve so much more."

Was she melting in his lap? Each word made her heart clench and she was greedy for more. They were almost as good as if he'd said he loved her. She clasped his head to her chest, running her hands down the soft bristles of cropped hair. If only they were in his bed with the cell phone turned off and the sheets rumpled.

Would he confess to loving her?

Chapter Thirty-Six

J.T. wanted to take her now, but preferably in his soft bed, not in the exposed front seat of an official vehicle. He'd planned to search the house one more time for any clues they'd missed the last hundred times it was searched.

He hadn't planned on making out.

If only there was a way to keep his hands off her.

Movement out of the corner of his eye caught his attention. He lifted his head and looked at the house over Molly's shoulder. A curtain fluttered in a second-story window. The house's electricity was off, so no air conditioning. From the darkness, a man stepped into the sunlight and stared off into the distance and then down at him before disappearing behind the curtains once again.

"Brandon," J.T. shouted at his brother.

He grabbed her shoulders.

"Keep the doors locked," he commanded as he lifted and placed her into the passenger's seat and slammed out of the SUV.

As he ran, part of his brain said he was insane, it was a

mirage, his imagination. There was no way his brother was alive. In seconds, he arrived at the out-of-the-way exit Franny had shown him the other day. When no one came out, he made his way through the dark passage into the house, taking the steps two at a time to the second level, checking the rooms along the way. When he entered the corner bedroom, the room was empty like the rest of the house. Worried Molly could be freaking from his hurried departure, he looked out the same window to see her, arms crossed, sitting in the front seat, staring at the house. She appeared mad, but not upset or in a panic. So Brandon hadn't exited through the front door.

No way was he mistaken. That had been his brother in the window. He didn't believe in ghosts, especially ghosts who attacked elderly women. What game was his brother playing? How was he still alive? How was his presence connected to the agent's murder? Too much of a coincidence that he showed up in the same house the agent's body was found. Yet, nothing connected the two deaths.

As much as he wanted to continue to chase ghosts, he needed to stick with the one plausible lead to his deputy's death. There were two people in his department who he suspected knew more and he was determined to get answers.

Then he would return to ghost hunting.

Chapter Thirty-Seven

Molly tried to follow J.T. into his office, but Brooke grabbed her arm.

"Girl, what's going on? He looks fit to be tied." The beautiful deputy's gaze stayed on J.T.

First, the woman called her "girl." Molly was at least two years older than Brooke. Second, the woman seized her arm, plastic nails digging into her flesh, as she eyed Molly's man. Not just looked, but *leered* at her sheriff's gorgeous sex-toy-walking-worthy rear end.

One of the benefits in working a successful tractor-trailer was the development of muscles from tossing hundred-pound tarps over large loads. Molly grinned as she clutched the deputy's wrist and squeezed.

"Sugar, I guess you'll need to ask him."

"Ouch!" Brooke released her to rub her wrist. "I could arrest you for attacking an officer of the law."

"Oops, I don't know my own strength." She tossed her braid over her shoulder as she strode into J.T.'s office. That would teach Ms. Prissy Pants to not mess with a Hicks.

J.T. stood over his desk, talking on the phone. "Eddie, I

said get your butt in here now! Why not?" He paused, listening to what was an explanation. "Fuck. Get one of the other deputies to handle the accident. Yes, that's what I said." Another pause. "No. What?"

Spotting her, he motioned for her to shut the door.

With immense pleasure, she closed the door in Brooke's red face and drew the blinds. As a teenager, Molly had watched other girls like Brooke date one guy after another while she struggled to get one boy to take her to the prom. So it was understandable jealousy ate her up. J.T. belonged to her and she dared any woman to try something with her standing nearby.

Heat infused her body as she studied his well-muscled body and especially the masculine, hard face. Though his face was smooth from his morning shave, she knew stubble would be showing before dinner. She loved to run her palms over the roughness. His eyes always softened whenever she did.

He was his own man. And no matter what other women wanted, he would be loyal to the one he was interested in. Presently, she was the lucky one and she would absorb his attention as long as it lasted. It was a fact it would end. She never was good at keeping men happy.

Oh, she loved working at keeping that man happy. During her years away, she'd wanted to forget him, to move on. Yet, after being with him in every sense of the word, no other man would do.

She watched as he argued with Eddie over the phone. The uniform stretched across his shoulders and with each move muscles contracted and expanded, reminding her of what was beneath the sturdy material. Closing her eyes for a couple of seconds, she struggled to regain her composure. She needed to stay on an even keel around him. He didn't need an emotional woman worrying about his every word or clinging to him every day.

"Are you okay?" He'd hung up the phone. His gaze remained on hers as he stood and stepped nearer. His arms closed around her.

She nodded and wrapped her arms at his waist and clasped his butt.

He pecked the tip of her nose. "Listen, I know I said I would explain what happened back at the mansion but I need to talk with Eddie alone and see what he knows and why he's been hiding this from me. I'll see you later." His finger skimmed across her bottom lip.

The concerned look in his dark eyes caused her throat to close up. He was being so sweet. *Don't start crying like a nitwit.* She nodded, not trusting her voice.

He pressed a light kiss to her lips and released his hold. "Thank you for understanding."

She nodded, afraid to say anything or she would start bawling. Such a stupid reaction. Last thing he needed was for her to get emotional.

He reached out and brushed hair out of her eyes.

Keeping in mind what she'd thought about seconds earlier—not being clingy—she flashed a smile. "I need to check in with my parents. I'm not sure if they have my name or theirs on the insurance papers. Call me when you get a chance." She squeezed him.

There. She showed she was mature and independent.

"Molly?" He chuckled.

"Yeah?" Lordy, his lips were so lickable. The pit of her stomach clenched. How could she be so turned on by a simple manly chuckle?

"Let go of me," he whispered.

He smiled big and she dropped her hands from his ass.

Her face tingled with heat. Could he really blame a girl for enjoying the feel of such taut cheeks? She stepped away and hid her hands behind her back.

"Ah, I guess I'll get going." She reached for the door knob without looking and bumped into the blinds, making them rattle and swing on their brackets. Shaking her head, she gave him a weak smile, mortified he'd seen her true geekiness, and closed the door behind her.

The only time she felt on equal ground with J.T. was in bed. She wasn't as experienced as he was, but she had a great imagination and was not afraid to use it. Crap! Why was she thinking of him in bed? She needed to keep her mind on other things. Certainly not as pleasant, but hey, they kept her from acting as if she was riding the crazy train. Without looking in Brooke's direction once, Molly hurried across the room and stepped into the sunshine with a sigh of relief.

Chapter Thirty-Eight

J.T. rubbed his shoulder as he peeked between the slats of the blinds, watching Molly run out the front door. That woman was a bundle of contradictions: hard-headed and soft-hearted, femininity personified in bed and any man's equal on a big rig, self-assured when protecting others but vulnerable when protecting herself. It was hard not to like her. He chuckled as he adjusted himself. That was part of his problem. Every time the woman walked into the room, he grew hard as a crowbar and forgot all about what he needed to do. He sobered on the next thought: what if he liked her too much?

He frowned. It was time for him to rein in his wayward thoughts and decide how to handle Eddie and his negligence in not reporting an important piece of the case.

Two hours later, J.T. walked around the interrogation room table and sat in the chair across from a pale-faced Eddie. He should be worried; he'd impeded a murder investigation. Knowing how much the man loved being a deputy, firing him would be near to a death sentence.

"Tell me again what happened that night." They'd gone

over it twice already but often witnesses—his gut feeling said Eddie hadn't killed Mike—usually remembered something new on the retelling.

"He left my apartment that evening to go on patrol. Every second and fourth Saturday night was his turn to keep an eye on the Sandbox and the surrounding neighborhood, and answer any of their disturbance calls. It was my day off, so I stayed home. That's all I know." Eyes red-rimmed and hands trembling, he sniffed, swiping his nose with a handkerchief.

It saddened J.T. to see the young guy torn apart with grief and worry, but it was necessary. Eddie was the key to solving the murder, the truth would come out.

"Did anyone see Mike leave your place? Was someone waiting to talk with him outside?" J.T. folded his hands on the table between them.

"Not that I know of. Brooke lives next door but she was out with a friend." Eddie leaned back, looking at the ceiling, rapidly opening and closing his eyes, trying to keep the tears from falling again. "I don't know why anyone would kill Mike. Everyone liked him. You know how bad he was about letting people off with only a warning. The time he and Devlin argued was one of the few times he let his temper get away from him. Brooke said she never saw his face turn so red, it was almost purple."

"Brooke was at the Sandbox?" J.T. asked. That was new. Damn it, why hadn't she piped up and added her observations?

"Yeah. Off duty and having a drink. Why?" The young deputy shrugged his shoulders.

"I understand—though don't agree—why you kept your mouth shut, but we all know Brooke can't keep a secret worth a shit. So why didn't she tell us she was there when Mike and Devlin argued?"

"Maybe because you had several witnesses about Mike and Devlin's argument and she didn't have anything to add?" Eddie's tone suggested he didn't believe what he was saying. He was just trying to take up for his cousin.

Taking up for a sibling or any close relative or friend, he understood, but Brooke most often treated Eddie's feelings with careless disregard. Yet Eddie adored Brooke and gave her whatever she asked for.

Until he and Mike found something in common?

Hmm. When Eddie finally found someone to love him for himself, had that burnt Brooke's butt? Perhaps she thought Mike owed her for taking Eddie away from her immediate sphere of influence.

"When did you and Mike start your relationship?" Chances were he was wrong but it was something worth looking into.

Teary eyed, Eddie stared unseeing at the floor. "Ah, about a year ago. Not long after I joined the department. We've been talking about moving in together since February."

If he remembered correctly, Brooke had driven up in the Mustang around St. Valentine's Day. Everyone had speculated she had a rich boyfriend, but he now suspected something entirely different.

"Have you ever asked where Brooke got all the money to buy the fancy jewelry she's been wearing or her tricked-out Mustang?" he asked as he stood and reached for the doorknob.

"I've always assumed some boyfriend in Birmingham was buying all that stuff." Eddie's eyes widened as he came to the same conclusion as J.T. had already. "She was blackmailing Mike. She'd asked me several times why Mike was coming over so early in the morning." He blushed when he realized how much more he'd revealed. "I thought she was just being nosey like usual. Most times she respected my privacy more than that. We're cousins and best buddies for crying out loud. I knew she suspected but I never thought she'd use it against me...or Mike."

J.T. opened the door. "Hey, Brooke, come in here."

"She's gone." The dispatcher, Karen, shifted in her desk chair with one arm crooked over the back.

"Where did she go?" J.T. asked.

"She didn't say, but I overheard her on the phone to Nina over at the bank, something about a safe deposit box." The woman remained still, waiting for any further questions.

"Eddie, come with me." He started toward the front door. "Karen, call my cell if Brooke shows up here. Don't tell her I'm looking for her."

What in the world did she have in a safe deposit box?

Chapter Thirty-Nine

olly had never seen Brooke in such a hurry. The deputy was actually rude to Nina, the small, blonde bank clerk, when it took a little while to find the keys for the safe deposit vault.

A couple of steps to the side gave Molly a clear path through the bank's lobby as she watched Brooke follow Nina into a barred-off room at the end of a hall. Between the bars, Molly could see the clerk unlock a box from the wall and place it in a small alcove for privacy. Then Nina said something to the deputy and whatever Brooke answered in return caused Nina to pull her head back and turn on her heels in indignation. With a sniff, she closed and locked the gate behind the deputy.

Before Molly could stop the woman and ask what the heck was going on, J.T. and Eddie came marching into the bank. J.T. had his official, closed look on his face. The same one she'd seen up close and personal when she'd shot him. Eddie's eyes were swollen and as red as his nose, as if he'd been on a crying jag.

J.T. spotted her and shook his head, holding her off from

coming toward him. He placed a hand on Nina's back and led the blonde back to the gate. The woman nodded with a glint in her eyes and unlocked the gate, letting in the sheriff and his deputy. Only a few minutes passed before Eddie, holding Brooke's arm, came out of the safe deposit vault.

"You little weasel! What did you tell your hero?" Brooke harangued Eddie all the way through the bank and out the front door. "Did you tell him all about doing the nasty deed with Mike?"

Several of the customers stared wide-eyed as they put their heads together, whispering the latest scandal.

J.T. spoke to Nina and a man in a three-piece suit who looked to be William Peabody, Sand City Bank's president and manager, for a few minutes before he stopped next to Molly.

"What are you doing here?" He had what Molly assumed was Brooke's safe deposit box under his arm.

"The usual type of bank stuff," she answered. "What's going on with Brooke?"

"We're taking her in for questioning," he said and then added, "I've got to wait for the judge to issue a court order allowing me to open this box."

Her eyebrows lifted. Was this J.T. Rogan providing her with an explanation without her prying it out of him? Was the world coming to an end?

He stepped closer. In a public place like this, she normally didn't like anyone invading her space, but J.T.'s firm, big body was the exception.

"What for?" She grabbed his hand and absentmindedly traced the little bit of tattoo revealed near the cuff of his shirt.

"Later." He cleared his throat as he turned his hand, slipping a key into hers. "Be at my house tonight, nine o'clock sharp. Ready and willing." He reminded her of the promise she'd made the other night.

Her pussy clenched with the thought of being *ready and willing* as he ordered. It wouldn't be a problem. She grinned. Tonight he would get more than what he asked for. There were a couple fantasies she wanted to play out with J.T. She only wondered if he was up to it.

Chapter Forty

J.T. doubted Brooke would ever break. Then at eight-thirty, he finally got the court order allowing him to open the safe deposit box with the bank's president, vice president, and her lawyer in attendance. Inside were pictures she'd taken of Mike and Eddie. J.T. quickly moved them out of sight—no need to upset Eddie—and then found a copy of the letter she'd given Mike outlining what would keep her quiet. Underneath other papers, including copies of emails, he found three monthly statements with a Birmingham bank's logo on the pages. From the looks of it, Mike had paid her nearly seventy-two-thousand dollars from February through April and nothing the last two months before Mike's death. Probably had wiped out the man's life savings, leaving Mike with nothing more to keep Brooke happy and quiet.

J.T. reminded Brooke she'd better confess and get life without parole as Alabama wasn't afraid to use the death penalty, especially for cops who killed their own. Then she finally admitted she'd shot Mike during an argument behind the Sandbox. Mike had decided to tell everyone the truth about being gay and she saw any possibility of more black-mail money going bye-bye.

Pleased one case was solved, J.T. was still saddened by the waste of two lives: Brooke had ruined her future and took the life of a good man for the love of money.

Tired beyond belief, he rubbed his eyes as he sat slumped behind his desk. Though solving Mike's murder helped take some of the weight off his shoulders, he still had one more murder to solve. When he asked Brooke about the body in the Farley place, the surprise on her face was too real. He had questioned her further, just in case, if she had known the man was a special agent and had been involved in his death. She had nothing, only the information the sheriff's and FBI offices had. By the end of the interrogation, her emotions were raw and near the surface to the point that if he'd asked about any tests she'd cheated on in high school, she would've confessed to them all.

Her only concern was what benefited her and nothing pointed to her guilt in the special agent's death. That confirmed he had another murderer on his hands somewhere.

Tomorrow, he'd call Special Agent Reese along with Devlin Hicks's family with the news. Big Joe would probably make J.T.'s life a misery, holding the accusation of his son's arrest over his head for a long time.

The drive home helped clear some of the cobwebs in his brain. He turned into his drive and parked the SUV to the side. His garage had room for only his gym equipment and his personal truck that he'd worked on the other day and hadn't returned to the outside. As he stepped out of the SUV, he spotted Molly's Jeep. It was nearly eleven o'clock. He was glad she'd stayed. His grin widened. She'd backed the Jeep in behind his garage, trying to hide in the shadows.

She still worried about what the neighbors thought. He grinned at the rather endearing trait.

He tossed his hat on the kitchen table and loosened his tie, unbuckling and unsnapping the duty belt. After he placed his gun in its safe, the glow from his bedroom lit his way down the hallway. As he strode into the bedroom, he noticed two things: One, candles were placed on every conceivable surface; two, all the blood had left his upper body.

Molly was on his bed without a stitch on except for a hat like his on her head and a fake duty belt minus gun strapped low around her hips. She came to her knees, pushing the hat low, covering her eyes.

"Mister, I believe I need to strip search you for hidden weapons," she said in a husky voice. She placed her arms akimbo, thrusting her beautiful breasts toward him.

Chapter Forty-One

Molly blinked. Had she messed up big time?

J.T. stood in the middle of the room without saying a word or making a move toward her. Had she overstepped some law enforcement boundary by wearing his spare hat and belt?

She'd gotten the crazy idea while waiting two hours in his bedroom and wanting it to be a memorable night.

She was about to apologize when he began unbuttoning his shirt and toeing off his shoes. In seconds, he was naked and stalking her across the bed to the other side. Her heartbeat sped up on seeing every beautiful, masculine inch of him. He grabbed her hat and tossed it to a chair. Without slowing, he expertly unbuckled her belt and tossed it to the floor as he pushed her onto her back. His hard cock pressed between her legs.

Oh, yes, her performance certainly got his attention.

Relieved he had liked it so well, her body craved his in ways she'd never imagined. She wanted him to do more than satisfy her. She wanted him to fill the emptiness inside. A feeling like desperation brought her legs against his waist and her arms around his neck as she tried to force him to hurry and enter her. She pressed her nose into his neck, savoring the masculine musky smell with a faint sweetness of soap. Home. She belonged in his arms.

"Shh, what's wrong, baby?" He began rocking her as he cradled her in his arms and rubbed her back.

That was when she realized tears dripped off her cheeks. She was crying. Oh, mercy, what was wrong with her?

"I'm so sorry." She sniffled as she grabbed a corner of the top sheet and patted at her face. Thankfully, she hadn't worn more than mascara. "I don't understand why I did that. I swear I was so turned on. You're so gorgeous. Everything I ever dreamed about." Warmth trickled down her face. "Oh, no, I can't stop." She covered her face and tried to move away, to hide, to go anywhere to recover from the embarrassment.

He held on tight, rocking and shushing her in an attempt to give her comfort.

"You have nothing to be embarrassed about." One broad hand smoothed her hair down her back, while the other braced her waist. She felt wrapped around by him. She felt safe.

Yes, he was nearly perfect.

She kissed his neck. He stopped moving. She wiggled enough to straddle his lap. The next kiss landed on his earlobe and she couldn't resist sucking on the flesh. His groan vibrated through her body. Her tongue licked the tender spot behind his ear, bringing a growl. Unable to resist, she giggled as she dropped her mouth to the heartbeat on his neck and sucked hard.

"Damn, Molly, stop!" He jerked away and glowered.

"The old ladies would have a field day if I show up with a hickey."

"You're too late. Tell them you had a dull blade. You've got a pretty, dime-sized one." She giggled again. From tears to giggles. She felt like she was on a rollercoaster. Her heart pounded with excitement. She couldn't stop smiling.

"You're going to pay big time." He held her down on the bed and scraped his rough chin across hers.

"You stinker." She dropped her hands and dug her fingers into his sides. He jerked away from her and grabbed for her hands. "Ah-ha! I forgot you're ticklish! I love it!" She giggled. Warmth from his big body pulled her closer to him, if that was even possible.

They wrestled, rubbing hard and soft spots until they both were panting. When he pushed into her heat, she stilled and gasped. About time. She wanted him inside of her every hour on the hour.

"Feel as good for you too?" He breathed into her ear.

She nodded and clasped his face to kiss him. Unable to resist the allure of those pouty masculine lips, she nipped them and pulled as her tongue savored the trapped flesh. She released him at the same time his fingers tweaked a taut nipple and she groaned. The sweet pleasure edged near to pain. She trusted J.T. not to go too far.

His tongue filled her mouth with a need she could assuage only by sucking and massaging it. He responded by thrusting into her with long strokes, staking his claim on her body in every way he could. With a roar, he moved from her mouth and bent over her breast and took a nipple between his teeth, flicking his tongue across the sensitive nub.

"Ahh!" Oh, yes. The man knew how to make a woman scream. Thank goodness he hadn't tried any of his special tricks on her in her parents' house. She'd had a difficult enough time keeping quiet then.

His hands cupped her breasts, squeezing them to make them tighter and harder as he gave the other one the same treatment. She grabbed his head and rubbed her palms along the sides, letting him know how much she liked what he was doing.

No longer able to withstand his special attention to her breasts, she dug her nails into his buttocks, encouraging him to go faster, more forcefully. With each plunge the bed shook and they grunted in unison, driving, plowing toward their mutual satisfaction. Then their bodies released the tension, bringing wave on wave of what they had never truly felt with anyone else before, total and complete fulfillment.

Molly stared wide-eyed at the ceiling as she caught her breath. She was going to be so sore tomorrow. She grinned.

Within minutes, her eyelids began to drift close and a muscular arm pulled her closer. The scent of sex and man surrounded her and she rested against his big body. She sighed. She never wanted to move again.

Maybe tomorrow he'd ask her to stay. Forever.

Chapter Forty-Two

A true Southern breakfast was one of the few meals Molly knew how to cook. Biscuits, gravy, grits, bacon and sausage with fluffy scrambled eggs along with strawberry jam on the side. She'd brought all the ingredients, knowing that most men rarely cooked in. Especially men who worked long hours like J.T., and she'd planned to stay the night if everything had gone right. And, mercy, had it ever.

Checking the biscuits for the hundredth time, she bent down to peek through the glass panel.

"Good smells and a beautiful view. What more can a man ask for?"

She stood and turned with a big smile. J.T waited in the doorway of the kitchen, barefoot and shirtless, with his arms braced along the doorframe. He was grinning ear-to-ear.

Wasn't it interesting how good a person felt in the morning after amazing sex?

She barely held back the verbal ah, but instead exhaled loudly. He was so damn hot. She could stare at him all day. Plus she was happy he wasn't one of those men who panicked when a woman cooked breakfast the morning after making love all night.

"I hope you don't mind. Figured a good breakfast wouldn't hurt either of us," she said. Chances were he could still panic. So she crossed her fingers for good luck and then returned to the oven. She slid out a pan of biscuits and quickly lifted a couple to his already-full plate, topping the biscuits off with gravy before placing it on the table nearest where he lingered.

J.T. reached into the laundry nook and pulled on a clean, blue T-shirt and then sat where she'd placed his food. "This looks great. Thanks, Molly."

Warmth came to her cheeks as she prepared her plate. "I'm glad you like it."

By the way he tucked into the meal, she could tell he meant it. Yet, he ate like a gentleman, napkin and one hand in his lap while holding the fork with the other. Perfect manners. Probably his mother's influence before she left— correct that, died.

The thought reminded her of another death. "Did Brooke know anything about the man who died in the Farley house?" J.T. had told her last night about Brooke's confession. She'd been so relieved that all doubt about her brother's innocence had been cleared up, she hadn't thought to ask.

"No. We still have another murderer out there along with whoever set your truck on fire." J.T. took a bite of the eggs. "This is good."

"So they've decided it was set?" Mercy, who in the world would want her dead?

"Sorry, sweetheart."

She pushed her plate to the side. "What do we do now?"

"You do nothing," he said in a firm voice. "You'll tell me if anyone comes to mind of who could want to hurt you."

"There's no one." She shook her head.

He took another bite and chewed as he kept his gaze on her.

She shifted in her seat, feeling uneasy by his stare. Why was he looking at her like that? There was something about a man in law enforcement staring a person down that made the person confess to about anything to make him stop. Doing her best to ignore his fierce scrutiny, she pulled the plate back and concentrated on her food. The previous night's exercise had burned up a week's worth of calories and she needed the fuel, no matter how uptight she felt.

"What were you doing in the bank?" he asked.

Her shoulders tensed. Someone was trying to kill her or J.T. and he wanted to know why she was in the bank? She really didn't want to talk about it, but the expression on his face said he wouldn't let her do anything else. She sighed and took her last bite.

"I was filling out paperwork for a loan." She rose from her chair and picked up the empty plate.

"What would a Hicks need with a loan?" J.T. pushed his plate away and leaned back in his chair, holding the cup of coffee between his hands.

With a shake of her head, she avoided looking his way as she loaded the dishwasher. Sure, she was a Hicks, but it was her father who had the money, not her. Before she knew it, J.T. had grabbed her shoulders and turned her toward him.

"Are you in trouble? Is there something you need to tell me?" He smoothed hair out of her face.

Was he asking because he was a cop? Or was it concern

for someone special? She sure hoped it was the latter. She needed it to be concern and not suspicion.

"No. I'm not in trouble. The insurance company is taking its time to pay me and I need a down payment for a new truck. Not counting the cost and six-month wait for a custom sleeper." She wrapped her arms around him, resting her head against his neck, inhaling his all-male scent. He was better than any nerve-pill prescription.

"What about your parents?"

"They don't approve of my job and wouldn't loan me a dime if I was stupid enough to ask." She slipped her hand underneath his T-shirt and rubbed his chest. "I don't need their help. In three months, I'll have the loan for the down payment paid off and surely the insurance money will be in and cover the major part of a new rig. I have some in savings and a few CDs I can cash to cover the rest if I need to. Worse gets to worst, I can borrow against my share of the trucking company." She leaned back a little and eyed his guarded expression. "Sam told me about a deal he brokered with a local manufacturer that has a large job in Seattle. I can use one of his older rigs. It'll be good money." She waited for him to ask her to stay. She would for him.

"When do you leave?" he asked in an even tone.

The air left the room. She stopped her caresses. She was surprised her heart didn't stop beating.

His hand covered hers. The closed look remained on his face.

"In two days." She stepped back, dropping her hand away from his. What had she expected? For him to admit he cared for her? Was she asking for too much?

"Well, I hope you have a good trip." He crossed his arms, his gaze steady, not leaving her face.

Why was his nonreaction a surprise? Everything she'd

done last night and this morning was to prove she wouldn't bore him. That she could be interesting and sexy. Maybe mind-blowing sex was an every woman occurrence to him. Maybe she was boring and nothing different or special like the other women in his past.

She'd really hoped he would beg her to stay. Instead he acted all cold and unfeeling. Didn't he feel anything for her at all? Didn't he want her to stay? Once again, had she made more out of their attraction than what it was? When would she ever learn not to wish for what she would never have?

Probably never. She'd always been a bit of a gambler.

She'd gambled on winning his affection by becoming interesting in bed and hoped to press him into making a declaration of some sort when she mentioned the job. Then she remembered the reason she hated to gamble. Losing sucked.

Chapter Forty-Three

J.T. expected more out of Molly. Last night had been special. He hoped it had been the same for her. Why was he surprised she wanted to end their relationship? Why was he hurting? Why did it matter? He was just another cock in a port for her.

Fuck. Was that fair? He'd never seen her flirt with other men. There was no evidence of other men in her life. Sam being an exception.

He tightened his fists to keep from reaching for her. One thing was for sure, he never begged a woman to stay and he wasn't about to start now.

"I'll be sure to call you when the official written report comes in from the fire marshal on your truck."

Keep it on an even keel. That was what he needed to do.

The glitter in her eyes confused him. She actually looked like she was about to cry. Damn. He massaged his temple and turned from her. What did she want him to say? That he would worry about her and she needed to be careful with so many psychos out there.

For fuck sake. Someone wanted her dead.

"Okay." Her voice was soft, as if it was difficult to talk.

He nodded and mind-numbing chill encased him as he walked out of the kitchen. He found himself blindly staring at his mussed bed when he heard the front door slam shut and the Jeep start. Then he questioned everything. Had he'd royally screwed up? She had walked out on him, but his pride had pushed her away. What had he expected? He was the one who had indicated they were friends with benefits only.

He rubbed his head—damn it hurt—and clasped his fingers on top.

She'd be all right. In less than fifteen minutes she would be with her parents, safe and sound. She wasn't leaving for a couple of days. He'd check on her tomorrow. She would be fine.

Time to get his mind back off of Molly. He pulled out an unwrinkled uniform shirt and pants from the closet. It was time to get to work.

Was Franny as crazy as everyone said and only imagined his brother was alive and had attacked her? He'd seen the mushroom of blood on his brother's shirt the day he'd died. He'd watched as his brother landed on the floor, motionless. He'd been there when the EMTs pronounced him dead. The ashes. Whose ashes had he spread near the lake they'd swam as boys? No. He was dead and Franny was losing it. And Molly was leaving him.

He closed his eyes and took a deep breath. Damn, he needed to keep his mind on his job.

How did he account for seeing Brandon in the same window of the second floor's corner bedroom? Maybe Franny's story had triggered his imagination.

Ignoring the rumpled bed and how it got that way, he

walked into his bathroom to take a quick shower. By the time he'd dressed and strolled out the door, he decided the woman was crazy and stress had made him imagine seeing his brother. He might be going crazy himself for he especially needed to keep his mind and hands off of Molly. That was apparently what she'd wanted. Everyone knew Hicks and Rogans didn't mix well.

He turned off Main Street, a block from headquarters, and saw the first sign of trouble. A large, white truck with a local station number plastered on the side was surrounded by a huge crowd of people. As soon as he parked, the nearby Birmingham news stations wanted all the bent details of one officer being arrested for another officer's death and blocked parts of the sidewalk into the building.

"Sheriff Rogan, was your female deputy blackmailing the deputy to have an affair with her?"

"Sheriff, is it true your female deputy had affairs with several of the other deputies?"

"Were you having an affair with your deputy?"

The shouted questions became crazier with each outburst. He weaved his way through the jostling crowd, promising information later in the day. His fists clenched as he held tight on his control. The walking nightmare continued when he broke up a fight between two of his deputies, with reporters taking snapshots and egging them on. Once the door closed behind him, he came face-to-face with the mayor and several city councilors.

Hell, he was living in hell.

Chapter Forty-Four

Molly frowned at Raymond the Weasel who was busy going through her dad's desk drawers.

"Do you have any idea how screwed you're going to be when Daddy hears about this?" She leaned against the doorframe with her arms and ankles crossed.

"Now why would you do that when your daddy sent me to look for some papers?" Raymond might be a good liar in court, but she'd grown up with him. The flush on his face made her think of a little boy caught playing with himself.

"Daddy is rather particular in where he leaves his files and he would tell you exactly where to find them. So you need to work on a better explanation." If not for the seriousness of the situation, Molly would be laughing.

Raymond slammed the drawer closed. "You know, you and your brother always thought you were too good for the likes of me. Considering what I know about your father, you better stay on my good side or I might be tempted to put him away for life."

Molly stood straight. "And I would make sure you were sitting next to him in prison."

He narrowed his beady little eyes. "I don't think your daddy would last long in there."

With a tug at his lapels, he headed toward the doorway. Not wanting to take a chance of his brushing up against her, she stepped to the side to let him pass. He stopped in front of her, his gaze sweeping over her breasts.

She crossed her arms over her chest and glared. "Get out."

"I'll be back and you'll welcome me with open arms," he threatened.

"Over my dead body," she hissed.

He smiled and finally his gaze lifted to her face. "That's your father's area of expertise."

Before she could ask what he meant by that, he was gone. She needed a shower to get rid of the rat stench.

"Miss Molly, are you all right?" Willy stood in the hallway, peering in.

"I'm fine. Daddy's lawyer is a creep." Remembering how she'd found Weasel rummaging through her dad's study, she touched Willy's arm. "Where is Daddy?"

"He and Miss Lisa went to pick up Mr. Devlin." He eyed her with concern. "Is there something I can help you with?"

"No, thank you. I needed to talk to him." Actually she wanted to cry on his shoulder. Once more she'd been too pushy and instead of pushing herself into J.T.'s life, she got pushed out. Before she started crying again, she changed the subject. "Does Weasel help himself in Dad's office often?"

"I believe Mr. Joe asked for Mr. Beauregard to fax over some papers that he'd forgotten. They're to help in the release of Mr. Devlin from the state's authority now that he's been declared innocent of all charges. Or something like that." Willy grinned, obviously happy about Devlin's return home.

Molly was too, but she worried he hadn't been in rehab long enough. Her parents ignoring her brother's terrible drinking problem was typical of the way they handled anything negative to do with Devlin. And Willy's assurance Weasel had a real reason to be in her dad's study still didn't settle the uneasy feeling in her stomach.

She turned and headed toward the den, planning to watch television until her parents returned home. Something mindless to keep her thoughts off J.T. was better than being uneasy about what Weasel had really been up to in her dad's study. Anything to numb her feelings and keep her from thinking about this morning. She thumbed the remote, looking for a movie when she heard the back-door slam. The murmurs confirmed her parents were home.

"Where's Devlin?" Molly stopped next to the kitchen's breakfast bar and rested a hip on one of the stools.

"He said he wanted to pay his bill off at the Sandbox and would find a way home later." Her dad gave her a curious look. "Don't give me that look, girl. He's a grown man. He has to learn on his own to say no to that first drink."

"Do you really think dropping him off at the neighborhood bar would help him stay sober?" She shook her head as she rubbed her temples. Dealing with her parents brought on a headache faster than a hit to the head.

"Young lady, your daddy knows what's best for Devlin. Your brother's aware it's time he accepts his responsibilities." Her mom shook a finger at her and then turned to place the pizza they brought on the table. The older woman turned to the refrigerator and pulled a head of lettuce out.

Molly knew if she didn't get out of there quick, they would begin a lecture on her own life, especially on settling down and quitting that monstrous truck. They certainly would be none too happy with her news of leaving. Though normally at odds with her parents, she knew they enjoyed having both of their children nearby. With her parents glaring as if she'd stolen the prettiest pig in the poke, she decided to retreat and go look for her brother. She had two days to make sure her brother would be okay, tell her parents she was leaving, and at the same time, avoid J.T. She wasn't a coward, but she was afraid if she saw him again, she would do something stupid like beg him to take her back. Or shoot him again. The ignorant jerk.

Molly took a deep breath. First, her brother, and then she'd worry about the rest.

Sam had returned to Atlanta and promised to be back with the borrowed truck day after tomorrow. She could only hope her brother wasn't backsliding into an alcoholic haze and could give her a sympathetic ear. Maybe she could persuade him into returning to Bradford Rehab.

"I have an errand to run."

Yes. Maybe she was a coward. And thankfully, worrying about her brother took her mind off her own troubles. At the way her parents eyed her, if she started to cry on her father's shoulder, she would only reinforce their belief she needed a steady man and that her choice of a living was too much for her.

"Willy said you wanted to talk with me." Her dad placed his arm around her shoulder. She wanted to enjoy the rare attention, but all she wondered was, what was he up to? Never the type of dad to offer comfort for a skinned knee, he was more apt to say, "Don't be a wimp. Walk it off." Maybe his dose of reality was what she needed.

"Did you send Raymond to pull some papers from your office?" she asked, the words spilling out before she could stop them. Willy may be wrong.

"Yeah. He faxed some papers to the courthouse. Why?"

The fine lines around her dad's mouth and eyes reminded her he was sixty. His years of working outside and making a living doing everything from farming to running construction companies were catching up with him.

"I caught him rummaging through your desk drawers," she said.

His arm tightened on her shoulder and quickly relaxed. That was interesting. He was working at hiding his irritation.

"Which drawer?" he asked.

"He was straightening up when I walked in. So I would say he looked at the bottom right one." She craned her neck to look him in the eyes.

"The right one as you're facing the door?" His eyes narrowed.

"Yeah. Why? What's going on, Dad?" She stepped out from under his arm and looked him in the eyes.

"Nothing, Sugar. Just curious." He pursed his lips and stared off.

Before she could say anything, he glanced back at her and then he walked to the kitchen table. Her mom slid a salad and two slices of pizza in front of him as he sat. He looked her way again. His eyes opened wide with simulated innocence which didn't fool Molly. He was up to something and also knew well what Weasel was up to.

Frustrated that he wouldn't answer truthfully, she snapped, "Okay. Be that way." As soon as she said it, she knew her mom wouldn't let her get away with the smart-aleck attitude.

"Now, Missy, you better watch yourself. Your dad doesn't have to explain anything. Either you sit down and eat with us or you go and check on your brother and see why he's not home yet." With penciled eyebrows raised, her mom waited for her decision.

What was going on with her parents? And why was she still trying to understand them? She had to be adopted.

"I'll head over to the Sandbox and see what's holding him up." As she reached the kitchen door, she looked back. Her parents were leaning toward each other, whispering. She wanted her and J.T. to be like that one day. Tears welled in her eyes. Her parents were so lucky to have each other.

But really, what could a couple, married for thirty-five years, have to talk about that their grown daughter shouldn't hear?

Chapter Forty-Five

"I told you Raymond was no different from his slimy father." Lisa narrowed her eyes. "I never knew what you saw in that man."

"Now, Sugarplum, his daddy was one of the best lawyers in the state and with the extra incentive I provided, he got us out of several tight squeezes over the years. Junior asked me to look after his son and give him a good living." Joe would always keep the late Raymond Beauregard Junior's secret.

Raymond Beauregard III's daddy's death due to AIDS had been a result of enjoying the favors of the cheapest whores offered in Birmingham and Atlanta, and Joe made sure he had plenty of the skankiest. Just the way Junior liked them. As soon as Raymond Junior had received the test results, he'd called Joe into his office and told him what he planned. Just as J.T.'s dad had done.

Joe mentally shook his head. Why in the hell did men confide in him about their plans for death? Two days after receiving the dreaded results, Junior, filled with self pride, had shot himself. Such hypocrisy. He'd rather go to hell for suicide than to heaven in forgiveness.

"Then what's he up to?" She grasped his hand.

"I have no idea. Better safe than sorry. I'll move Harry's papers to another place." He kissed the back of her hand.

"Why don't we let J.T. have his dad's papers?" she asked.

"It's not time yet. We're still waiting for Harry's last wish to be fulfilled and then all will be as it should." Joe only hoped no one else died in the meanwhile.

Chapter Forty-Six

Molly couldn't believe what the bartender had told her when she reached the Sandbox. At least she hadn't until she walked into the Sand City Community Center and peeked into meeting room number fifteen. There was her brother sitting with his sandy-blond hair caught beneath his button-up shirt collar, wearing paint-stained pants, and with head bowed as if in prayer. The meeting adjourned and several people raced to a table loaded down with donuts and large, silver urns of coffee and hot water for tea. She stepped out of the way as others streamed into the hallway.

"Psst! Brother." A few raised eyebrows turned toward her and she smiled, pointing to Devlin.

When she looked back to her brother, she found his seat empty. On the other side of the podium, a door swung back and forth as if someone had just pushed through. By the time she caught up with him, he'd reached the street.

"Devlin! Didn't you hear me calling you?" She clasped his arm, jerking him to a stop to face her.

"Actually I did, Sis. Did you ever stop to think I was

trying to avoid you?" he asked in a gruff voice, his eyes red and puffy.

If she didn't know better, she'd swear he'd been crying. He lifted his shoulder and rubbed his face against his upper arm. Oh no, he had.

"I'm sorry." She stepped nearer and placed her arms around his waist. "Oh, Devlin, I'm so sorry."

His big body began to shudder. He squeezed her tight as he pressed her cheek to his neck.

"There's nothing to be sorry for. I brought this on myself." Inhaling deeply, he released her and moved away. "I thought drinking would help me get over constantly disappointing Dad. But instead I've let everyone down." He wobbled and caught her arm to regain his balance.

"Let's sit over here." Molly pointed to a bench under a large oak tree. The small park area next to the Center was a perfect setting for the brother and sister to have a heart-to-heart talk. "Well, I know all about disappointing Mom and Dad."

Lids halfway closed, he looked at her. "Aren't we a pair? I drink and you run." He flopped next to her.

"I don't—"

"That's what you did five years ago. And from the way you're squirming on the bench, I got a hunch you're about to leave again. Is that why you came looking for me?" He leaned forward, elbows on his knees as he clasped his hands, looking at the ground.

She could feel his loneliness. Blinking her eyes like a butterfly flapping its wings, she held back the tears. He was right. She ran whenever the going got tough.

"Yeah. I guess I do." She scooted next to him and stretched an arm across his back, resting her chin on a broad shoulder. "That meeting you were in, it was an AA meeting, wasn't it?"

He took a deep breath and slowly released it. "Yep. I'm tired of waking up and not remembering what I did the night before." A stillness came over him. "Dad offered to back me on buying the old Monroe place."

Wow, that was a surprise. From the way his hands were clenched, he waited for her opinion.

Choosing her words carefully, she asked, "You want to be a farmer?"

"Hell, no." He shrugged off her hold and stood, pacing in front of her. His restlessness didn't hurt her feelings. She understood perfectly. He continued. "Not that there's anything wrong with being a farmer. I just have some ideas of raising longhorn cattle."

"In Alabama?" She was sure the alcohol had pickled his brain. The mulish look on his face told her she'd been tactless. "I'm sorry. I'm sure you have a good reason and the Monroe farm is as large as Magnolia Farms, if not larger."

"Larger. Though some of it is hills and needs a lot of work. Others in the state have raised longhorns. May sound strange, but they're known for having less saturated fat." He nodded his head as if in answer to an unasked question. "This is the right thing to do. I know if I don't do it, I might as well curl into a ball and die. Dad promised to handle it like a loan to a stranger and not interfere with my decisions. I've been taking some online classes on breeding and business management."

The haunted look in his eyes told her he was hanging on by a thread. What else could a loving sister do?

"I think it's a great idea. When I come back to visit, you'd better save a guest room for me. You know once you have a house, I'll finally have an excuse not to stay with Mom and Dad."

Lines fell away from his face and his eyes smiled along with his mouth. Some days she had enough sense to say the right thing. Sure, she worried about him, but at least he appeared to have a purpose now.

"So, when are you leaving?" he asked with resignation.

"Day after tomorrow." She glanced down the street in the direction of the sheriff's office. Her chest squeezed. "Maybe."

"Maybe, huh? What did J.T. have to say about it?" Devlin leaned back next to her again and stretched out his long legs.

"He said to have a good trip." Even a gulp of air didn't hold back the tears. She was such a ninny, crying over a man who didn't care about her.

"Did you tell him you were leaving, or did you ask him if he wanted you to stay?"

"Now why would I ask...oh. I guess I didn't give him a choice." The dull feeling she'd been carrying around since the day before lifted.

"Men think in black and white, doofus. Reading between the lines isn't something we're good at." He crossed his arms. "You need to give him a chance." His crooked grin was good to see. She didn't even mind his teasing. It was like the old days.

He was right. So simple. Why did she make everything so complicated? How could she have been so stupid? Pride mixed with self-doubt. She'd been so certain he couldn't want her, she didn't let him have a chance to say he did. There was a good possibility she was a closet masochist but she had to find out.

"Excuse me, but I've got to see J.T." She kissed his cheek.

She was marching down the sidewalk when she heard Devlin say, "Good luck!"

Molly ducked into an alleyway as soon as she spotted the vans and SUVs of about a dozen reporters in front of the sheriff's office.

Maybe she should feel sorry for J.T, but with the cold way he'd dismissed her that morning, she felt he only got what he deserved, at least until he apologized to her. As she was about to take a step out of the alley to find another way to get to J.T., she heard Rachael's voice raised in anger. Thankfully, a large, green dumpster hid her from the mayor's view.

"I don't give a damn what you think. You go back tomorrow and get those papers, mister!" Rachael lowered her voice but was still loud enough for Molly to hear. "Do I have to tell you again? If we have the evidence, we'll have Big Joe in our pocket. The sneaky bastard has a meeting tomorrow with someone at the old Farley place. That will be the perfect time to sneak in and do what you should've already done."

Molly leaned toward the corner of the building, hoping they wouldn't see her. A sniff of the cheap cologne clouding the air was a dead giveaway of who the mayor was hollering at. Raymond. Knowing her dad, he'd already moved whatever papers as soon as she mentioned Raymond searching through his desk.

So why was her dad meeting someone at the Farley place?

Worried they might see her any minute, she stepped back. A hand covered her mouth, jerking her up against a warm, large body.

Crap! Who else were they working with?

"You can find yourself in a heap of trouble that way." The familiar, deep voice warned her as he slowly dropped his hand.

"Sam! What are you doing here?" she whispered back.

"I brought you the rig I promised. Who were you listening to?" He craned his neck, trying to see around the dumpster. "You're lucky I saw you from the street when I passed by and not a reporter. Who are you spying on?"

Not wanting to risk catching Rachael's attention, Molly pulled Sam along with her closer to the street and the rear exit of the nearest building.

"The mayor and Weasel. They're plotting something against my dad." She opened the back door that led to Bill's Diner's kitchen. "I'll tell you more in just a minute."

"For living in such a small town, you sure have a lot of drama going on." Sam followed her inside.

Molly grimaced and mouthed, "I'm sorry," when Bill gave them an angry look for disturbing his staff. Thank goodness Bill was an understanding sort. It wasn't like she did this every day.

They continued to the front door and stepped out on the sidewalk, hoping to miss the big crowd near the Sheriff's.

"Once I find out what Dad's hiding, I'll leave without worrying about my family." Well, as much as she could while leaving an alcoholic brother behind. And...it depended on what J.T. said.

"Girl, you'll always worry about your family. You love them. No matter what you think they think of you. They love you. You really need to consider finding yourself a new job. Even I saw how much you missed this town and your family. As dysfunctional as they are, they need you and vice versa."

She sighed. Sam was the second man in her life to point out the obvious. She'd been running away for five years. She missed her family no matter how they might feel or didn't feel about her. She loved this crazy town. And she was desperately in love with the sheriff.

"Thanks. I can't argue with you about it. You know, if you were straight I'd be all over you like white on rice." She grinned.

His cheeks flushed. She couldn't recall seeing the big hunk blush in all their years working together.

After clearing his throat, he asked, "Do you need the truck?"

A glance at the crowd of reporters indicated J.T. would be busy for most of the evening.

"I'll let you know tomorrow. Sorry. Is that okay? I need to talk with him again but I'll have to wait for the media to thin out. Then I have an appointment to find out what my dad's up to."

"I'd stay around and help, but Eddie promised me a ride back to Birmingham tonight." Sam's big grin lit up the evening. "He can always bring me back tomorrow to pick up the truck, if you decide you don't need it."

"Oh, it's that way." She chuckled and hooked her arm in his, squeezing. "You be careful, and like I said, I'll call you tomorrow and let you know my decision."

Chapter Forty-Seven

It was nearly midnight before J.T. returned home. The only good part of the day was that he'd been too busy to think about Molly. Once his mind had a chance to quit racing with everything that had happened in the last twenty-four hours, he would examine their non-argument. He did know he was frustrated with how it ended. Part of it was his fault. He wasn't used to talking about his feelings. From the way she acted, she wasn't in the habit of it either.

How did they get angry without one heated word? How did women do that? He shook his head. He was too tired to think about it, and too exhausted to eat. He stripped and dropped across his bed, promptly falling asleep.

Later, he would shake off the dream as a product of the emotional rollercoaster he'd ridden since Molly's return. He should be accustomed to it. Since he was a kid, whenever he was under stress, he'd replayed one significant fight of his parents'. They had fought often, but this one was when his dad hit his mom for the first time.

Out drinking as usual, his dad had staggered back home

and his mom started crying and yelling. J.T. had awoken from a sound sleep in his bunk bed above his little brother's.

"I can't keep living like this!" she'd said, sobbing so loud her words were almost incoherent.

"Then leave. But you ain't taking the boys." His dad's slurred words warned J.T. the arguing would continue. Then he heard someone knock over or throw what sounded like one of the rickety kitchen chairs.

"Look at yourself. What kind of life is it for the boys with a dad that drank himself into a stupor over a woman? A woman who rejected you for your best friend," his mom accused.

Then the strange sound like someone thumping a watermelon woke J.T., pulling him out of the nightmare, struggling not to throw up. Sweaty and twisted in his sheet, he took several deep breaths and jerked the cloth off to let the night air cool his body.

The next day his mom had sat at the breakfast table with a swollen nose and shadows beneath her eyes. She'd plastered makeup over the areas, hoping to hide the bruising, but J.T. knew. His dad had hit her and broken her nose, one of the many bruises and broken bones over the next few years until she disappeared.

From that night on, along with many more arguments he overheard, he'd slowly understood his dad was in love with Molly's mom. While his mom begged for her husband's love, and his dad drank and beat her, Big Joe Hicks grew richer, keeping his wife in luxury, ignoring his old friend. The Hicks's children lived a fairytale life compared to J.T. and his brother, plus they had their mother. In a child's mind, the name Hicks represented all that was wrong in the world. Enough of a reason to keep any Hicks at arm's length.

He rolled over and inhaled Molly's scent still lingering on the pillow's slip cover. Tossing the pillow off his bed, he worked at pushing Molly out of his head and life. She'd be leaving soon. And he'd sworn he would never care for a woman who could leave him without a backward glance.

He covered his eyes, chuckling in self-derision. All those years he'd pushed away one woman after another in fear they would become a crucial part of his life and then leave him as his mother had left her family. Now he knew the lie his father had told, and yet he still held women away, especially a certain special woman, despite having an asshole for a father. Being older now, he understood why Big Joe had done what he had. But she was leaving *him*. No way would he ask her to stay. He wouldn't beg. He didn't want a woman who refused to work on a relationship.

Yet, every time he and Molly were together, it felt as if the sun had been shining bright. How could one person who aggravated the hell out of him make him feel so fucking happy? And then, bam! She made him feel as if he'd fallen into a dark pit. Even the darkness in the room was only part of the darkness he felt surrounding him.

Unable to fall asleep again—fearing he would dream once more about his childhood—he stared at the ceiling.

Rubbing his chest, he tried to ease the ache inside. The pain brought on by letting down his guard around Molly. Looking into her gentle eyes always helped him forget the past, making it harder to fight his attraction for this one certain Hicks. He reached for the pillow on the floor and smoothed the material, inhaling her scent again. Then realization hit him.

He was in love with her.

Chapter Forty-Eight

Molly pushed hair from her eyes as she tossed a bag full of clothes from the consignment shop into the back of the Jeep. She'd barely made a dent in replacing all her stuff destroyed in the fire. The thought of asking her parents for more money had crossed her mind a time or two, but the cost of a new truck would be too much already. She never liked owing anything to anybody, including her family.

After swiping off the sweat beading on her forehead with the back of her hand, she glared up at the sky. Clouds swirled overhead, trapping the heat. Even the wind and dust peppering her face was hot. A tropical storm hitting the Gulf Coast was expected to come through that evening, and in the meantime, the heat was dragging her down. She was looking forward to the rain and the ensuing cool weather.

A flash of color near Bill's Diner caught her attention. What in the world was Franny up to? The woman, dressed in a purple sarong, a green silk blouse, and yellow leotards, had her dyed black hair twisted in a knot topped off with a big, orange bow. She stood in front of a large window, poodle in one hand, waving frantically with the other to someone inside.

Worried for the woman, Molly headed across the street just as the diner's door opened and J.T. walked out.

"Sheriff! I'm so sorry. I would've gone inside, but Bill acts so funny when I bring Snowball with me. Like my sweetie's going to hike his leg on one of his customers. Leaving Frosty should've been enough." Franny huffed and squeezed the little poodle to her ample chest.

"What's going on?" Though he spoke to the older woman, his attention was caught on Molly. She liked how his gaze traveled down her body and back with a hunger that sent pleasurable shivers over her skin. Good. He should see what he was missing, how he screwed up. Maybe he'd...

She cringed inside. No. It was best she was leaving. She was hitting the road to protect what little self-respect she had left. She didn't need a man. Yeah, right. That was why she dressed like she was on the hunt for one.

This morning she'd put on a new pair of jeans and a red blouse, all molded to her body in the best way to show off her figure. With her hair loose around her shoulders, she hoped he remembered how the strands fell around them as they'd made love the last time.

She couldn't help admiring him in return. His khakis, pressed and creased, molded to those buttocks she loved holding as he thrust into her. They were so taut she bet she could bounce a quarter off them. The shirt stretched across shoulders she knew could hold more than their weight. He was a handsome and decent man.

Oh, man, she loved him so much.

"Your brother's back. This morning before the sun was completely up, I'd let Snowball and Frosty out to tinkle and that's when I saw them." The excitement rolling off Franny filled the air.

Molly had forgotten about Franny's claims from the other day. Why was she talking again about Brandon being alive?

"Them?" J.T. prompted, his attention now on the older woman.

"The lights. I saw lights on at the old Farley place." Franny buried her face into the poodle's fur.

"Thank you, Franny. I'll go and check the place."

"You be careful, Sheriff. I have a feeling he knew I would see so many lights on and go running to you."

"Why didn't you call it in?" His forehead wrinkled in concern.

"I know how your deputies feel about my complaints. I thought it best to tell you face-to-face."

Molly understood the deputies' feelings, but after the attack the other day, she felt they would've believed her this time. But then again, she was imagining the sheriff's brother was alive.

"Franny, do you have someone you can stay with for a few days while I figure out what the hell is going on at the Farley place?" he asked.

"No one's running me out of my home. I'll double lock the doors." She shifted the poodle to her other arm. "Just be careful. There're not enough good-looking hunks like you around to keep my eyes happy."

Franny fluttered her fingers and headed down the street, leaving a trail of heavy perfume behind her.

From what Franny said, Brandon would have to be the one her father was meeting today. Brandon? J.T.'s brother was actually alive? Obviously, Franny believed so and J.T. wasn't denying it. So he knew? Was that who he saw at the

Farley house the other day? Was Brandon or whoever pretended to be him meeting her dad? How was her dad involved with J.T.'s used-to-be-dead brother?

She looked back at J.T. to see him head toward his SUV parked in front of the diner. When he opened the driver's door, without wasting a second longer, Molly hopped into the passenger side.

"No, Molly." Glaring, he pointed for her to exit the automobile.

"I'm going with you. My father's going there to meet someone and I think it's your brother," she explained.

"The crazy women in town are driving me insane." J.T. shook his head and slammed his door. "I really need to learn to lock that door."

"Just as you're concerned about your brother, I'm concerned about my dad." She fastened the seatbelt and folded her arms. He would need a crowbar to move her.

He frowned at her for a few seconds. "I'm not concerned about my brother. He's already proven he can take care of himself, if it's really him. Not many people can resurrect themselves. Now I'm worried about what your father has cooked up with whoever he's meeting."

Then it clicked. His distrust of her dad was the reason he wouldn't let his guard down. She'd thought he held a grudge against her for getting him kicked out of Sand City all those years ago. But it went further back than that. Big Joe's hard-ass, well-deserved reputation had always been the bane of Molly's existence.

"Besides the time he ran you out of town, what do you have against my dad?" she asked, trying to keep her emotions out of the question.

His eyes narrowed. "Where in the hell did that come from? And what makes you think it's anything more?"

"You have to admit leaving Sand City was the best thing that happened to you. You graduated college and then were recruited by the FBI. There has to be a better reason for you to hate my dad."

What in the world had her dad done to make J.T. refuse to care for her? What if she was wrong? What if he just wasn't into her? A man only needed to feel lust for a woman to sleep with her. She couldn't stand the thought he didn't at least like her for her.

"I don't have time for this," he said between gritted teeth as he shifted into drive and floored the gas pedal.

She almost grinned. At least she got a reaction out of him.

"Fine. But we *will* talk about us. You bet your pea-picking heart we will." Fiddling with the birthstone ring on her left hand, she caught his curious glance out of the corner of her eye.

"You know chances are they'll be long gone by the time we show up." His knuckles whitened as he squeezed the steering wheel and stared at the road ahead. "And that's the only reason you can come with me."

Except for the occasional call over the police radio, the ride was a silent one. Molly sensed every breath he took, and she soaked in his massive presence. She curled her fingers, fisting her hand, anything to stop her from reaching over to him. The mixture of masculine soap and the mere presence of J.T. brought back memories of kissing every inch of his delectable body. She'd never been the type to be so touchy-feely, but with J.T. she was different. Would she ever get enough of having his warm skin sliding along hers?

The tightness between her shoulders loosened when they parked down the street, behind some overgrown bushes. Anyone already in the house would be hard-pressed to see them. No cars. No lights. Maybe her dad had come and gone.

A shiver ran down her back as she stared at the rundown, abandoned house. The lawn was mowed, probably by a frustrated neighbor, but the bushes were overgrown and leaves piled in the gutters. Trees swayed in the wind from the oncoming storm. The place looked deserted and creepy, perfect for ghosts.

Good thing she didn't believe in ghosts.

Chapter Forty-Nine

"Stay here." J.T. exited the SUV and tramped across the large front yard. When the FBI had finished their investigation at the house, they had left the key with his office, but he didn't think to pick it up. So first rule, check the easiest way in. He tested the front door. Unsuccessful. Next, he looked into the nearest window. No one in that room.

"Do you see anyone?" Molly whispered over his shoulder.

Barely containing his jump of surprise, J.T. clenched his jaw. Why in the hell did he think she would obey him?

He turned to face her. "You really need to stay in the SUV."

"If my dad's in there, I want to be there too."

What logic was that? A Hicks's logic was the simple answer.

"Molly, I'm not playing around this time. You've got to stop following me and interfering with what you don't understand or are unqualified to handle."

Time for her to recognize he meant business. He

grabbed her wrist and brought the arm behind her back, making sure not to twist too hard. At the same time, he covered her mouth with his other hand, being careful to keep his thumb beneath her chin, pressing her head back so she couldn't bite him when he kept her a little off-balance.

"I'm serious. Brandon was always unpredictable and I doubt that he's changed. I can't take a chance of you being hurt." He dodged her backward kick. Feisty women always revved his engine.

He goose-stepped her all the way to the SUV and moved his hand from her mouth as he spun her against the driver's door. Her hair was mussed and her dark eyes flashed between the strands. Damn if she didn't look like she needed to be kissed and he was the man to do it.

"You son of a—"

His mouth covered hers. He closed his eyes for a second. She tasted so sweet. He shouldn't have kissed her, but he couldn't resist one last time. Damn, he hated what he had to do next. She sure would hate him for it.

With a move he'd learned at Quantico, he turned her before she could take another breath to scream. Then he pressed his lower body against hers, holding her tight to the side of the SUV, and handcuffed one wrist.

"What are you doing?"

He ignored her question.

She gasped in exasperation when he jerked opened the door and shoved her into the back passenger's seat, locking the other handcuff to the bar dividing the backseat, made specifically to restrain prisoners. And the doors were on child lock, stopping anyone from opening them from the inside.

"Unlock it right now!"

The rattling of the chains assured J.T. she would stay put.

"I'll crank the car and leave the air running. Behave. Best not to scream. You'll only embarrass yourself." He leaned into the SUV's front seat and pressed the gas as he started the engine, adjusting the fan to high. "That should keep you cool."

He was a sick bastard, but damn, if watching her didn't turn him on. Hair flying around her shoulders as she fought the handcuffs and her face rosy from anger were as sexy as seeing her buck naked on his bed wearing his hat.

Palm open, he slapped the doors closed, cutting off the tirade of obscenities. Wow, he'd never seen her this mad before. She did have a mouth on her.

Only he had better uses for those luscious lips.

With a shake of his head—he had to keep his mind off her—he walked back to the mansion and started his search for his psycho brother.

J.T. started by breaking a window in the basement and crawling through. He worked his way up. Twenty-two minutes passed, no sign of anyone so far until he came to the last room. Again, no one. The upstairs master bedroom opened onto a balcony about sixteen feet by ten with small curving steps leading down to the empty pool area. He unlocked and opened the French doors, stepping out to look into the massive backyard.

Earlier in the year, a tornado had come through and thinned the tree line at the end of the lawn. And with the new storm coming in, the remaining trees swayed and twirled, clearing views he normally wouldn't see. A movement between a couple of tall pines caught his attention. He moved a few steps to the right and then saw the end of a small building, red brick with white shutters. Either a guest house or studio sat in the woods.

Without wasting time, he ran down the steps, keeping to the side of the yard, away from the building's windows. He wanted to creep through the dead flower bed, but a thick line of bushes blocked his way and dry leaves on the ground would crunch loudly. He doubted the wind would cover his progress. So he eased along the path until he was even with the front porch of the small house. Then ducking down he stepped between two bushes and peeked inside.

"Damn!" J.T. spit out beneath his breath.

In the middle of an old kitchen, Molly's hands were handcuffed behind her as she sat in a chair with what looked to be a hand towel shoved in her mouth and the ends tied at the back of her head, effectively muzzling her. The vivid bruise on her cheek brought a rush of heated anger.

Whoever touched her would pay.

Chapter Fifty

"Hello there, brother. So you're finally here to say hi to your girlfriend." Brandon opened the screen door and grinned as if greeting J.T. for Sunday brunch.

J.T. almost didn't recognize him. His blond hair dyed black made his face look pasty white. The damp wind lifted the fringe across his brow, exposing a receding hairline. Wrinkles spidering from the corners of his eyes and the bags beneath them betrayed how much a life on the run could age a person. A stranger would never have guessed Brandon to be two years younger.

"What do you have planned, brother? You had everyone believing you were dead. You could've gone anywhere and no one the wiser." J.T. stepped a little closer. Was someone helping Brandon? "Why involve Molly?"

He clenched his fists, ready to teach his brother a lesson or two about touching his woman.

At that moment, the storm blowing in from the southwest kicked up, rustling leaves at his feet. The wind yanked the screen door out of Brandon's hand and slammed it behind him. A loud crack and then the falling of a tree limb nearby pulled J.T.'s attention to the treetops. The tips stirred to the left and then right. That wasn't good.

"Yo, big bro?"

J.T.'s gaze returned to his brother. "What the fuck are you up to?

Brandon opened the screen door again and, with a smirk on his face, leaned a shoulder against the frame, blocking the entrance. He acted as if he had all the time in the world.

"What do you think?" His brother shook his head. "As always. You never were the smart one, always coloring in the lines." Each word was filled with derision.

J.T. shifted his stance, trying to see around Brandon. Were others inside? He needed to persuade his brother to let Molly go. One thing was for certain, her dad hadn't arrived yet. Even Big Joe wouldn't let anyone touch her like that. At least, J.T. hoped so.

"I deserve an answer," J.T. said to keep him talking.

"Sure, sure. It's like this. That asshole Hart spent every cent I had socked away in the islands. So there I was stuck without any money. But I taught him to never betray me, didn't I, big brother?" Without waiting for a reply, he continued. "So I need more. I deserve to have as much as I want." Brandon raised a gun, pointing the muzzle at J.T.'s chest. "Throw your guns into the bushes."

He spread out his fingers and slowly lifted his gun from its holster. "So Special Agent Hart was your partner in crime?" His brother merely stared at him. J.T. continued. "What little I have would only keep you happy for a couple days." Taking his time, not wanting to push his brother into doing anything rash, he tossed it onto some leaves. Brandon had already shown his true colors. So J.T. figured, between faking his own death and killing friends and FBI agents, murdering a brother would be no different.

"Come on. One more. You always carried one at your ankle, like some stupid-ass hero." He opened the door wider. "Quit wasting my time. Pull up your pant legs."

"I don't anymore. Not since I became sheriff." J.T. didn't see anyone inside the doorway. While keeping his eyes on his brother, he lifted one pant leg after the other, showing only brown socks and skin above them.

"That doesn't surprise me. Actually, knowing how much you liked watching that hokey show about the unarmed sheriff, I wouldn't put it past you if you tried going without one at all." Brandon waved his gun, indicating for him to go inside.

When they were kids they loved watching old black-and-white reruns of *The Andy Griffith Show* together. Both of them wishing their father had been Sheriff Andy Taylor, the hero of the series.

He paused as he walked by his brother into the house, taking a second to stare into his face. Brandon's pupils were dilated and his gaze appeared unfocused, his attention jerking from one spot to the next. Was the wildness in his brother's eyes from drugs? Or was it more like something ate at his insides and he didn't want J.T. to guess? Something wasn't right. J.T. was deeply worried for everyone's safety.

Holding back the urge to pounce on his brother, J.T. walked into a small living room, taking his time, scanning every shadow, every dark corner. Until he knew for sure his brother was alone, J.T.'s hands were tied. He couldn't take the chance someone waited in the kitchen with Molly, ready to harm her if he attacked Brandon.

Dust motes floated through the air as he headed toward the kitchen. Musty from being closed up, the faded curtains and heavy furniture appeared to be from twenty years ago.

Eyes wide but dry, Molly stared at J.T. and then at Brandon. What was going through her mind? At least, she was keeping her cool. The woman was something. He winced when his gaze came to the bruise on her cheekbone, such a stark contrast to her paleness. Despite her overall calmness, her body trembled. It might be from the storm and drop in temperature or from fear, J.T. wasn't sure. But one thing he did know was before the evening was over either he or his brother would be prone on the floor in a pool of blood.

"Handcuffing her, was it necessary? You—" he bit off the last. *Keep calm, J.T.* No need to antagonize him further. His brother always loved to irritate the hell out of him as kids. This was most likely another way to go about it. "Are you hoping I'll do whatever you want because she's here?"

"Once again, you think it's all about you." Brandon pulled out a cushioned metal chair and slid it across the floor toward him. "This time, big brother, you're not the main attraction. And you'll see soon enough why I need her. Sit down."

As J.T. eased into the chair, his gaze traveled over her once more, making sure the bruise was her only injury. Her large, brown eyes softened, but then she looked from him to Brandon and back. Her obvious concern warmed his heart. No matter how afraid she was, she still worried about him. He wished he could console her and let her know his brother wouldn't hurt her again, but he'd be lying. The year before Brandon died, he'd been erratic and, after years on the run, who could say if anyone was safe from his psycho brother?

"I didn't hurt your little woman much. She's a wild one.

Took all my concentration to hold her down and handcuff her and shut her up before she could warn you." He walked over to Molly and placed the muzzle of the gun to the side of her neck, running the barrel up and down. "But you are a lousy boyfriend, leaving her handcuffed in the backseat like that. Tsk, tsk, tsk. Lucky for her I know where you keep the spare key. You're as rigid as ever. Shit! I bet you only fuck mission-style." His free hand dropped down and cupped a breast.

J.T. jumped out of the chair and was only a step away when Brandon warned, "Better sit back down or your girl-friend will have a nasty scar." He jabbed the gun to her cheek.

"Get your damn gun away from her! She's not part of any of this." Afraid if he moved closer, his brother would pull the trigger, J.T. remained in the same spot, fists opening and closing, wanting to smash in his brother's face more than ever.

"Sit down. Our visitor's here and you'll have your answers." Brandon moved away and leaned against the kitchen counter, keeping the gun pointed at Molly.

Some things never changed. His brother still enjoyed creating drama. J.T. returned to the chair, glancing over to check on Molly to see how she was holding up. The white of her eyes glowed in the dim lighting. If only he could reach her, touch her, comfort her. Then again he had no one to blame but himself for her being in this situation. Damn, why had he let her come with him? And saying it was because he'd missed her, wasn't enough.

The front door rattled and Big Joe shouted, "Hey, asshole, what do you want? The storm is picking up and tornado warnings have been issued."

"Come on and join the party, Joe." Brandon grinned at the older man as he cautiously entered the kitchen with a large Smith and Wesson drawn.

"What's my daughter doing here?" Big Joe's hand trembled.

J.T. was glad he was right about the old man. Big Joe cared enough for his daughter to not want her involved in this mess.

"She's insurance that you'll tell me where Harry Rogan is." Brandon stood straight and rested the muzzle against Molly's head. "Drop your cannon there." Nodding to the floor, he waited for the old man to comply.

"Do you think I'm stupid? You'll kill us all." Big Joe glanced over to J.T. "What part do you play in this?"

"Me? Trying to talk some sense into my crazy brother." J.T. caught the twitch at the corner of his brother's eye. So he didn't like to be called crazy. *Isn't that a shame?*

"Enough! Tell me where Harry is." In a flash, Brandon had Molly by the hair, shaking her as he pressed the gun into her temple. She gave a muffled squeak when the sight on the gun scratched and broke her skin. Blood streamed down her cheek.

"Let go of her." J.T. jumped to his feet, his chair crashing against the wall. Thunder reverberated in the distance as if even the heavens protested with him.

"Big Joe better tell me what I want!" Saliva sprinkled the air in front of Brandon, his face red with rage.

"What do you want with your father?" Big Joe asked as he edged a little closer to Molly.

The older man had guts but J.T. really wished he'd do as his brother said. Molly's life was more important than pride.

"Did you know, dear Molly's Daddy, your best friend

beat the shit out of us regularly after Mom disappeared? The drinking and losing jobs, not paying the bills, making people pity us were not as bad as the beatings he gave? He owes me." He shook Molly as if she was a stew bone clamped in a dog's mouth.

"Fuck, Brandon, let her go. She's not a part of this." J.T. pleaded. He wanted to beat his brother to a pulp.

J.T. wasn't sure if he'd gotten to his brother's better side or Brandon thought he was harmless, but Brandon pushed Molly into J.T.'s lap.

"Here. Say goodbye to your sweetheart while I finish up with her daddy."

"Are you okay?" He jerked off the gag, using it to smooth the blood from her face, noting the angry red scratch was already clotting. "He'll pay for that."

"He's loony," she whispered back. "He blames my dad for everything that happened to you two." Her breath tickled his ear as her body leaned against his.

Her quaking body told him how much it was costing her to hold back her fear. Slipping the small key from his pocket he unlocked one cuff and placed the key into her hand. "Hold on to the cuff. Don't let it make any noise." He whispered as he pressed her wrists together to let her know she still needed to pretend.

The man he called brother had changed so much. Or it could be the real monster had come out to play. Even as a kid he'd been rougher in play than necessary, always in trouble for slugging those who wouldn't do what he wanted, when he wanted.

They had been good friends most times growing up. A little competitive but willing to help each other. Could he remind his brother of those times and keep him from hurting anyone else?

Especially Molly. Whatever it took to protect her, he would do it. His brother had to understand that. So why was Brandon pushing him? Did he have a death wish?

251

Chapter Fifty-One

Molly was happy to have J.T. holding her. As soon as he'd walked into the room, she knew everything would work out. Maybe she was kidding herself. She'd been terrified each time Brandon had placed his gun to her head, but she knew J.T. would save her if there was a way.

"He's dead," Big Joe roughly blurted. Everyone turned to stare at her dad.

"What?" J.T. stood, moving her into his chair.

She struggled to keep her hands hidden.

Big Joe lifted his chin. "He was dying of cancer and refused treatment. I offered to help, but he wouldn't hear of it. A week before he died, he told me where he'd buried Paige. I had her dug up and moved to a little meadow near Cold Springs. Your dad is buried next to her. He'd never forgiven himself for killing her. He swore to me until the day he'd died he didn't remember doing it." His shoulders slumped as if he'd finally released a terrible load.

How hard was it for her dad to carry such a burden alone, knowing his friend had been a murderer? And he then helped the man with his dying wish. The actions would cause any man to question their morality.

She jumped in fright when Brandon began laughing hysterically, tears streaming down his red face. All the while he kept his gun pointed in her direction. Her stomach churned with the vile possibilities. She prayed he didn't forget to keep his grip light.

J.T. stepped closer to Big Joe. "You knew where my mother was buried all this time and didn't let me know. Who gave you the right to decide? My father didn't deserve any consideration." J.T.'s pain-filled voice remained steady.

"He loved your mother," Big Joe stated without any explanation. "Willy helped me bury them." The older man's forehead wrinkled as he watched Brandon. "What's so funny, son?"

"Don't call me son, asshole!" Brandon pointed the gun at her father.

She tried to keep her mouth shut but a frustrated scream escaped. For an old man, her dad exploded into action, diving for his gun on the floor.

During their argument, the sky had darkened, bringing a moist thickness in the air. A loud crash of thunder shook the house. The lights flickered and then with a click went out. Before her eyes could adjust, several shots resounded in the small space, throwing bursts of light into the darkness. J.T. shoved Molly off the chair and onto the floor, covering her with his body. Shouting and a grunt was all she heard before it became eerily quiet again.

Lightning brightened the room momentarily, allowing Molly to see Brandon standing, limp arms at his sides, his gun pointing down as he stared at her dad's body on the floor.

Disbelief filled her with numbness. Was her dad dead?

He couldn't be. She refused to believe it. Would Brandon shoot her next and then his own brother? Her nails dug into J.T.'s arms, afraid to move.

"Shit! That was the old man's secret." Another flash of lightning outside revealed Weasel in the doorway. The Beretta in his soft manicured hand looked out of place.

"Hey, Weasel. You're late." Brandon shoved her father with his foot. Big Joe didn't make a sound.

She couldn't take her eyes off her father's body. Molly had never seen a dead person before, especially one she loved. Just moments ago he'd been full of life, trying to protect her.

He couldn't be dead. He couldn't be dead. He couldn't be dead.

"Molly, shhh. Baby, I'm here. We're not out of this yet," J.T. whispered, giving her a squeeze.

She hadn't realized she'd been repeating out loud her hopeful mantra, tears streaming down her face. With a gentle lift, he helped her back into the chair.

A pop and then a hum preceded the lights being restored as the thunder rattled the house followed by the hard patter of rain hitting the windows. Molly couldn't decide if being outside was as dangerous as inside. Between the electricity crackling and the storm letting loose, it was all a gamble.

"For some reason, asshole's son showed up wanting to talk about his acquirement of some property." For all of Raymond's bravado, his face was as white as the long-sleeved shirt he wore. He looked down at Big Joe. "Is he dead?"

"Hell, what do I care? I still have his little girl and I'm sure she can find a way to get her daddy's money." Brandon stepped toward her.

"You leave Molly out of this." J.T. moved in front of her. "With Big Joe dead, it won't be a problem getting his money." Was he trying to pull his brother's attention away from her? Or had she screwed up? Were the brothers in this together? No, no. She would see it, right?

Chapter Fifty-Two

J.T. needed to give Molly some time to pull herself together. She was too quiet. Hell! How could anyone pull themselves together after seeing a parent killed in front of them? He glanced back at her. She was glaring at Brandon, tears still flowing, yet she had herself under control.

For that matter, it was taking most of his control not to go mental on their asses.

Raymond waved his gun toward J.T.

"What do you want to do with him?" Raymond grinned at Brandon. "You know your brother thinks he's Andy Taylor or something."

Brandon chuckled. "See, brother, I'm not the only one who sees it. You're such a dumb ass. So many times I pulled the wool over your eyes and your gullibility made it so easy. You couldn't imagine your own brother would extort, cheat, or kill for money." His face hardened as he leaned toward J.T. "I did whatever it takes to make my life better. I refused to live like we did growing up. The hand-to-mouth existence is bullshit."

"Oh, I knew you were capable of anything. But I had thought you were on the straight and narrow until that last day when you faked your death. Now I know you're a liar. Your whole life was a lie."

J.T. kept his hands at his sides, unmoving, trying not to provoke the two men. Brandon looked at him as if he expected more to be said. A nagging feeling came over J.T. Then a smirk came to his brother's lips. What had his brother done?

"What the fuck? So I'm a liar. And my favorite type of lie is when I don't have to say a word. A secret that allows others to take the blame for what I did. I learned that the day Mom died."

A horrible thought bloomed to full life. Brandon was only ten when their mother had died. What ten-year-old could be so evil?

"That day you were shot, you told us that Dad had killed Mom. You never explained how you knew." His stomach boiled and churned as he realized how long his brother had been crazy.

"When Mom took her last breath, I was there in the kitchen. That day I understood how someone's death could give me power. A power that took me years to regain." Brandon raised his gun, leveling it at J.T. "A power that I enjoy."

A cold sweat broke over J.T.'s entire body. He hoped to God his brother wasn't saying what it sounded like. The evil chuckle Brandon had perfected rolled down J.T.'s back.

"You need to explain." J.T.'s throat tightened. He hoped he was wrong.

"You always were thick-headed. Our sainted mother was whining at Dad about how he loved Lisa Hicks and not her. The usual day-in, day-out crap we heard as kids. She got on my last nerve. It was pathetic. So while good old Dad was passed out, I hit her with the frying pan. People would blame our low-down drunk of a dad and he wouldn't be able to deny it, being black-out drunk. I couldn't believe how easy it was. I remembered how surprised I was when she went down with the first blow. Her head burst open—"

"You bastard!" As J.T. was reaching for Brandon, three things happened at once: a loud crack like splintering wood shook the house, a large, red mushroom shape formed on his brother's chest, and Molly screamed.

J.T. turned and looked at Raymond. The lawyer's hand shook as he aimed his gun at J.T.

"Hey, you couldn't expect me to trust him after he confessed to killing his own ma. What would keep him from killing me later when I got the money?" Raymond's voice sounded hollow as if he were on autopilot.

"Put the gun down. We can say it was self-defense." J.T. knew it was unlikely he would take the bait but could only hope. He slowly stepped in front of Molly. He couldn't take a chance Raymond would kill them all.

Raymond stared at J.T. for a few seconds. The wind continued to howl and whistle through the attic.

"You forget. I'm a fucking lawyer. Sure, I work with corporate law, but even I know a few things about criminal. This wasn't self-defense." His eyes looked empty as if no one was at home and he was ready to clean house. The lawyer knew all witnesses needed to be done away with.

"Then you can use an insanity plea," J.T. said in an even tone.

Before J.T. could say anything more, another crack echoed through the house, followed by snapping wood and clinking of glass crashing as pieces of the ceiling fell in on top of them. J.T. turned and dived toward Molly, once more covering her with his body as he pulled her off the chair. A tree fell through the roof, and then the lights flickered and went out.

"Don't think you and the bitch can get away," Raymond shouted.

J.T. covered her mouth. Beneath his hand he felt her gritting her teeth, trying to regain control of her trembling, but she quickly understood the only way to get out alive was to leave before Raymond found them. One arm over her shoulders, he moved her toward the large hole made by the tree. They ducked underneath the branches, pushing their way through wet pine needles and splintered wood until they escaped outside.

He headed toward what he expected was the mansion. Between the dark and rain, and exiting the little house through a wall, he was turned around. The electricity was out in the whole neighborhood. Damn, he'd forgotten how dark it could be in the country with no street lights. A shout from the house behind them had J.T. running faster, hoping the noise of their feet splattering through the mud puddles was muffled by the wind and leaves. The rain fell so heavily J.T. felt as if they were running across the ocean floor.

Whether from fear or cold, Molly's shoulders shook beneath his arm and he pulled her closer and tugged her down with him behind a bush, giving her as much of his body heat as he could without losing their balance. They needed to be on their toes and prepared to dash in any direction. For now, he needed time to regain his sense of direction.

Her elbow jabbed into his side. He looked down. She was holding out the key to her handcuffs. From the way her hands were trembling, she was having a hard time unlocking the remaining bracelet. He brought her wrist to his mouth and kissed the area most likely bruised by the metal. In seconds, he unlocked the last bracelet and tucked them one-handed into its case on his duty belt.

J.T. looked for Raymond and the direction they needed to walk to reach the mansion, but the rain was as thick as a mountain waterfall. Sheets streamed down his face blurring his vision further. Just when he was sure they would drown, the rain and wind stopped as if someone had shut a valve. In seconds, the warm ground began steaming, creating a fog about a foot deep. The atmosphere of the woods was like one of the old B-rated horror flicks he loved. Maybe he'd reconsider his taste in movies.

After the constant pounding of wind and rain, the occasional drip of water slapping the saturated ground and the shrill singing of the cicadas were magnified in the stillness. J.T. and Molly held their breaths, waiting for Raymond to jump out at them.

"Where is he?" Molly whispered.

J.T. shrugged. His legs began to cramp from the uncomfortable position. She shifted. Obviously, she was hurting too.

"Get ready to move and be prepared to run," he said with his mouth to her ear.

Chapter Fifty-Three

everish skin and clammy clothes. Molly felt like she'd been placed in a hot dryer someone had forgotten to turn on. She'd always heard shock meant chills, so she wasn't experiencing that. Maybe instead this was a nightmare she needed to wake up from. That had to be it.

"J.T., are we having the same nightmare?"

Just then the clouds separated and the moon's glow created shadows through the trees. She looked into J.T.'s silhouetted face. Even in the partial darkness she could tell he was determined to protect her. His arm had remained around her since the moment they had escaped.

"I wish I could tell you different, sweetheart, but I'll do my best to make sure it doesn't get worse." He hauled her against his chest, wrapping his arms around her.

Though he radiated heat she didn't need, the sensation of having someone to protect her was a wonderful feeling.

"Now isn't this sweet?" Raymond stepped from behind a tree. The determined look in the man's eyes told her they wouldn't see any mercy from her dad's lawyer. He lifted his gun, aiming it at J.T. but his hand shook so badly, he brought up his other hand to hold it steady. "The newspaper is going to have a field day. Sheriff in a rampage shoots his younger brother and the town's most respected citizen along with his daughter before committing suicide. While I comfort the grieving widow, assuring her I'll take care of all the finances, I'll have everything changed over to my name. In no time, I'll be the richest man in Sand County."

She cringed thinking how Raymond would mistreat her mother. Especially after her mother told him no to his plans. Lisa was no one's fool.

"What about your partner?" Molly asked, curious if he would admit the mayor was his partner in crime.

"Partner? Oh, you mean Rachael. The stupid bitch wanted to blackmail Big Joe. I knew the old man would have us killed before we could enjoy any of his money. He might as well have been the Teflon man. Every crime he'd ever committed, he'd gotten away with. Money will do that for you and it will do the same for me." Hair sleeked back from the rain, Raymond still looked greasy. "Enough talking. Time to get rid of the two things holding me back from taking over Big Joe's area."

No way would she let that bastard hurt J.T. or her mother. Without thinking it through, she tried to push J.T. to the side, but he tightened his grip on her arm as if he'd guessed her intentions. He swung her around and brought her down with him. She landed on the ground and his long, big body rested on top of hers once again.

Did the man have an exhibitionist fetish? The stray off-color question zipped through her mind.

The pop of Raymond's pistol stopped the cicadas' noise. Then a loud bang broke the silence followed by a grunt and a thud.

She looked up as J.T. scrambled to his feet. Ignoring his command to stay—wouldn't he ever learn?—she followed and came to an abrupt stop.

Her brother stood over Raymond as the man held his leg, rolling back and forth, crying and whimpering.

"You stupid son of a bitch!" Devlin snarled. "What makes you believe I would let you get away with hurting my sister or stealing from my mom and dad?" Devlin held one of their dad's prized possessions, the matching Smith and Wesson Magnum 357 to the one that was probably still lying next to their dad's body. Their dad had always called it a true man's weapon.

Molly jumped when bright lights shone from several directions. Shouts and the roar of a hundred feet trampling through the woods pushed her into panic mode. Strong arms grabbed her and pressed her cheek into a firm, wet-shirt-covered chest. She inhaled the familiar scent of J.T. and safety.

"Shh, honey. I got you. It's the alphabet cavalry." J.T.'s soothing words helped calm her down.

She huffed at his reference to the men and women with the letters "FBI" on their vests scrambling around them. Closing her eyes, she let J.T. carry her to one of the ambulances.

It seemed forever when she ended up in a deputy's car with the heater blasting and a blanket covering every inch of her. Shock or something had set in for she couldn't get warm enough. The paramedics had treated her numerous cuts and bruises, the worst being the ones on her cheek and across her forehead. She couldn't remember when she got the last one but guessed a tree limb had done the damage.

Molly leaned against the window, crying while keeping watch for the paramedics as they should be bringing her father's body out of the house any minute. The ambulance with Raymond had left over thirty minutes earlier with a deputy riding with him in the back. Being a coward, she decided to wait before calling her mother. No way could she ever tell her what happened tonight. Why hadn't she done something to stop her dad?

She heard the raised voices and then a gurney was being pushed onto the drive toward the ambulance. As it passed the car, she noticed her dad's face wasn't covered. She scrambled out of the door and caught the side of the gurney. His face was bloody and a large bruise cupped his chin. But the rising and falling of his chest was the most beautiful sight.

He was alive?

"Daddy, oh, Daddy! They're taking you to the hospital and I'll be right behind you." Tears rolled down her cheeks. She wanted to giggle and dance around. "Daddy, I love you."

His swollen lids fluttered and a small grin bowed his lips.

J.T. clasped her shoulders and pulled her away. "Let the guys take your dad and get on down the road."

She leaned back, taking comfort from his embrace. The overalls he'd borrowed from another officer were well-worn and soft as she held his arms beneath her breasts. She realized he'd held her more in the last few hours than he had in the weeks they were lovers. She liked it. A lot.

"Is he going to be okay? I thought he was dead." She hated saying "dead" out loud but she needed to know.

"He's got a long recovery from losing a good bit of blood. From what they could see, no vital organs were hit. They believe when he was struck by the bullet, he landed on the floor chin first, which knocked him out," he said in an even soft voice.

She wanted to turn around and stretch her body across his to soak up his strength and the feeling of being safe. But too many people were milling around and they were already receiving their fair share of raised eyebrows.

"What about Rachael? Has she been arrested?" As soon as she asked the questions, J.T.'s body tightened.

"No. When I sent one of the deputies over to question her, her house was empty. She's left town." His voice was gruff as if he was prepared for a fight.

"Good riddance I say. She can sleaze up someone else's town." She almost giggled when his body relaxed. It was good to have a man unsure how you'll react to news about other women. Kept him on his toes and prevented her from being boring and predictable.

With a guilty start, she jumped in J.T.'s arms when another gurney bumped over the grass and then onto the drive. The body was completely covered in a body bag. She'd forgotten about J.T.'s brother. How he could've slipped her mind she wasn't sure, but the evidence of his sibling's betrayal would be hard on J.T.

She turned in his arms and cupped his face. His mouth stretched tight and eyes filled with pain told her so much.

"I'm sorry your brother was crazy. At least, you understand what your dad was going through. When my dad recovers somewhat, we'll get him to tell us where they're buried. We can move them or leave them, place markers, whatever you want. You know now it wasn't your dad." She was talking too much, but she wanted to see something good come out of this craziness.

Chapter Fifty-Four

J.T. resisted the urge to pick up his brother's body and beat every inch. The disappointment of knowing he not only lost a brother again but also his father reopened the wound of losing his mother by a loved one's hands. She'd loved her sons more than anything. Like many women who were abused by their husbands, she was unsure of how to get out of the situation.

He had to admit, his dad's death hadn't been much of a surprise. J.T. really didn't want to examine how he felt about it. Too many beatings as a kid, even death couldn't make things right between them. His family had been so screwed up. That type of life could wreck a man's mind. He wondered if he deserved to be sheriff.

Hell, in a sick way, he was relieved his brother and dad were gone. Not that he'd ever wished them dead, but he'd worried about the two for years. They never deserved his concern.

He looked down into Molly's sweet face. What kind of man did she see in him?

"Molly, I...you're more important to me than keeping

your father safe. I had to protect you." He lifted her the few inches to his mouth and told her the only way he knew how sorry he was.

Her lips were so soft and warm. He delved into her heat, tasting and taking the comfort he needed and she was willing to give. Her hip brushed his groin, and moans escaped them both as he squeezed her soft body. Hard and throbbing, he liked how her pelvis rocked against him.

"You two need to get a room." Franny walked by with her two little white poodles on leashes as if all the activity was a daily occurrence.

J.T. and Molly jumped apart.

He took a deep breath and waved over a deputy.

"Hey, take Molly home." He turned his attention back to her. "The special agent in charge said if he had any more questions for you, he'd been in contact. So go. Take a warm bath, get some dry clothes on. I'll be here for a while."

He raised her wrists to his mouth, kissing the black and blue lines near delicate bones. "I can tell you're anxious about your dad. You've got to tell your mom what happened. She'll need you." He brushed her hair off her bandaged forehead. "It'll be a couple more hours before we'll release your brother."

As she opened her mouth to offer her opinion, he stopped her with a shake of his, just as an unmarked federal car pulled up and Special Agent Reese stepped out.

"It was self-defense and he saved the two of us. They'll let him go," he assured her.

His big hand cupped her cheek, his thumb smoothing her other bandage. He hated seeing her hurting. If he could find a way to make all the bruises and cuts disappear he would. "Don't worry. Here, take my cell phone. I'll borrow one from my deputies and call you later."

Chapter Fifty-Five

Molly placed her hand over his, holding his strong fingers to her mouth, and closed her eyes. When she opened them, the look he gave her took her breath away. Was it love? She believed so, though she'd never seen it in a man's eyes before. Not a man looking at her.

"We've got to talk," she said.

Her brother had been right. If she didn't at least tell him how she felt, she wouldn't do anything but run for the rest of her life. Living with regrets was more torture than living with a broken heart.

"Okay. We need to do that, but not until I take care of this mess."

He bent down and brushed his lips against hers. Then he moved away, nodding to Special Agent Reese to follow.

"He won't be long, ma'am." Reese grinned and in a long-legged stride caught up with the sheriff.

Molly ignored the deputy patting his foot next to his marked car. Funny, all these years whenever emotions bubbled to the top she ran away. There she was, happy to stay in Sand City and find out if he loved her. Though she wasn't sure if J.T. could come to terms with being in love with a Hicks, she knew he was stuck with her.

Chapter Fifty-Six

Sunlight streamed through the windows of the hospital's lobby, warming Molly's face and arms as she stretched out across three chairs. She'd given up her seat in the way-too-crowded and stuffy sitting room on the seventh floor, and found the roomier lobby to her liking until her dad could be placed in a room. With luck on his side, the surgery had gone well. All major organs had been missed, and he was resting in recovery. He'd have a nice scar to show off with the long pale one made by a knife when he was younger. The man did have some wild stories to tell if he ever decided to share.

Her mom had fussed, ranted, and cried when Molly told her what had happened. They arrived at the hospital an hour after her dad, and learned within minutes of walking into the emergency room he'd been taken immediately for tests, x-rays, and then prepared for surgery. Twice, Molly had to grab her mom from going in search of him. As the night progressed, the nurses, afraid of her mom, would motion Molly to come over to give her the updates.

The sun shining through the large window felt good

against her skin, maybe even doing a little healing of her soul. Throughout the night, she comforted her mom as they paced and fretted over what was taking so long. The surgery had gone longer than expected and Molly was about to pull her hair out when in walked her brother. Her mom had collapsed in his arms.

Certainly she'd been happy to see him, but for the first time in her life, she felt sorry for Devlin. Maybe she finally understood why he drank. Her parents could be a handful for sure and she'd always left him to handle them alone. He'd never received a break from their schemes and dramatics.

She rubbed her eyes and looked around. The foot traffic through the lobby was growing as the morning progressed. She dropped her feet to the floor, sat up straight, and stretched. The elevator doors opened and closed with regularity, dinging each time. Looking out the tall glass panes past the drive leading to the turnaround in front, Molly took in the beauty of the patterns the large water feature produced every few minutes.

"Molly?"

She turned and shielded her eyes from the morning sun coming in the windows behind him. All she could see was a silhouette of a man. The broad shoulders, trim hips, and military short hair were dead giveaways. When he moved closer, she noticed he wore a clean uniform but the thick five o'clock shadow on his face told her he hadn't made time to shave. When she finally looked into J.T.'s eyes, she was surprised to see the same expression she'd seen last night. She'd convinced herself during the night that the way he'd looked at her was merely fond affection and concern from the hell they'd endured and nothing more. But she'd been wrong.

"J.T." Her heart lurched.

She'd always thought people were full of crap when they said their heart ached at the sight of someone they loved, but it was true. Hers ached for him something fierce. She wanted to call him hers. Forever.

"Are you still leaving today?" His face closed down, hiding his feelings. He was all sheriff again, fulfilling an obligation. Was that all she was to him? An obligation?

"Dad's on the road to recovery." She stepped back as he came closer.

"Do you plan to be on the road yourself?" he asked in a dark, angry, almost dangerous tone she'd never heard from him before, even when his brother or Raymond had aimed a gun at him.

She didn't like him invading her space with that attitude. She took a deep breath and stopped when his fingers dove into her hair, cupping the back of her head. His mouth was hot as his tongue swept inside. In seconds, she forgot about the rapidly filling lobby, his attitude, all of her obligations, and what he'd asked. She clasped his shoulders as she rose to her tiptoes to show him she could give back as good as he gave.

A burst of clapping pulled her back to reality. A small crowd stood nearby watching the show they were putting on. Before she moved away, J.T. grabbed her hands.

"Stay. I love you, Molly Hicks. Stay in Sand City and marry me."

Seconds, it took only seconds for tears to stream down her face. She couldn't believe it. He loved her. She'd waited for years to hear those words out of his mouth.

"Are you sure?" Molly asked. What was she saying? *Don't give him a chance to change his mind!*

"Yes. I'm sure," he replied as his eyes narrowed. Then

quickly a tender grin broke across his face. That clinched it. She believed him.

But more questions ate at her confidence. What type of wife would she be? Would she run for the road after their first argument? He was waiting for her to answer. Lord, she wanted to say yes.

When he shifted as if he was about to walk away from her, she held tight to his hands, refusing to let go, to let him leave her. But instead of moving away, he knelt down.

"Maybe this will make you believe I'm sure. No other woman has ever gotten me on my knees on a regular basis like you do." His gorgeous face watched her. Remembering the last time he was on his knees in front of her, she blushed. "That's much better. I'd rather you blush instead of wearing that scared look on your face, like you're about to run for the door. So marry me."

She stared at him in disbelief. Happy beyond words, she wanted this moment imprinted on her brain.

"Answer him, girl! Don't let such a good-looking one get away. The boy's waiting," said a white-haired woman, standing nearby with the crowd, back straight, clasping a cane in front of her.

"Yes!" Molly shouted and then followed with a quieter, "Yes, I'll marry you. I've loved you for so long and never dreamed...expected you to love me in return."

"You silly woman. I guess I'll need to prove it to you every day of our lives."

The roar of clapping and shouting echoed in the huge lobby. Molly wrapped her arms around his strong neck as he shot to his feet. He squeezed her tight, swinging her around. Good thing the crowd had the sense to stand back.

"What is going on here?"

Chapter Fifty-Seven

J.T. stopped, releasing Molly to greet her mother. The older woman was eyeing him in a way that made him want to look down and check his fly.

"Mom, J.T. asked me to marry him and I accepted." Molly's face radiated happiness, making her freckles stand out.

She brought a freshness to his life he'd never known he'd been missing until she told him she was leaving. After a hellacious night, he'd decided no matter what her family tried, he was going to marry her. He was so thankful she'd said yes.

He glanced over to Mrs. Hicks, expecting her to protest. Instead, she was smiling with tears in her eyes.

"I'm so happy. I only wish Harry could've been here. He'd've been so proud of you, J.T. I can't tell you how many times he bragged about the work you did with the FBI and then working for the county. He told Big Joe often he thought it would be great if you married Molly. It was his dying wish to see you two together. I have to admit, since Molly's return, Big Joe and I worked hard to throw you two together as much as possible. I'm glad you grew up to be such a good man." She hugged her daughter and then J.T.

His dad wanted him to marry Molly? Always before, he'd assumed his dad hated the Hicks. But his dad had asked Big Joe to help in hiding his wife's body and then later his own. Such a request was evidence enough his dad held no grudge against Big Joe. If nothing else, Molly's dad proved what a good friend he was to his dad. Maybe his dad had realized the past was gone and nothing could be changed.

Mrs. Hicks looked up at J.T. "You know your mom would've been real proud with how you turned out. She loved you very much."

Damn, the woman was going to make him cry like a baby if she kept this up. Molly giggled beside him and then stopped when he glanced at her.

"What?" he asked.

Molly covered her mouth when another giggle almost escaped. "At least I understand why Mom and Dad insisted on me being with you. I had thought they'd lost their minds. But I'm glad they did. That is, insist." She smiled big and added, "And you look scared as if Mom had threatened to take a switch to you."

"Keep teasing him, Molly. You can't take a chance of them becoming full of themselves. It's hard for a man as gorgeous and independent as J.T. to admit he's in love and willing to marry. They're so bursting with pride, thinking they don't need a woman full-time in their lives. They need a woman to keep them humble." The older woman leaned her head on Molly's shoulder and grinned. The same grin that was on her daughter's face.

Looking at Mrs. Hicks standing next to her daughter, he could understand how two men had fought over her in her youth. He would fight the devil himself to keep Molly. J.T. had a sneaking suspicion he would need to stay on his toes to keep ahead of those two.

Molly stepped toward him and cupped his cheek. "Are you okay?"

There was so much he wanted to tell her. Like how he missed her in his bed, hearing her laugh, and how she looked at him with love in her eyes.

"Yeah. I am now."

Chapter Fifty-Eight

One Year Later

Molly stood in the back of the church waiting for her cue to walk down the aisle. Her dad leaned on his rosewood cane and peeked into the sanctuary where the pews were packed with Sand City's best.

"Lordy, she looks so beautiful sitting in that rose-colored dress." He claimed he couldn't keep his eyes off her mom, but she had a sneaky suspicion he was worried J.T. would back out at the last minute.

She had no worries. Earlier J.T. had called her to describe the bed-and-breakfast in St. Augustine where they would spend their honeymoon. How it was right across from the bay and where they could rent a carriage ride, and how he was bringing his extra handcuffs just in case she got cold feet. That last comment was more to remind her he was out to get her back for the little stunt she'd pulled the week before.

She fanned her reddened cheeks with the bouquet of daisies. In the name of keeping J.T. interested, she'd handcuffed him to his bed and then tortured him for hours. He'd warned her payback was hell. Considering what she'd done to him and what he promised to do to her, she couldn't wait for payment.

"Daddy, they're about to play the Wedding March. Hurry. J.T.'s already standing at the altar, isn't he?"

She smoothed the candlelight satin of her simple wedding dress. No frou-frous for her. A straight skirt to her ankles with a tantalizing slit up the side and matching buttoned-up jacket hinting at ample cleavage to draw J.T.'s eyes to the deep shadows when she walked down the aisle was enough for her.

"Yeah. The boy knows when he's getting something special." Her dad straightened and limped over to her. The bullet had missed vital organs, but the fall had damaged his knee. In another week, surgery was planned to take out chipped cartilage and repair the knee.

He kissed her cheek and placed her hand on his arm. The doors opened wide and the wedding planner gave the signal for one more minute.

Sam stood at the altar too, as her man of honor. She had to do some fast talking to convince J.T. that her partner was the only one for the job. Not that she needed his permission, but this was J.T.'s day too, and she wanted it to be special for both of them. Besides, there was no one else she was as close to other than J.T. and her brother, and J.T. had already asked her brother to stand in as the best man. If anything, her wedding was as interesting as the rest of her life would be with J.T.

"Doesn't Devlin look handsome?" Molly was worried about her brother. He'd fallen off the sobriety wagon twice in the last year though he appeared to be sober this afternoon.

"Yeah. If we could keep him from that Landings girl," her father snarled.

"Mark Landings's daughter?" Molly remembered the girl about five years or so younger than her. The poor girl had always looked rumpled with her hair sticking out every which-a-way. Her father owned the salvage yard outside of town and was known for making moonshine as an extra income. That explained why Devlin said Mark had threatened to shoot him if he showed up there again.

He nodded. "Let's just hope he doesn't knock her up. Can you imagine having the Landings in our family?" He took a step forward when the planner waved at them as the Wedding March began.

"I don't know. Considering we're so squeaky clean and such upstanding citizens," she whispered, teasing her dad.

About halfway down the aisle, their conversation was forgotten as she looked into the eyes of the man she loved more than life. J.T. filled out the tux better than any man had a right to. Broad shoulders and long legs encased in dark grey. He'd even let his hair grow out a little and had brushed it back, giving him a dangerous James Bond look. She liked the new style, but she had a feeling next spring she would be talking him into cutting it military style again. Oh, yeah. Having the big, bad sheriff in her bed was a huge turn on.

She floated down the aisle and ignored whatever her father and the minister said to each other when she reached the altar. When she stepped into J.T.'s arms, he leaned down to her ear.

"You're beautiful. I love you." His deep voice rumbled, sending warm vibrations down her body.

Tears in her eyes, she croaked, "I love you too."

That sexy grin reassured her. They both were doing what was right by tying their hearts to each other.

She was finally marrying her hero.

280

About the Author

Carla Swafford loves romance novels, action/adventure movies, and men, and her books reflect that. And on top of it all, she's crazy about hockey, and thankfully, no one has made her turn in her Southern Belle card.

So, it's no surprise she writes spicy romantic suspense filled with mercenaries, motorcycle one-percenters, and southern criminals. And in the last few years, she's included sexy hockey players in books without suspense, except for the kind that asks, how will they ever find their happily ever after?

Also by Carla Swafford

The Circle Organization

Circle of Desire

Circle of Danger

Circle of Deception

Circle of Dishonor (Novella)

Circle of Defiance (Novella

Kidnapped For A Day (Short Story)

A Southern Crime Family Novels

Jake

Sen (coming soon)

Ethan (coming soon)

Brothers of Mayhem Novels

Hidden Heat

Full Heat

Naked Heat

Atlanta Edge Hockey Romance

Crossing The Line

Fake Play

Love In A Small Town Novels

Loving The Small-Town Preacher's Son

Loving The Small-Town Hero